Stepbrother Charming:

A Billionaire Bad Boy

Romance

Nicole Snow

Description

NOBODY WARNED ME CHARMING MEANS
INFURIATING, INTENSE, AND IRRESISTIBLE...

CLAIRE

I'm ready to slap my new step-brother clean across the
face.

Brash, arrogant, and stinking rich doesn't begin to
describe Ty Sterner. He's also sinfully sexy, and wicked
talented at making my blood boil.

Ty thinks it's funny to chase me around like I'm the next
notch in his bedpost. He lives to piss me off. But that isn't
why my heart skips a dozen beats every time I look at him.

What happens if his crude jokes about us hooking up
go too far? What if I admit I actually want this filthy
talking playboy, and one little misstep lands me in Prince
Not-So-Charming's bed for real?

TY

I can't decide whether to laugh my ass off or kiss her 'til
her panties ignite. Little Miss Perfect's too hot and uptight
for her own good. Knowing she's off limits just makes me
want her more.

There's a twisted thrill to flirting underneath our

parents' roof. And I want a whole lot more than teasing her cheeks red, or watching her eyes pop when I'm strutting around half-naked. I want to rock her world into a screaming mess and leave her soft lips breathless.

Too bad this is the summer I'm supposed to get my crap together to build the family fortune. That's a distraction I don't need when all I really want to do is find out how perfect Claire feels between the sheets...

I: Hit the Floor (Claire)

Visiting Club Zing is supposed to be my last hurrah, a post-college escape before the long summer falls across Seattle, and ushers me into grown up land. It's supposed to be my last girl's night out before distance makes things a whole lot harder.

So, why the hell can't I keep my eyes off *him?*

"What's up, Claire? You're nursing that thing like you're about to go away to Saudi Arabia for a year!" My best friend Dana points to my Long Island iced tea and lifts her own. "Come on! Put it down and keep up with me, girl. This is *our* night!"

Sighing, I raise my glass and clink it against hers. "Cheers," we both echo.

Somehow, I'm not feeling it. I've never liked goodbyes. And I *really* don't like this other bastard stealing away the attention my bestie deserves, even if he's moving around the club like he owns the place, sculpted to leave more than a few pairs of panties scorched.

Who am I kidding? Is this seriously how it ends?

By now, I'd normally be holding back the tears and hugging Dana's shoulders while she takes her stompy

1

boots out to the dance floor. I don't understand how she wears those things so gracefully – they look like something German soldiers used to march in – but they always make her the center of attention when she busts her moves.

I'm going to miss her stupid purple hair and how she can't let go of the goth look, even though she's pushing twenty-two, just like me. Hell, I'm going to miss this place. Mostly, I'm going to regret wasting this precious time with my eyes glued to the devil by the bar, the giant towering above everybody else.

It's so obvious I can't hide it anymore. Dana grins at me after a long, dizzying sip on her drink. She spins around and follows my eyes.

"Jesusss, Claire! Don't tell me you've never seen the owner before? Haven't you seen him?"

"Nope, never." I shake my head. "That's the boss man? He's so young..."

My friend waves a hand, flashing the bright purple nails that match her hair dye. "Pssh. You'd own this place if your daddy was a billionaire too. That's Tyler Sterner. Playboy for life and easy on the eyes when he's actually here doing his job."

My brow furrows. Seriously? This guy barely looks older than we are. It's even more amazing I haven't seen him around campus or here on our earlier outings. He's got the kinda body any woman with a beating heart would notice *anywhere*.

He's at the end of the bar, slapping some older, balding man on the back and laughing. Two plastic looking girls are at his side in short skirts, their ruby red lips and pearly white teeth grinning at him like statues.

Massive is a gross understatement. He puts everybody else in his shadow, even the other well-built guys next to him.

He looks like something from another age in the neat suit jacket wrapped around his broad shoulders. An aristocrat, maybe, remembering all the paintings I studied for my art history minor.

Except country gentlemen didn't get this built in the old days taking strolls through the hills and chasing after foxes. No way. Mister – what's his face? – Sterner looks like he's been pumping serious iron and eating big to get big in all the right ways.

The harpies next to him step aside for drinks, and I get a view of his tight packed torso. He's a Greek god from head to toe, a six foot something goliath with a beast of a jaw and blue eyes that look like they're there to put out the fires he's bound to spark in every girl who looks at him. The quirk in his lips and the messy wave in the dark hair on his head matches the self-assured way he's leaning back against the stool.

Something tells me looks are deceptive, as they usually are. This Tyler might look like Prince Charming, but I have a crazy feeling he's more like the ultimate rogue with the way these chicks are eyeing him.

"Hey!" Dana reaches up and snaps her fingers in my face. "Seattle to Claire Frost – come in!"

It's nothing new, she's done it a million times before

when I space out. I always push her hand away and get annoyed. Tonight, I just smile, knowing how much I'm going to miss her crap.

"There are plenty more hotties here who'd actually give us the time of day, if that's how you want to roll this evening," she says with a grin. "Check out that one!"

I follow her finger to the dance floor. There's an edgy looking boy with a few too many piercings and a swirl of thick ink around his eye that makes him look like an Amazon warrior.

Ugh. Just her type – not mine.

I'm all for edge and ink, but I like to be able to feel a man's bare skin too beneath his decorations. I nod, take a long swig of my tea, feeling the delicious vodka and rum bathe my belly in fire.

"You go on. Looks like he's eager for a dance," I say, flipping my wavy hair back.

"Oh, no, you don't!" Dana wags a finger. "Come on! Shake your pretty ass. It'll be fun now that you've got the good stuff in your system!"

"Dana, Dana, Dana!" I keep calling her name as she jerks me out of my seat and pulls me toward the dance floor, but nothing's going to stop her tonight.

It's our last good night at our favorite club. I'm heading north tomorrow to take a few weeks off at my mom's house before the big internship begins. I landed a paid gig with Cascades Now!, an environmental lobby with an amazing reputation for landing awesome consulting work. It's half of the equation I need to jumpstart my career –

the other fifty-percent is coming from my mom, former three-term Congresswoman, Amanda Frost.

As for Dana, she's off to Portland for her MBA. Really, I think she just wants to embrace the city's weirdness. There's no doubt whatsoever she'll fit in great with Portland's eccentric scene and endless supply of food trucks.

I'm trying not to think about the future. It's uncertain and exciting and so damned unnerving sometimes I feel my stomach churn. Thankfully, the alcohol hits right as we step onto the floor, numbing everything in its sweet fire. Everything is a glorious distraction up there, and it's easy to see why my friend is a dance-o-holic.

"Go, go go! Shake it like you're going blind!" she chirps.

I laugh, wondering how many drinks Dana had before I showed up. We're definitely going to need a taxi home after tonight.

I move my hips, mimicking her movements. The dress I've picked out is too tight to dance comfortably – or maybe I've just let all the senior year stress add a few too many inches to my butt. Regardless, I hit it hard, and the liquor in my system helps me feel like I'm not making a complete jackass of myself.

It feels good to move – especially when dancing helps me lose track of Prince Not-So-Charming. I don't even see his freakishly perfect jawline hovering over anyone now.

And I'm not the only one who's lost track. Nobody's paying attention to me, as usual. Several eyes are on Dana, though, including the grown up emo kid who's been circling us on the floor like a shark, his silhouette whirling through the throbbing bass and neon lights.

"Hey, little mama, you got a name to go with those moves?" He finally sneaks past me, and he's hitting on her so obviously I start to laugh.

"I'm nobody's mama!" Dana pushes playfully against his chest, and then he grabs her with a grin, pulling her into his arms. "If you want to dance with a grown woman, then step the fuck up. Don't give me that crap. Show me you've got some skills yourself!"

I watch them whirl and twitch in each other's arms. Dana flashes me a drunken wink while I try to cut in with the small talk. That's the cue we've worked out for each other to make ourselves scarce, but it's always been Dana who makes off pretty. Or should I say makes out? Fucks and moves on?

Nobody ever dances with me for more than a minute before I freeze up or shrug the idiot off as a complete asshole.

I've never been into easy, forgettable dick like my best friend. Ugh, and she's already grinding up against him. For a second, bright red jealously burns in my veins. I wonder how it comes so naturally to her – she's had a gift for free, uncomplicated lovin' ever since our freshman year in the dorms.

Whatever. I hope to God my grown up desire to play the dating field seriously before I jump into bed with some bastard will pay adult dividends. They've got to, right? I need to believe all this waiting around for the perfect man isn't for nothing...

I'm spinning, listening to people blabber drunkenly and laugh. The hard rock switches over to some techno stuff, and the lights go insane, doubling their speed. I'm not even wearing heels and I stumble, nearly losing my damned grip on the floor.

Plowing into the huge shadow in front of me feels like slamming into a brick wall. He reacts quickly.

His arms are around me in an instant. My cheeks burn first, and I've got about three seconds to figure out how I'm going to apologize for smacking into him before I look up. When I finally do, my heart stops.

It should've been predictable as hell, yeah, but when it happens, it doesn't soften the blow one bit.

I'm staring into Tyler Sterner's glacier blue eyes.

He looks at me for what feels like a whole minute as I start to stammer and tumble back. His lips – those evil, kissable, suckable lips! – pull up like horns, exposing some adorable dimples on his cheeks. Who knew Prince Charming had the devil's smile?

"Shit, babe, you look like you've never been out on the club floor before. You had one too many, or what?" He steps close to me again, throws his hands around my waist, and jerks me close like we've already been intimate. "What's the matter? Don't tell me I'm right. Can't believe an ass like yours doesn't have a few good moves."

My mouth drops. I try to speak, but the words won't come. Flushed, stunned, infuriated doesn't begin to describe the shock turning my blood to ice.

I can't believe these are his first words to me – his *only* words – if I have anything to say about it.

"Come the fuck on," he growls, starting to grind and sway with the music. "Move with me, baby. I wanna see *everything* shake through that thing you've got on. I like to see what I'll be bouncing later when I'm balls deep inside you."

Jesus, and here I thought Dana's new buddy was way too forward. My brain can't process what's happening, and my confusion rolls out in a laugh.

I start laughing and try to double over, but he's holding me too tight. I hate admitting the asshole's hands feel good on me, but I guess that's part of the charm. If you can call it that – my Prince is about as charismatic as a swamp toad.

Does he seriously think he's too good to skip cheesy pickup lines? Does he always just jump right into how he's going to fuck a girl?

"What's so goddamned funny?" He says, that stupid sexy smile on his face finally pointing down. "Don't tell me you've been hitting E or some crap. We don't allow that shit here. Listen, I'll toss your ass out and find whoever the fuck sold it to you if that's why you're laughing your damned ass –"

I slap his chest. "I'm laughing at *you*, idiot. And I've had exactly one Long Island iced tea this evening. Not exactly an illegal substance, last time I checked."

"Whatever. You here to laugh your pretty head off or dance? I'll even forgive the idiot remark if you shake it like I think you can. You've got the right stuff, babe." He stares me up and down like I'm a piece of meat, making zero effort to stop his eyes from lingering on my cleavage.

He bends me around in his arms, making me do a turn so he can get a perfect view of my ass. I've never felt completely *undressed* by a man until now.

The smart thing to do is target his face with my next slap. But his hands zip down my back and cup my ass, giving it a sharp squeeze, perfectly timed to the way the music starts to throb again.

Asshole! I shoot him a furious look, but it's really directed inward. I can't believe my body purrs happily with the raw, caveman way he's grabbing my goods. I don't understand what the hell he's doing to me.

I jerk backward, breaking his grip. Tyler laughs, marches forward, and grabs me by the wrist as I'm trying to get away. "Okay, okay. We'll take it slower, beautiful. Give me another try. I'll keep my hands off anything hanging like ripe fruit while we're on the floor. Promise. That shit can wait 'til later when I've got you all alone."

My hand twitches in his, hungry to deliver the slap that'll get me the hell out of this place. Of course, I don't do it. His smile draws me in, and I catch Dana out of the corner of my eye, pressed up against the emo boy with her lips on his.

Sigh. I slip back into his kinder, gentler grip and start to sway my hips, about the most conservative tempo anybody can keep to match the song. I try to keep my breasts and hips well away from direct contact with his washboard body.

9

"I'm Ty," he says after a minute. "This place belongs to the family, in case you didn't know why everybody's making room for us."

I blink and look around while he folds his arms around me. Crap, I hadn't even noticed. It's true. Half the people are gawking right at us, like we're skating on ice. Half the guys look fearful, or else so jealous they're about to hit the ground and worship us.

I shrug, trying to hide the heavy weight on my shoulders. "Well, I guess a nice, private dance won't hurt."

He laughs. It's rich baritone and it resonates deep in my ears, turning my blood to lava. "Babe, this isn't exactly what I'd call private or dancing. Now, we can do the horizontal dance in my personal suite later if you want. You don't know it, but I've had my fucking eyeballs glued to you all night, and they're gonna melt right outta their sockets if I don't see you naked. I'll bet you turn into a fucking whore when those panties come off..."

His voice drifts into a growl. God damn. How does he do it? I thought my anthropology class taught me Neanderthals were extinct. Except, now there's one with his arms around me, talking dirty in my ear, keeping his hands low enough to be polite – but still so fucking close to my ass.

Too close. And having them one inch away from crude and uncivilized makes me think savage thoughts to match.

What will I do if he puts his hands there again? How will I react if he goes further, pulls me into him, grinds his undoubtedly huge cock shamelessly between my legs? Who the *hell* am I becoming in this man's filthy grip?

I jump. The music stops. He swoops in like he's aiming for a kiss, and I fight like hell to break his grasp. I need to get him off me before I lose my mind.

This is officially too much.

It's just as well too. Out of nowhere, two plastic looking bimbos come trotting up and grab his shoulders. There's one on each side massaging him with their long, bright nails.

The redhead on his left leans over, and I let out a little gasp as she touches the tip of her tongue to his earlobe. "You said you'd be off the dance floor by now, babyyy," she whines. "Is this girl joining in or no?"

"Hold up. I need another minute." He jerks out of their grip and steps up to me.

I don't know how the hell I manage to keep my palms folded down instead of hitting him, but I do. He's shown his true colors several times over tonight. But it's not hard to see it's who he is – a rich jackass who's made Club Zing his personal kingdom – just like Dana told me.

I feel like a fucking idiot for dancing with him. Jesus, I *let* him put his hands where nobody else's have ever gone before, even when I'd started to get hot and heavy with a few college guys.

"Babe, come on..."

No. I run the instant I hear his voice. I hop off the dance floor and push through tight crowds on my way to the table. Halfway there, I look over my shoulder and do a double take. The psycho bastard is actually *chasing* me.

I can't believe he won't take the hint. Or maybe he doesn't want to. Maybe he can't believe someone is actually saying no, showing him what a disgusting pig he really is.

Reaching for my glass in the unlikely event I need a weapon, I spin around and face him, just as he reaches my table. "Look, Ty, I don't give a crap if you run this place. Stop following me. I'm *not* interested in you."

I almost choke when I say the last part. My brain agrees, but my body twists, calls me out as a liar.

"Hold up. I'm sorry we went too fast. I didn't mean to make you scared. I just figured you were used to the business that goes down here between a man and a woman on a good night like this." He runs a hand through his dark hair. "There's something I gotta ask you..."

For some reason, the gesture softens my heart a little. He looks genuinely hurt. I shouldn't be hearing another thing he has to say, but I sigh and lean in, letting him bring his lips close to my ear.

"There's room for one more in my private suite, babe. You wanna be part of my first foursome?" He reaches around and cups my ass. "I wanna make these other sluts jealous when they see what we do. I'll fuck you 'til you scream and break their fucking eardrums."

That's when I lose it. My hand flies up and lands on his powerful jaw. I slap him as hard as I fucking can. Giving in to the urge feels incredible.

I can hear the crack over all the club noises. His lips twitch and he steps backward, drawing one hand to the hot red welt blossoming on his cheek. It's like time locks up.

For a second, we stare at each other. I swallow, knowing I'm in deep shit. But I wouldn't take it back for anything. *Nobody* treats me like this – especially not this pompous, strange prick who's obviously used to getting his way too much for his own good.

Ty tips his head back and starts to laugh. I think I let a growl slip past my lips, wondering if he's some kinda sociopath. Nothing seems to get to him. Absolutely fucking nothing.

"Asshole!" It tears out of my throat. Too bad it doesn't stop him.

He's still going, chuckling dark and deep like I just leaned in and whispered the world's dirtiest joke.

When he finally recovers, wiping his eyes, he reaches into his pocket and slams something down on the table. "Thanks for the laugh. You enjoy your evening, baby. Door's open upstairs anytime if you change your mind about that foursome."

He turns smartly and disappears back into the crowd. It's good he moves fast. I swear, one more second and I would've whipped the glass right at his stupid smug face. My heart's racing like mad, probably faster than it has since I gave up tennis my sophomore year.

I need to sit. Sliding back into the seat, I set down my glass and reach for whatever he's left behind. I don't know why I bother.

It's an envelope. When I crack it open, I gasp. Inside, there's at least three crisp one hundreds and a bunch of smaller bills. I consider stuffing it into my purse and taking off, leaving Dana a text to explain my disappearance whenever she's done with lover boy. But I promised we'd go home together, and I really don't want Ty the Jackass to ruin my last night clubbing with my best friend.

I hold up a hand, waving a server over. Ten minutes later, I've got two fresh Long Island teas in front of me and a couple shots of high end vodka.

"Fuck you, Mister-Asshole-Sterner," I whisper, lifting the first crisp shot to my lips.

I don't stop until the entire club is spinning.

"Claire, holy shit!" Dana hisses. "You look like *hell*, girl."

I crack my eyes open and feel a cool compress sliding over my forehead. The first thing I smell is Dana's perfume, now mingled with the thorny scent of the emo kid. I look up and see her hair. It's all messed up.

In my dumb state, there's a pang of jealousy. Why can't I walk out of a place like this just once with Dana's sex hair? Then I remember the only asshole who wanted to fuck me tonight, plus two other girls simultaneously.

My head jerks. Dana leans down, wiping my brow like a concerned sister. I suppose she is.

"Jesus! Take it easy." She frowns. "Don't tell me you've been sitting here alone all night drinking?"

"What time is it?" I groan.

"Quarter to two. The bar's about to close. Hang on, I'm going to see if I can still get you some water!"

I yell out to her, but she's moving too fast. Jesus, my head keeps pounding. I know I've been out at least an

14

hour. Fastest, swiftest hangover in the world – just my luck, right?

My stomach lurches as I stand up. I try to make it to the bathroom before she gets back, but it feels like my knees are jelly.

I manage to make it just in time. The bathroom is halfway down a long hall with a big fancy burgundy door at the very end – probably leading to the kitchen or some VIP lounge. I wash my hands and stumble out, but not before I crash into the second asshole of the night.

I look up. They say karma's a bitch, but I think it's deja vu.

Ty's huge chest stops me like concrete, except this time it's almost bare. He's got a robe halfway open and draped around his shoulders. I catch a glimpse of some wild geometric designs going around his neck, above what looks like a tiger or panther in full roar on his breast.

"Fucking shit. Didn't think I'd run into you again tonight, babe."

I barely stop myself from sticking my tongue out. "I didn't think so either – and I'm really sorry that I did."

Predictably, the bastard laughs. God damn it. The laugh I loved at first now just sounds like nails on chalkboard. Well, if scraping an old blackboard could be deep, sexy, resonating –

Stop. I can't let myself think another positive thing about this royal dick.

"Christ. I can smell the booze rolling off you, babe. You need a ride home or something?"

15

I shake my head furiously. Big mistake. It only makes the pounding in my head worse. While I'm frozen, he reaches up and tucks a few stray hairs back against my ears.

I'm drunk and hungover, but I'm not dead. My hand shoots up, pinches his forearm, and I rake my nails down him. Just like a feral cat.

"Fucking hell!" Ty growls, steps back, and hits the wall. "Don't be a bitch. I was just trying to make sure you're –"

"What? Okay? Yeah, I was, until you decided to get in my face tonight. You fucked up my last night in this city with my best friend!"

He tries reaching for my shoulder, but I dodge him. Looks like I'm not the only one drunk tonight. Except there's the unmistakable smell of women all over him. Sickly sweet sex and perfume. He must've fucked them for hours.

My stupid brain wants to think about it too, but I won't let it. I try to get away as fast as my feet will carry me.

Then my heel catches on an unwieldy step going up the short staircase and I tumble.

I brace myself for a lot more pain when I hit the floor – except it never comes.

I fall right into his huge arms like a damned fairy tale. Okay, now I'm *really* pissed.

Ty flattens me against the wall as I fling my elbows against his hard abs, screaming my frustration. It doesn't faze him.

"Shhh. Quiet, babe. Just relax." His voice rolls low, soothing, dangerously close to my ear. "Let me walk you out for a taxi. Just need to get a shirt on. I never got your name."

"No!" Hellfire flows through my elbows again, and I stab him in the guts, as hard as I can.

I can't even hope to hurt him. I don't care if he's trying to help. I don't trust this jackass, and I need to get away before he drives me insane. I shove my elbows into his rock hard abs two more times, squirming like a madwoman.

He's just stunned enough to let me go, and I practically crawl up the stairs. For some dumb reason, I stop and look back, using the banister to get back on my feet.

There's a wicked sneer twisting his lips. He looks at me like something he's just stepped in, shakes his head, and shrugs. "Fine, babe, do it your way. Go the fuck home. Get some sleep."

My stomach heaves. I'm terrified I'm about to lose the liquor left in my belly all over the place. I fight back the urge to vomit and watch him stomping back to his room.

I feel like total shit. I've made an ass of myself way too many times tonight, even if it was partially this dickhead's fault. I call out to him and stumble forward, back down the stairs, before I know what I'm doing.

"Wait!" My voice echoes down the long corridor.

He stops when he's almost to the burgundy door and turns, waiting for me. "Is there any way I can hit you back for the money? I spent it, and I shouldn't have."

Brutal guilt. Shame. Typical for a Frost girl, especially one who grew up seeing her mom slandered every two years for re-election. But I don't want to owe this fucker a dime, even if we're talking about my own internal good karma counter instead of money.

"You don't owe me shit," he growls. "I paid you for the laugh, just like I said. No different than any other entertainment tonight. You wanna give me something? Go home and rest like I told you. You're not Club Zing material."

"You're not my boss." I try not to shake my head, though it's impossible when this ham-fisted apology is the dumbest idea in the world. "I just want you to know I'm not a bitch. I'm not a bad person."

He looks me up and down. Slowly. His eyes zero in on my cleavage, and I flush.

"Does that mean you changed your mind about the foursome?" He steps close, and next thing I know, I'm back against the wall. Fighting but not really fighting as he moves in for a kiss. "Shit, I'd settle for one on one at this point. Drunk and pissed, you're still fucking hot."

Hot. Nobody's ever called me that before. It's the only explanation for why I let his vile lips connect with mine.

This isn't a kiss. This is a fucking explosion on my lips. My entire body tenses up, muscles clench, everything below the waist writhes like I'm made of snakes. I moan just as he presses his tongue in my mouth.

Of course, I've read about sexual tension in books and seen it on the big screen. I just didn't think it really happened, not like this animal spark igniting between us.

His tongue twines with mine and his lips move rougher,

faster. My palms are on his back and my fingers go jagged, tearing at the skin underneath his thin robe. I can't decide if I want to hurt him or make him fuck me.

The unbelievable hard-on I feel grinding on my thigh definitely says he's willing.

I'm about to come completely undone when my legs kick hard. I knock my knees on his and shove my hands to the wall, twisting and flattening myself, crazy to get away before I do something I'll *really* regret. The other shit that's happened tonight is an afternoon sprinkle compared to this hurricane staring me down.

"Don't!" I yell, pushing against him when he comes close. "Really. I mean it. This was all a mistake...I need to go."

"That's not what your body says, babe. I know a girl who wants to fuck when I see one. Hell, I can *taste* how bad you want it."

I run. This time, I don't stop. I'm like a hummingbird darting up the stairs and through the bar, grabbing Dana by the wrist.

"Hey! I've been wondering where the hell you went. I've got your water if you want to down it before they –"

"We need to go. Right now, Dana. *Now, now, now,*" I whisper, urgent as all hell. "Let's find a cab."

The rest of the night happens in a blur. Dana makes me crash at her apartment, and she doesn't let me sleep until I take a multivitamin and swallow three huge glasses of water.

I keep telling her I'm okay. I whisper something about a

guy being too aggressive, too close to me when I'm drunk off my ass.

I don't dare tell her it's Ty, or that I practically invited the last collision with the sex-crazed jackass.

I'm already stuck in enough crap. I can't imagine telling her how good his lips tasted on mine.

At some point, she stops interrogating me and throws a blanket over me as I'm lying on her couch. I pass out and sleep like the dead until my phone screams me awake in late morning.

"Claire, it's Mom. Just making sure we're still on for lunch?"

Of course we are. The universe has decided to make me pay for last night.

I inwardly groan, wishing I could pass out for a few more hours. I'm alone in Dana's place. My friend went out shopping and left me an extra key to lock up if I decide to leave, as the note on the counter says.

"Yes, mom. I'll be there."

"Oh, good!" her high, almost sing-song voice makes my ears ring. "Don't be late. I've got some *huge* news to tell you."

Huge? As if *big* isn't enough? I hope to God she isn't going to say she's launching her Senate run early. I can't deal with the stress of that, especially the media storm it'll bring, when my first summer as a real adult has barely started.

"Honey, what's wrong?" Mom pauses, oh-so-concerned.

I'm surprised she can't smell the vodka through the phone.

"Late night with Dana. Nothing to worry about. I'm just shaking off all the fun."

"*Claaaire.*" She clucks her tongue in that haughty, disapproving way she's always done. "You need to start taking better care of yourself. You're out of college now. When I was your age, I was struggling just to keep my head above water. I didn't have time for all night drunken —"

Blah, blah. Fuck you. And blah.

Shaking my head, I slam my phone at the edge of the sink and wash up, listening to her lecture me about all the thrills and dangers of being a young woman. I want to cut the speaker phone, or else drown the fucking thing in the sink.

"Mom, I know. I hear you. Let's not talk about this, okay? I really want to have lunch and figure out the ride back to Tacoma. I haven't seen you for a while, and I actually want to. I just don't want you treating me like a total idiot."

"Yes, Tacoma..." She trails off oddly, and I don't really understand why.

Maybe admitting she actually counts freezes her cold in her tracks. Mom and I haven't really been close since I was a teenager. Her last couple terms in Congress were a blur. There wasn't much hanging out with her staying in DC half the year while I was stuck here for school.

Then when she left the US House and came home, she was always busy with something, and I can't say the desire to reconnect has been crazy pressing until now.

"All right. You know I'm only hard on you because I love you."

"I know. So, Carbonari's at one?"

"No, no. I thought we'd try something new. There's this great new wine bar a little north of the city."

She gives me the name and I almost fall over. It's a budget buster for me, and way beyond anything my frugal-minded mom normally indulges too.

Damn, now I really know she's contemplating that early Senate campaign. She's going to bribe me to soften the blow.

"Okay, I'll be there. Uh, you're paying, right?"

I exhale relief when she says yes, because I'd be going home hungry if she wasn't. It's a miracle I'm not ass deep in loans like my friends, but hitting the classes hard hasn't left me much time to work, and my bank account looks really pale.

Slipping out of Dana's apartment, I lock up and slide the key back underneath the door. Then I'm in my car, struggling for oversized shades to blot out the blinding sun.

My eyes don't want to let go of what happened last night. They're throbbing like mad, making me re-live all the stupid memories at Club Zing. My mind won't get off him the whole way to the wine bar.

I can't believe I kissed a total asshole. And I *definitely* can't believe I let him put his hands all over me, however brief. Jesus, what would've happened if I'd been so fucking drunk I said *yes* to Ty's gross advances?

Shaking my head makes my eyes feel better, so I'm practically swaying to the music buzzing out my radio the whole trip. Last night needs to be my last big drinking binge ever. A tall order, I know, because right now a glass or two of wine sounds awfully good, if only to take the edge off.

The place is even fancier than I thought. If it's not the Senate campaign, I wonder if she hit big in Vegas. Mom was gone there for a whole month up until my graduation. She's a gambler by nature, which I guess is what makes politics so appealing.

I can't say I'm immune to the same adrenaline rush – and certainly not to finer things. When I walk into the place, it's heavenly. The light potpourri of high-end wines blends with well-cooked steaks and starters. My stomach growls something fierce, reminding me I haven't eaten since a quick dinner last night, before meeting up with Dana.

"Honey! There you are!"

I turn toward Mom's voice and see her sitting in a stylish tall booth. And – what the hell? – she's not alone.

I can't get a good look at the guy next to her until I slide into the free seat. When I do, he looks vaguely familiar, but my brain can't place him. He's about her age, broad shouldered and generally well built with just a hint of a gut. His face is nice, except he's rocking some thick ass glasses that make him look like my Chem 101 professor.

"Claire, this is –"

"Gary Sterner." He smiles, jabs his hand toward me. I take it, and he gives me a powerful shake. "I sincerely hope this isn't too rattling for you. Your mother assured me this would be the best way to make an introduction, so...here I am!"

I can tell by the way he's talking that this guy is a blend of distinguished rich guy and slightly awkward nerd. My stomach starts to tighten up when I think about why the hell's he's here at all.

"Don't tell me...this is your new campaign manager?" I blurt it out and guzzle water. Jesus, my throat's so dry from last night.

I just want to get this disaster over with, and find out how royally fucked our family's going to be for the next year.

Mom laughs, loud and a little childish. She gives my question a big fat no by wrapping her arms tight around the rich geek's neck – way closer than anything that would be professional or platonic.

I frown. Mom hasn't dated in ages. Hell, being a strong single woman who survived after being left by the anonymous deadbeat who made me was always a big part of her election narrative.

"No, honey. Gary's much more special than that." She pauses and looks at him. Talk about puppy love. "I...I don't know how else to say this..."

Holy shit. I'm sitting up so straight my spine hurts. Mom's never at a loss for words.

"Claire, your mother's a married woman now," Gary

finishes for her. "I know it's sudden —"

"So sudden!" Mom squeals, squeezing his arm with her hands. "We didn't want to make a big spectacle. Gary's got way more cameras to worry about than I do. Claire, I cut my trip to Vegas short for this. As soon as he proposed, we headed up to Alaska on his jet. Had ourselves a small, private ceremony in Denali Park. It wasn't even a ceremony, really — just us and a priest, maybe a few grizzlies roaming around behind us. It was beautiful."

No joke, I can feel my heartbeat in my eyeballs. It's like they're about to explode. I grab my water and swallow the whole thing, tipping the glass up high so it blocks my view of them.

"Claire, honey? Are you okay?"

I don't answer until my cup empties. The glass bangs the table hard when I set it down. I shake my head for like the hundredth time today.

"I'm...Jesus Christ, Mom! Married? I didn't even know you were seeing anyone!"

She frowns. It pains my heart to see the big smile melting like that.

Fuck. I don't like it, but I can't bring myself to totally ruin this special moment. I reach past Gary's hairy arm and pinch Mom's.

"It's okay. I'll get over it. It's just going to take some getting used to, that's all." I try to be reassuring.

Gary clears his throat. "Yes, well, I apologize again for dropping this on you without any formal notice. It was a whirlwind, Claire. One thing I'm never going to be sorry for is putting a ring on this little lady's finger. I hope you understand — we're really in love. I'm going to take the very best care of your mother."

They lean in and kiss. There's that stupid head shake again. My prim, upbeat, and always guarded mother is acting like a goddamned teenager. It's seriously freaking me out.

I lift my hand and summon the waiter over for more water while the two love birds are at it. Mom doesn't even look up while I order a glass of good Malbec and another pitcher. Like, an entire pitcher of water, just for me.

"I don't get it," I say, stopping until they're both looking at me again. "Gary, you mentioned something about media? Jesus, I thought this whole thing was about my mom's Senate campaign."

Mom smiles and pushes a finger to her lips. "That's our little secret, baby. And it's one I'm not ready for quite yet myself."

Gary looks at her and winks. "Come on, Mandy. I think I know all about your ambitions, and I'm right behind you all the way. You're going to make us all proud."

Mandy — fucking Mandy? Is he serious? Nobody's called my mom anything besides Amanda or Miss Frost or Representative for as long as I can remember!

"Gary!" Mom clucks her tongue.

"Just teasing, dear, I'm sure that decision's a few years off. Your mother was talking about my own little paparazzi issues, Claire," Gary says as I start massaging my temples. "Since 1997, I've been the founder and CEO of —"

"Spree," I cut in. "Fucking Spree. Of course."

Mom gives me a stern look at my language. Whatever. It's just as well because my wine shows up along with two other glasses they must've ordered before I arrived. Perfect distraction.

"We've been using your site since I was a kid," I continue. "God. Your company's a household name. That must mean you're loaded, right?"

Mom's mouth drops open. Gary laughs and clinks his glass gently against hers, giving the sparkly champagne inside it a swirl. "It's okay, Mandy. The girl deserves some slack. It's not every day your mother marries a billionaire online mogul without warning."

Christ. He can say that again. I have to stop and drink half my Malbec before I'm able to speak again.

"So, how long have you guys been dating?"

"It's been – what? – seven or eight months?" Mom looks at Gary and smiles. "We actually met at the big industry dinner in DC about a year ago. Gary came to me personally for some help moving things forward in Washington. I was on my way out and happy to take some risk with his drive to grow Spree because it meant more jobs and more revenue. One thing led to another and...well, here we are today."

Yeah, here we are. Just where the hell is *here*?

I can't place myself in this reality anymore after they both set off this bombshell in my face. What's really insane is how sure and lovey-dovey they seem. At first, I thought it might be a marriage of convenience, something

27

old people with years in business and government do. America doesn't have blue bloods, but it definitely has aristocrats.

And yet, the man sitting across from me with his brilliant features and graying hair is a *much* different kind of royalty than anything we've ever been. A Congresswoman's salary doesn't mean insta-millionaire, especially when she's not taking kickbacks. Mom stayed fairly clean for a politician.

Her new hubby, on the other hand, is a billionaire. Billion with a capital B. I can't fathom it, but I'm going to have to try.

This is the new normal, isn't it?

"Claire, are you sure you're okay?" Gary's tone is almost fatherly.

Holy shit. Fatherly. That's right – he's officially my new step-*father*, something that didn't hit me in the face until now. Staring at the huge diamonds on Mom's finger helps drive it home too when she turns her hand and they catch the light.

"I'm fine. I'll be okay, I mean. It's just a lot to take in after a long night out."

"Of course it is, honey. Don't worry. We'll all mull this over at a big family dinner soon enough. I just wanted to give you a chance to find out in a nice, relaxed atmosphere."

Ha ha, Mom's so funny today. The way my heart's beating, I'm not sure I'll ever be able to relax again. I look at Gary, narrowing my eyes.

"So, what's your story? I hope Mom isn't like your fourth wife? Have you been married before, Gary?"

Another scolding look from Mom. I feel kinda bad, but there's no fucking way I can be polite. Not when my whole world keeps crashing to smithereens. My brain racing a trillion miles an hour strips away the mind-to-mouth filter. Naturally, that makes me think of the asshole and his smothering kiss last night.

Gary laughs, patting my mom's hand. "It's okay, Mandy. Really. I like curiosity. Claire, you'll be pleased to know your mother's only the second woman I've ever called my wife. And I intend to make sure she's the last."

I raise an eyebrow, breathing an inward sigh of relief as more water shows up. I pour it and start sucking it down. My body needs it, plus it might just keep the nuclear reactions inside me from going off.

"What happened to number one?" I ask in between sips.

"Skiing accident. It was terrible. I still think about those times – where does it all go?" Gary shakes his head. Finally, someone else's turn to do it. "I was a young man with a startup and a five year old son in those days. There wasn't time to mourn. The only saving grace is I wasn't such a popular guy then – the media left my family alone. I wasn't on their radar yet. It was up to me to raise my son alone while I built my company. I'm pleased to say it all worked out. Mostly, anyway."

I nod. Okay, maybe Gary's not such a weirdo with a silver spoon hanging out of his mouth after all. I gnaw on some bread while they make goo-goo eyes at each other again.

Shit. I hope the spark wears off at some point like all relationships. It's going to be a *long* fucking summer if I have to see this all the time.

Munching isn't helping my stomach much. I have to really focus on drinking my water and trying to remember what Dana taught me about meditation from her yoga classes to keep from spitting wine up all over the table.

"Honey, you're *sure* you're okay?" Mom gives me the look of death, demanding I tell her the truth.

"I think I need to rest. Let my brain recuperate after it's been blown right out my ears. I hope you don't mind if I cut this a little short. I just want to go home."

Gary laughs and looks at me. "You're perfectly welcome to join us at our new home, Claire."

New home? Oh, shit. I hadn't even considered that, but it does make a scary kinda sense.

Mom nods. "It's way better than our old condo. I think you'll like the house – Gary had his maid set up a room for you, Claire. You'll find everything you need there, and if anything's missing, just shout. I'll be putting the old place in Tacoma on the market soon too – it's peak buying season, after all."

I throw down my napkin and stand up. I really want to whip it right at them and scream until every wine glass in this fucking restaurant breaks.

It's one thing to have my whole world turned upside down, but now they're telling me the only thing I can really count on – *home* – is somewhere else?

"Don't worry about driving. We'll take care of your car," Gary says. "I already told my driver to wait for you out front. I figured you'd need a little time to be alone and get settled in. You'll find my place in Bellingham very comfortable, Claire. My chauffeur will have you home and be back here to pick us up in no time."

Jesus. Bellingham's like an hour north on a good day. They must be planning to sit here for a good long while and drink, maybe make out or something nasty I definitely don't want to see

I do the only thing I can in this situation. I plaster on my biggest, fakest grin and shake Gary's hand.

"That actually sounds good right now. Are you sure you'll be okay getting my stuff home? Everything I brought off campus is in the trunk."

Mom beams – probably relieved I'm making a graceful exit instead of an explosive one. "Of course! We'll take care of everything, baby. Gary's a good man. When he proposed, I told him you're my number one. Our marriage doesn't change that."

"And I told her I want the whole enchilada," Gary says, reaching for my hand. "Mandy's family is mine now, Claire. I know it's going to take some time, but give me a few months, and you'll see I'm right. I always am."

I give him one more weak smile and get the hell away before I'm drowned in their affection or the billionaire's arrogance. True to his word, there's a sleek black sedan waiting out front with a neat looking driver, who gets out and opens the door for me as soon as he sees me coming.

31

My only regret as I slip into the car is that I didn't have more water, and more wine.

One thing's for sure – Mom and new Step-dad aren't bullshitting about the size of the house. When the car rolls through a gate that's like twice as tall as I am, I know I'm in trouble.

There's a guard shack. An honest-to-God security checkpoint just for billionaire Gary, and I guess that includes Mom and me too.

The man in the guard shack smiles and waves us through, just as friendly and perfectly behaved as the driver. The place looks like a modern castle sitting on the coast. Powerful waves churn just over the hills, and I see one of the cleanest Washington beaches ever below.

On the other side, it's flanked by the most blinding, beautiful green the Pacific Northwest has to offer. The incredible foliage hanging around the house reminds me all our rain has its advantages.

"Miss Frost," the driver says, almost like he's about to salute me when we pull up. I step out through the door he's holding, gawking at the monstrous palace for a good thirty seconds.

Then my stomach twists again, and I'm forced to move, if only to get inside and use the bathroom.

The key Gary gave me works. It's a card, just like at a hotel, and apparently there's an app to let your phone unlock the door too. I wouldn't expect anything less from a tech mogul.

Luckily, there's a bathroom nearby. It has about all the fine finishes I expect. I do my business, wash up, and run cold water over my face. What little I've seen of the house so far makes me feel like I need to purify myself just to be here.

When I step out in the hall, the first thing I hear are footsteps. Thinking I'm alone, I jump. But that's stupid, I tell myself. I already know Gary has a housekeeper and who the hell knows what else – and I'd better get used to it awfully fast since this is my new home now.

He also mentioned a son...and didn't really say much else about him. Is he living here too?

I head down a long hall with these awesome murals, hoping it brings me to the kitchen. It does. The massive refrigerator has a whole shelf filled with drinks – mineral water, fancy juices, kombucha, and some other tasty looking imports I've never seen before. It all looks good, but I know I need more water.

Always more. My stomach won't forgive me until I've replenished everything the last two days have drained from my system.

I head through the other opening in the kitchen, ready to explore at least this little part of the mansion. There's a dining room, and then a hallway leading to what looks like an awesome living room. There's leather furniture, the biggest glass windows with a perfect view of the ocean, and –

Oh, hell. There's a young man standing right in the middle of the room, dripping wet from a workout, shirtless. He's ripped and tattooed as all hell. It looks like he's just come in from a run, or maybe using the gym — wherever that is.

I set my drink down on the nearby counter nervously and hold my hand up to wave. If he's Gary's son, I never thought I'd be meeting him like this. I hope it's not too awkward.

Only one way to find out.

"Hi, there. I'm Claire."

The boy turns around. His piercing blue eyes dart right through me like a bullet to the head.

"Fucking shit," Ty says, breaking into a princely smile.

Fucking shit is right. I barely have time to reach out and catch myself next to my drink before I go crashing to the floor.

II: Little Miss Perfect (Ty)

I can't believe this chick's standing in my living room.
It's living proof that there's a god in heaven, and
apparently he wants me to fuck this girl right through the
floor. Nothing else explains why the only woman who ever
said no to me in my own club is here, looking at me like I
just stepped off a UFO.

I'm about to give her some serious shit for walking in on
me like this, but her knees are shaking. I know a woman
who's fainting when I see her. Our poor housekeeper,
Joan, used to have the same damned problem before she
got her insulin under control.

I rush over just in time before she crashes on Dad's
Turkish rug. I gotta suppress a smile as I catch her. She
feels too fucking good against my almost naked body.
Obviously, I don't wanna upset Little Miss Perfect
anymore while she's reeling, but fuck, I've already done
that just by standing here.

She's comatose in my arms. Not exactly how I wanted
to feel those sweet curves against me again, but what-the-
hell-ever. I reach for the mineral water next to her,
unscrew the cap, and splash it right in her face.

That wakes her up.

"What the hell do you think you're doing?!" She screams, batting me away.

When I'm sure she's able to stand on her own two feet again, I let go, and give her the space she's flipping her shit over. "Making sure you don't bruise your pretty face on the damned floor. It's harder than it looks, even with the rugs. Trust me, I've slipped on my ass here before."

Watching her face, it's like a fuse in slow burn. When it hits the charge, I see the explosion in her eyes, the horrible realization about who I am and why I'm standing in front of her.

Believe me, it's a disaster for my sorry ass too. I knew dad remarried some former Congress queen, and I'm supposed to meet the new family soon. I knew the woman had a daughter.

But I didn't expect it to be this delectable piece of ass that got away from me last night. Having a step-sister this hot introduces me to some sick torture I'm just starting to comprehend.

Fuck me. Maybe it's not a miracle she's in my house after all. Maybe it's a devil's curse – Old Scratch come to collect my karmic debt for all the girls I've fucked and walked away from.

"Sterner. *Sterner.*" She repeats my last name over and over, stretching a hand across her face like her skin's boiling. "Jesus Christ. How could I be so stupid? Why didn't I put it together until now?"

I smile, shrug, and mimic her gesture. There's still a lotta sweat dripping all over me after my workout downstairs.

Training always leaves me beat and damp when I do it right, and this chick's the reason I hit it extra fucking hard this evening.

"Why the fuck didn't you tell me your name last night? I was trying to help, you know. We could've avoided this embarrassment."

"You were trying to fuck me!" she screams, getting up in my face.

Those sweet tits beneath her shirt plump up and bounce real nice. She looks good enough to slam against the wall and devour with my hands, my mouth, my dick, no matter what she's wearing. And that's rare, especially when I've been on a strict diet of club girls who just wanna suck me off because I'm hung and rich.

And in the cold light of day, some of those chicks are a lot less fuckable.

Not the one in front of me, cursing my name, though. It's not even possible. She's hot twenty-four-seven, morning or night, rain or shine. My dick twitches, thinking about all the shit it wants to do to her in all those conditions.

Claire. I burn her name into my memory, wondering why the hell it's landed in my lap when I tried so hard to squeeze it outta her at the club.

She's shaking her chestnut hair, blinking those big brown eyes to match, the same way I've seen her do like ten times by now. "I can't believe this."

I step up and extend a hand, trying to give her a proper handshake. She slowly takes it and looks sick, but of course I'm not gonna let her off that easy.

"I know, babe. I can't believe we're never gonna fuck. Somebody's got a sick sense of humor to bring our parents together. That's for damned sure. Can you believe your new step-brother's a badass motherfucker, *Sis*?" I flex my muscles and rub myself against her.

She jumps back like I'm on fire. I can't help but laugh. Humor's all I've got to take the crazy fucking edge off — not that it helps much when I feel how hard her nipples are.

"Don't you dare call me that!" Claire purses her lips and wags a finger. "Jesus. Are you always so crude?"

I turn around and shrug, crossing the room for the Gatorade I left sitting by the window. "Maybe, if you're a fucking prude all the time. Shit, I was hoping you'd lighten up and come alive outside the club. Guess you carry that stick up your ass wherever you go, huh?"

Her eyeball twitches. The girl looks like she's gonna explode.

"You're...you're..." It's cute. She's really at a loss for words.

Go ahead and say it. Yeah, I'm a rat bastard, and I'm easily entertained too. I'm pushing her to her fucking limits and loving every second.

I stand behind the sofa, hiding the savage wood I've got popping in my shorts. It wants inside her like a battering ram. My dick's dumb — it can't comprehend there's a major taboo blocking us from getting down and dirty. Or maybe I'm the idiot for just now seeing a few more fireworks when I think about holding her down and slamming my cock as deep as it'll go.

Step-sis or not, there's no damned way I'm letting her see how much she turns me on. This attraction's just a game as long as she's in this house, and I'm the one in control.

"Well, spit it out. I'm what, babe? The biggest swinging dick who ever crashed into your life?"

Fuck it. I wanna set her off. I step past the couch sporting my massive boner, but she's too pissed to look below the waist.

"I was going to say the biggest piece of shit I've ever met." The words come out like she's foaming at the mouth.

"Well, we're in the cesspool together now. Better get used to it," I tell her. I've had my fun, and now it's time to diffuse the situation before she bolts the fuck outta here and never comes back. "Tell you what, Claire, you forget about the last two brushes we've had and I'll do the same overnight. I'll give Dad the cozy little family breakfast he wants tomorrow morning. You'll settle in and do the same."

"I'm not listening to *your* suggestions," she snaps. "I'll do whatever I want."

I shrug long and hard. Not just to brush her the fuck off, but because it feels damned good after a heavy workout.

"Your funeral. I'm just trying to make the most of a shitty situation, and I'm not hearing any good ideas from you."

"Shitty situation!?" She screams, balling her little fists at her sides, shaking them like rattlers. "Stay the hell away from me. I don't care what's going on between our parents, Ty. Let me make this loud and clear, right now – I'll *never* be family to you. I don't even want to your friend. We've spent all of half an hour together, and you're the last guy I ever want to deal with."

"Cool." She blinks in surprise as I take a long pull from the blue juice in my bottle. "No, really. You're bitchy. Direct. Honest. I like that. I'm not much for bullshit. I threw my cards on the table, and so did you. Now that we've got that shit outta the way, we can figure out how we're gonna live under the same roof without driving each other absolutely fucking loco."

"Argh!" She punches the air one time with both her hands and turns.

She's had it with my shit, and I'm not real inclined to deal with her either. Seeing her flip her back and give me a nice view of that hot little ass as she stomps away feels a helluva lot better than more talk anyway.

I follow her, keeping my distance, watching as she stops by the main entrance and freezes. I wanna bust another gut, laugh in her perfect face, but I don't. I stand there and wait, feeling the sweat drying on my body.

With a heavy sigh, she spins, knowing I'm there. "Are you going to point the way to my room, or do I have to figure it out myself?"

I stick my thumb out. "Down one floor. You'll see a big

door for the laundry room. That's where you wanna turn, and then go all the way around the corner to the next hall. You've got the one with the purple walls and the beach view, right next to mine."

"Huh? We're neighbors? In this huge of a house?" She croaks, and I half expect to see her wither right in front of me. "Jesus Christ."

Surprisingly, she takes it in stride, and I watch her sashay angrily down the steps. She pulls open the door to the lower floor and her footsteps are softer, fading 'til it's hard to believe she was really right in front of me at all.

I don't follow her down there to my room because I've got to shower and wrap up some other shit.

It's a little too warm in the house. I need to find Joan to make sure the temperature controls are set just right. This place is so fucking big it always takes an adjustment or two when the seasons are shifting.

For the first time this year, I'm actually looking forward to summer. Having Claire behind my wall's gonna make it a lot more interesting.

The next day, I'm the first one in the dining room. Don't have a damned clue what time our parents got home.

Shit, *parents*. Plural.

It's been so fucking long since I've thought about that word. It's alien to everything I know. And whatever the hell happens, the prissy Congresswoman Dad married for reasons I'll never understand will never be my ma.

She died skiing on the slopes outside Olympia before I

barely knew her. There's never been anybody but Dad, busy CEO and father-of-the-year. Or at least that's the way he presents himself to the smiling reporters.

The real Gary Sterner raised me. I respect him the way a peasant pays respect to a hard ass tyrant.

Whatever. It's his right, I guess, and it's not his new lady's fault that she saw something in my old man. I swear I'm not gonna give her too much shit as I wash up and head down to the dining room.

I've got Claire for taking the brunt, after all. And you'd better believe I want to give her a whole lot more than total crap. I want to give her everything I got, hard and deep and raw. I want to fuck her breathless, fuck her 'til she's biting my shoulder, slam into her tight wet cunt 'til my dick's so numb I can't even feel it.

I stop and lean on the staircase's banister for a moment. Gotta collect myself. This thinking's dangerous, and I know it.

Wish I could figure out what the hell it is about this chick that keeps lighting me on fire. Every time we're in the same room, it's like there's a storm building underneath my skin, thunderheads so fierce and primal I'd be scared if it didn't make me tingle so damned good.

Love at first sight? Fuck no.

I don't believe in that shit. Lust at first sight, on the other hand, just might have some serious truth behind it.

My lungs pulse relief when I get downstairs and see she's not there yet. It's just Dad, sitting on his throne at the head of the table like he always does, and a dark haired lady at his side I can only assume is Amanda Frost.

No, Amanda Sterner. My new step-mom. Shit.

"Tyler!" She stands up when I come in like I'm the damned President or something. I wonder if it's the same way she bolted up at the State of the Union speeches back in DC. "We've been waiting for you kids. It's so good to finally meet you!"

She puts her hand out. Dad's watching me like an eagle about to swoop in on its kill.

I skip the handshake and give her a hug. She clings to me tight, pleasantly surprised by the gesture. I hope like hell my father's just as pleased — maybe he'll lay the fuck off and cut me some slack. It's gonna be hard as hell behaving myself with Little Miss Perfect due any time.

"Pleasure," I say. "How was Denali?"

"Ty, why don't you sit down and grab a plate?" Dad cuts in, before she can answer my question. "We don't need to stand around gabbing like rednecks when we've got this wonderful spread. Have you seen Claire?"

"I met her yesterday," I tell him, dropping into my seat. "She was tired. Seems like meeting you was a lot for her to take in."

His lips twitch. I smile, wondering who the fuck's really bottling shit up the most and practicing their best behavior. Not just me, apparently.

"Oh, I should've gone down myself to check on her," Amanda says. "Maybe I should anyway, just to make sure..."

She starts to get up, but Dad lays a protective hand over

hers. "Nonsense, Mandy. I'll send Joan to give her a wakeup call. I don't blame the poor girl for sleeping in. She's been under a lot of pressure."

Dad's about to tap the button for the intercom on the wall behind him to call our housekeeper, when Claire comes trotting in. She looks neater today. She's wearing some fresh shit her mom must've picked out and stashed in her room.

It's a nice white summer dress. I'll be fucked if it doesn't make her tits look like heaping scoops of vanilla ice cream. My dick's been reasonably well behaved this morning 'til now.

I'm fucked the minute I take a good long look. It instantly pops up and starts straining in my pants, giving me the mad desire to carry her outta the dining room, find a quiet spot to throw her on the floor, and bury my face between those perfect fucking globes while I piston between her legs.

"Claire!" Amanda jumps up again, beaming. "I'm so glad everybody's finally in the same place. Sit, sit. The food's nice and hot."

Nothing like a hot breakfast to smooth things over. I stack my plate high with pancakes, sausage, and extra scrambled eggs, watching Claire sitting across from me. She gingerly picks a few pieces of cantaloupe and slaps them onto her plate before she finally meets my eyes.

Brave girl. Sexy girl. Woman I can't resist.

"You always eat like a bird, or is it just the summer heat?" I stuff a bite into my mouth and point my fork at her.

"I'm still getting over my stomach trouble yesterday. Just having something light."

"Ty." Dad's evil eye twitches.

"He's right, honey," Amanda cuts in. "You really should have a little protein. I imagine you know a thing or two about eating healthy, Tyler."

"Ty. We don't do that Tyler shit around here." I tell her, soon as she looks at me. "Yeah, I try to keep it lean and healthy when I'm training. Other days, a guy's gotta eat. It's the best season for it, after all. Love my protein."

"Training?" Claire speaks her first word of the day to me, cautious and questioning. "What do you play?"

"I'm into this underground MMA shit. Nothing like getting up close and personal with some psycho fighter to test your strength. It's good for this body and great for my charity. My club hosts matches sometimes, with most of the proceeds going to a good causes."

"Good causes," Dad growls, stabbing at his food. "I think a better cause would be focusing on expanding your business, son. Do you realize how much more you'd be able to raise for folks in need if you made Club Zing a franchise?"

We lock eyes. It's the same goddamned shit we've been through before. On the surface, Dad wants me to make something of myself, become my own self-made millionaire so I'm not forever in his shadow.

But I know at the root it's the same bullshit. He wanted the perfect son. He thought he could raise one part-time, fill the gap left by ma's death with endless maids and tutors.

Obviously, it didn't fucking work.

He got me instead.

Drinker. Playboy. Fighter.

Not his little prince, hanging on his every word and jonesing at the chance to take over his multi-billion dollar empire.

I don't hide what I am. I get down and dirty in the ring when I'm not fucking some slut's brains out in the nearest room. Got no apologies about it neither – I've busted a few teeth and blooded noses in my time. I've left bruises on my opponents so hard they'll be feeling them for weeks. And I've taken my share of pain too.

Yeah, it's fucked up, but I'm not gonna stop. The bastard across the table can't make me with his guilt trip and fatherly glare, and neither will these two freaks joining the family. No, make that one tight wound freak and her *very* fuckable daughter.

"I know I'd raise a lot, and probably turn into a flabby old fucker too. Not interested, Dad. I'm planning to live a good long life and stay fit. Work hard, play hard. Don't tell me you wanna have this argument again?"

I watch his fingers writhe as he grabs his coffee and brings it to his lips. If we were alone, the cup would be half-depleted by now, losing half its shit on the table when he slams it down like a stone. I'd be grabbing my plate and running off to my room, leaving his sorry ass screaming after me, pouring out all the impotent rage I set off in his skull.

"I don't want any arguments today, Ty," he says, stuffing his emotions. "I wouldn't dream of ruining our first family breakfast together. We'll just have to agree to disagree."

Amanda plasters a big grin on her face. Yeah, she's a tough old bird, but she's got some of her girl's looks too. She must've been quite a number back when she was Claire's age.

"So, how about the Denali wedding? You got any pictures, or was it all just done on the fly?" I'm really pushing my old man's self-control.

He shoots us the biggest, fakest smile I've ever seen. "Only a few. You'll all see them later. Truth be told, we couldn't contain ourselves. There wasn't much time for a proper photographer. When Mandy said yes, it was right off to the park. We had to get it done."

"And it was perfect." Mandy slides her hand into my dad's.

Claire looks at me, an eyebrow raised, while they kiss. Little Miss Perfect and me are on the same side here – grossed out and seriously suspicious.

I can't figure out what the fuck's going on. Nothing about the insta-wedding computes. I want to believe the Congress queen's tapped some unseen, softer side of my dad that's been dead since I was a kid, but I'm not gonna fall for it yet.

"So, Amanda, tell us what it's like being in the belly of the beast," I say, changing the subject. "Is Congress really the clusterfuck we see all the time on TV?"

She blinks. Claire stifles a laugh. Dad looks at me like I've just moved up on his shit list.

"Ty, don't be rude."

"What? Don't say you're gonna blame me for taking a sudden interest in politics." I look around the table with the same bullshit look that used to drive my teachers crazy in high school.

Amanda shakes her head vigorously – another thing she's got in common with daughter dearest. "Trust me, I get it all the time. It's inevitable when you've served three long terms and survived the campaign trail. If I didn't have a thick skin by now, I'd be nothing but bones."

Her eyes flash bright and she flicks her hair back. "Honestly, Ty, the game we're playing isn't so different. I'm sure you understand after growing up with a powerful businessman for a father. Heck, you're managing a club yourself. You understand compromise, work, and good old fashioned 'getting things done.'"

I snort. "Wasn't that one of your campaign slogans?"

"Very good, young man. Looks like you're as smart and attentive as your father." She watches me shrug.

The weird compliment rolls off my back. Fuck, how hard is it to watch the news? It's not like there aren't a billion bullshit ads every two years while assholes are out politicking.

"You're on your way like my Claire. I'm so glad neither of the kids in this family are drunk on the youthful idealism that trips up so many young people."

"Mom..." Claire waits 'til she's got her mother's

attention. "You're being a little cynical, don't you think?"

"I think she's a realist. That's fine and fucking dandy by me."

Little Miss Perfect flips her face toward me and gives me a glare that says *I didn't ask you, asshole.* I don't even look at Dad because I know he's on his last warning stare right now.

"Come on. Don't let my language shock you, sis," I tease. "Surely, your ma's heard some serious shit talk on the campaign trail and up on the Hill. How many reps does New York send to Congress? Those fuckers alone talk like animals."

"God damn it, Ty!" Dad's fist hits the table, and everybody jumps. "One morning. That's all I asked for."

He wipes his brow and turns to his new wife. "I'm very sorry, Mandy. I warned you about my son. My biggest regret is never being able to get his potty-mouth under control. I'm sure the dirt goes straight to his head too. It's a shame I neglected to shove some soap in his mouth when he was little."

Amanda sniffs and smiles politely, like she's at a loss for words. Dad lingers a moment longer, then rips himself up off his seat, and goes stomping toward the stairs. He learned a long time ago that sending me to my room doesn't do shit – and it's not even an option since I hit my twenties.

"I'm afraid Claire isn't the only one who's been under some stress lately. This marriage is such a *huge* shift for everyone. I'd better go check on him." Amanda's chair scrapes the floor, and she stands up on her heels.

Well, at least she's not looking at me like I just took a dump on the table. Neither is Claire, surprisingly. The chick looks totally stunned, almost sympathetic.

I should be happy someone else finally sees my father for the jackass he is, but it doesn't matter. Her tight, twitchy little lips wrapped around my cock are all I can see when she looks at me like that.

"Hey, I'm so sorry to cut this short. It's wonderful to meet you, Ty. I'm sure we'll all get to know each other better once everything calms down. We've got the whole summer." Amanda nods apologetically, and then she's off like a bullet.

The woman catches herself before she crashes into Joan, who's come to clear the plates. The old maid gives me a sassy look. I'm lucky she finds my shit amusing and doesn't think I'm a total devil. She's the closest thing I've had to a mother since my real one died.

"I'm so sorry!" Amanda barks, steadying herself on the wall so she doesn't topple over on those tall black heels. "Kind of in a rush."

"No need to apologize, madam," Joan says, clearing a path for her.

"Oh, that reminds me – you kids both have the day off, don't you? Why don't you take some time to get to know each other? It's beautiful out there!"

I follow her smile to the window behind Dad's empty spot. She's right – it's really a gorgeous summer day. Blue skies, not a cloud in sight, the ocean rolling, stabbing a thousand middle fingers at the heavens.

Amanda trots off and heads upstairs. Claire and I are alone and quiet for about a minute, just listening to Joan hum gospel to herself while she clears the plates, loading them onto the nearby cart.

Damn do I love that woman and her music, even if I've never been the religious type. I let Joan's soft hymns float over me and don't dare look at Claire again 'til she's done. Even I have limits for how fucking awkward it would be to have my cock at full mast while I'm listening to the soft, sweet stuff that used to lull me to sleep.

"Well? What do you say, *Sis?*" I emphasize the word, loving the way her eyes spark with anger when she hears it. "How 'bout a little family bonding time?"

"No way." Claire's cheeks go red.

She's pissed off, embarrassed, confused. I can't blame her, but I sure hate having my ass turned down. I'm not used to no, and it sits about as well with me as a punch to the jaw.

Her chair screeches on the floor just like her mom's, and then she's up, taking her glass of orange juice with her.

"You're crazy if you think this breakfast changes anything. After seeing your dad blow up, I can kind of see where your crap comes from, Ty. I feel bad for you." She lowers her voice. "But let's just get this clear – there's *no fucking way* I want to spend any time with you. Certainly not alone. I saw what you're like at the club. You're a drunken, crazy, womanizing *creep.*"

Fucking shit. It stings more than I expect, lights a spark

I haven't felt since I was a goddamned gawky teenager asking out a senior chick to prom my sophomore year. The older girl said no, and she was the last one ever 'til today.

"Okay, Sis. You wanna treat me like a goddamned stalker criminal, then I'll fucking act like one!" I get up in her face for a second, flatten her against the wall as she gasps. "I read you loud and clear. This creep's gonna fuck right off. I thought it'd be nice to sort this shit out, maybe try to find some common ground. But you're absolutely right – we don't fucking need to, and I sure as hell don't need your shitty sympathy. You can shove it up your perfect ass and spend the day alone. I can do the evil eye too, Sis, and that's all you're gonna get from me all summer."

I let go. She blinks, and doesn't move a muscle. Turning sharply, I head into the hall.

I don't even feel bad about scaring the shit outta her for like the third time since we met.

The only thing that makes me burn is my own stupidity. I've been a fucking idiot to think I'll ever feel *anything* for this woman except a blinding urge to fuck her, or else rip her goddamned head off.

There's no common ground between us. There's nothing. The bitch is right – if it doesn't involve my dick pushing in her pussy, then we don't need to explore. We just need to stay the fuck outta each other's way.

III: Calm and Stormy Seas (Claire)

I didn't know whether to scream or slap him. He gets in my face, sad and scorned and angry all at once, and then he's gone in an instant, leaving me hating him more than ever. I also feel like the biggest bitch in history.

Guilt blossoms in my stomach like a heavy, bitter lump. But then I remind myself that Ty's used to getting his women on demand, however he likes. I won't oblige him. I'm not going to play nice when he hasn't given me one good fucking reason to.

I can't pretend. I'm not going to suck up to him and bring myself agonizingly closer to sucking what's probably a magnificent cock between his legs.

Just thinking about how close we've been the last few times makes me blush.

I head downstairs and sit at my laptop, trying to read some stuff my new boss has sent over. It's a nice escape for awhile, but I can't stop looking out the window.

The beautiful day lends a terrible distraction. Right now, I don't want to be reading about how fat cats are wrangling to bring down every inch of Cascadia's pristine wilderness. I want to be out in it, running along the shore, feeling the warm sand flush between my toes. Here in Washington, these are the rare days you're supposed to pluck from the tree, gorge on every golden second that breaks the eternal rainy gloom.

Damn it. I last about an hour, and then I can't take it. I'm going stir crazy.

Slamming my laptop shut, I grab a water bottle and head out to the huge twelve car garage. My rusty shitbox of a car looks as out of place as I feel in this house. It's a decaying tumor wedged between three shiny new Tesla cars. I wonder if they all belong to the billionaire, or if one of them is Ty's.

"Hey, what the fuck?" A gruff voice behind me makes me spin.

Ty's standing there in shorts and a wickedly tight t-shirt, an umbrella tucked underneath one arm, plus a bottle of sun screen. In the other, there's an open bottle of rum. I smell it on him, spicy and infuriating, the rum's natural hues blending with his rough, masculine scent.

"What're you doing out here? You're drunk."

He laughs like it's a joke. "I'm going to the fucking beach. Just like you, sis. Forget the bullshit I said earlier. I'll walk. Maybe we'll meet somewhere up ahead."

My mouth drops. With the way he's slurring his words, he's in no state to do anything, let alone navigate rugged patches of Pacific coast. He's putting me in an impossible position, doing a complete about-face from the venom he hit me with earlier.

So, you're not just an asshole, I think to myself, *but an asshole who likes mind games?*

For the millionth time since meeting Ty Sterner, I have to decide whether to shake my head or whack him across the cheek. Doing both sounds really good right about now.

"You can't go anywhere like this. Put the rum down and go back inside," I snap.

Instead, I just stand there, watching as the arrogant smirk on his lips melts and he turns around.

"Eh, what-the-fuck-ever. I tried, babe. See you on the flip side."

My eyeballs almost pop out as I watch him stagger over to one of the fancy electric cars. He pulls open the door to the shiny white Tesla car and crumples in the driver's seat. The asshole's drunk, but thankfully he's so wasted he can't even find the keys in his pocket. He swears when he realizes he doesn't even have them, and I start to laugh.

"What's so fucking funny?" he growls, stepping out and slamming the door behind him with a bang.

"You're such an irresponsible dumbass, Ty. I almost feel sorry for you. Almost."

"I told you I don't need your sympathy. What I need is a ride to the goddamned beach. Now, you gonna let me chill in your car, or are we gonna waste a perfectly clear Washington evening seeing who can piss the hardest?"

I sink my teeth into my lower lip. He's an asshole and an idiot.

I can't believe I'm about to do this, but leaving him here to roll around drunk or even hurt himself under the influence isn't something I want on my hands. Honestly, he's sad too, pulling on my hearstrings in a lost boy kinda way.

"Fine. Follow me and get in. I swear to God, if you touch anything in my car or lay another hand on me, you're out. I'll pull over and kick you to the curb. I don't care if you have to call up the chauffeur or fucking hitchhike home. You're only my problem as long as you behave yourself."

Grinning, he throws his hands up, gives them a shake, and then pushes them behind his back. "These hands have knocked twenty guys out cold. I know how to control them. You worry too much, Sis. I won't turn a single hair on that sexy brunette head gray."

Rolling my eyes, I get in my car and wait for him to lumber into the passenger seat. It takes a minute to make sure he's got his seat belt on, and then we're off.

Passing through the gate with the guard shack humiliates me just enough to forget about Ty's stupid antics for a second. Amazingly, the guard smiles, whispers a few pleasant words, and reveals nothing. I can't believe he isn't secretly wondering what this peasant girl with the old beater is doing on his billionaire boss' long driveway.

It's a ten minute drive down the sprawling coast. It's almost all part of Gary's estate. I can't believe how many miles of coastline this crazy family owns, but I'm beginning to figure out billions can buy just about anything.

So why can't they buy happiness? Is that old cliche really true?

I keep looking at Ty. I can't figure him out. He's either

an asshole wrapped in an enigma, or an enigma bound up in a total asshole.

He hasn't said a word since we got through the gate. He's staring out at the Pacific's roaring waves, little sailboats lining the distant horizon. The hand on his forehead tells me the rum is finally getting to him.

"Do you always drink like this?" I ask.

He shrugs. "I play hard when I can. Life's short, babe. Got my training in yesterday, and I'm all about relaxing now, especially after that fucked up family sit down this morning. I'd have needed a couple stiff drinks after that shit any day."

He's right about that. I'm feeling so much better just being out of the house.

"Is that why you stormed off this morning? Look, I didn't mean to be such a bitch. But I haven't gotten over what you said –"

He waves a hand. "You will, Sis. I don't say shit I don't mean. We're stuck in this fucking house together. Both of us are cursed to watch while our parents fuck up their lives with this stupid marriage. We can either learn to like it, or lump it all goddamned summer. All I know is, summers here are way too short for sulking. I wanna forget about this bullshit for the rest of the day and soak up some sun. You know I'm right."

Even as a drunken fool, he's too confident. I want to wipe that know-it-all look off his face.

Too bad the asshole's making sense too. Maybe it won't hurt to give him one more chance. He's obviously troubled.

Neither of us asked for this mess. We've been thrown together in the same box like two stray cats. I can't believe Mom didn't consider the tensions I'd have with this stepbrother I never asked for. Then again, it's not her fault I ran into this asshole before I knew he was even family, let him get his lips and hands all over me...

"Hey! Right there!" I'm snapped out of my thoughts by Ty leaning into me and pointing. "That's a perfect fucking spot. There's a little dock and some sweet views, better than the boathouse a couple miles back."

"Okay! You know I'm trying to drive here, right?" I shake him away off me, rolling my shoulders.

I turn onto a little service road and follow it up to the beach. Ty pops his door first and flops out, bouncing onto his feet and running toward the shore.

He's left me in the dust. Once again, I feel like a complete idiot, and then an even bigger one when I'm trying to catch up with him.

"Wait, wait, wait!" I call. He doesn't stop until he's just a small figure up ahead.

I can't decide if he's ignoring me or just unable to hear me over the ocean's roar. Shaking my head, I start to slow down, deciding to admire the beauty instead.

God, this is stupid. Worse than chasing after a loose dog.

It is, and I'm way past caring. If he wants to run right into the shimmering blue waves and let the sea carry him away, it's not my problem.

Oh, except I'll be more than a little liable if anything

happens to this drunken asshole. I doubt my brand new billionaire father with the explosive temper will let it go lightly if I brought his son to the sea to drown.

A couple seagulls squawk overhead. My cue to start running. I have to catch up.

There's plenty of sand between my toes now, but not like I expected. I never got a chance to change into my sandals before the dickhead took off.

Where the fuck is he?

He's disappeared into a long sandy path through some tall brush lining the hills overlooking the beach.

My heart's racing. I'm starting to get seriously freaked out. I follow it for what seems like forever and start to second-guess myself. It's getting narrower and a little more rocky, so I have to slow down, much to the relief of my poor lungs.

I haven't been working out like I should for the last year. I make a mental note to do something about it – assuming I can find this jackass.

He beats me to it. Ty comes up behind me when I'm not looking and tackles me to the ground. I hit the sand with an *oomph* and roll, slapping at his face.

"Asshole! You got us lost!"

He grabs my wrists like they're nothing and pins me to the ground. That brash, rage-inducing smile I'm starting to recognize as his trademark lightens his face.

There's something hard against my leg. It better not be his cock, or I'm going to scream. Mainly because it doesn't freak me out nearly as much as it should.

59

Apparently, my flesh still can't understand that such an amazing body belongs to a complete freak. I *hate* wanting him, and I don't care that it's all on a primal level I can't control. It's too fucking much.

I push against him as hard as I can. He falls backwards and lands on his butt, laughing. There's no way I managed to move him, he's just lost his balance. Lucky me.

"Lost? I come here all the fucking time. This is my spot. Perfect place for drinks too." He reaches into his pocket and fumbles around.

Heat flushes my cheeks when I see it's just another little bottle of rum. For a second, I wondered if it was a condom. He pops the cap and takes a long pull before handing it to me.

"What? Did you think I lured you out here to fuck my own sister?" The look on his face says he knows damned well what I was thinking. "Come on. Have a nip. I can't be a selfish prick if I like to share."

I rip the bottle out of his hands. The sharp stink hits my nostrils like pickle juice. For a rich boy, you'd think he'd be drinking something nicer.

It's disgusting, infuriating, and out of place. Just like him. Damn, just like us.

I wait until his eyes are locked to mine, and then I hold it out, tip it upside down, and empty every drop on the ground.

"Are you fucking kidding me?" His arm shoots out, rips the little bottle out of my hand, and throws it several feet away when he sees it's empty. "You're still treating me like a total asshole!"

"That's because you *are* one," I snarl, crossing my arms. "You scare the utter shit out of me, put your hands where they don't belong, and then you litter this nice beach to top it all off. Seriously, Ty, what the hell am I supposed to think? You're not acting like a Nobel prize winner."

Ty laughs while I'm shaking my head. Slapping him stupid doesn't seem like it'll do the job – I want to fucking punch him right between his gemstone blue eyes.

"I started to think there was another side to you this morning. Your dad treated you like crap at the table. But you're really the same – both of you! You've got his habits. You treat me with the same respect you've got for the rest of the world, I guess. None at all. You obviously don't care about anything around you." I point to the fallen bottle.

The playful smirk on his face melts. Those baby blues turn angry, dark and cold like an iceberg threatening to gut anything that comes too close.

"You can shut your mouth now, babe, 'cause you don't know shit. Come the fuck on, Claire. You think I need a lecture in your hippie enviro-shit? I did a charity fight last winter for conservation. Gave the money to a group that's got a brain in its head just to piss my old man off. You're just about to start interning for a bunch of crazy asshole idealists. You can't tell me you're a true believer in all this group's shit."

No, I'm not true blue. The bastard has me there.

Sure, I want to see the state's natural wonders preserved. I know Cascades Now! has a reputation for extremes.

Mostly, I'm excited because they're going to give me experience and throw a few bucks my way – everything I want out of my first post-college gig.

"Of course not," I hiss. "I don't believe in everything they do any more than you support everything your dad's done with Spree. Or maybe you *do* think it's okay to dump your crap out here when nobody's looking?"

That does it. Ty jumps up, stomps right past me, into the brush. He returns a second later, holding the empty glass flask in one hand.

"You wanna get personal, Sis? I can do that shit, yeah, but I'd rather just fucking go." Without asking, he reaches down, grabs my hand, and jerks me onto my feet.

I follow him down the windy path back toward the beach. The Pacific's churning waves should be a comfort, but it just puts me more on edge. Bright evening sun dances off the waters – too bright. It's reflective, blinding.

The asshole a few steps in front of me is the reason I forgot my sunglasses too.

"Personal?" What the hell are you talking about?"

He doesn't answer me until we stop next to a tall blue canister. He drops the glass bottle into it, and it hits the bottom with a resounding clap. Guess there aren't a lot of visitors on this private land.

He stops and stares at me, his arms folded over his huge chest. Jesus, I can't stop staring at him, even when I'm steaming mad. Ty's got an angel's body – a guardian angel's – and it takes so much effort not to let my eyes glide down him too long.

I shouldn't be so hot and bothered. Okay, maybe *bothered* because he's punched all my wrong buttons. But I know I'm in trouble when he steps up, closing the distance between us, and I can't stop sneaking little glances at his powerful hips.

The shorts he's wearing accent everything. His bare legs are as built and muscular as the rest of him, and I know that hard ass at the top lets him run like the wind.

Does he shake a girl straight down to her bones when he's between her legs, driving deep and hard? Fucking this animal must hurt. Probably in all the best ways I can imagine.

And believe me, my overactive, inexperienced virgin brain is going wild.

Ty stops with less than a couple inches between us. He must've seen me peeking because his eyes are all over me, lingering on my breasts. I'd regret not wearing something a little more conservative if I wasn't busy regretting this whole damned thing.

He reaches out and puts a hand on my shoulder, starts to turn me before I can protest. "Spin, babe. You've got sand all over your ass."

He gets two or three quick strokes down my back and over my butt before I dart away. *Fucker.*

I can't blame him for looking because I was doing the same, but I'm drawing the line at him ever getting his filthy hands on me again. "Don't be a pig."

Ty comes closer, his handsome face cast in arrogance again. "Pig? Let's talk about that shit for a second. You're right about one thing, Claire – my old man's an asshole. You won't hear me arguing otherwise. I always wondered what the fuck caused him to ride my ass so hard. Could never tell if it was just chasing money, or because losing Mom so young fucked him up."

My head tilts and I study his face, wondering where he's going with this. "Maybe you should worry more about the road you're going down, Ty. That's something you can control."

He breaks the gaze and walks right past me. I walk fast, trying to catch up, stepping into his footprints in the sand.

Did I actually hit a sore spot – or is he just waiting to jerk me around again?

"Before today, I thought my old man was one-of-a-kind. Greedy, narcissistic, cut throat. Willing to do anything to take the empire he's built with his bare hands to the next level. I'll never be the perfect son, and it's too fucking late for him to mold me. But he's got the rest of his life to mold Spree into what he wants."

"Why today? What changed?"

"Meeting Amanda. Straight up, your ma's different, lower on the totem pole in some respects. Still, that woman had to pull some seriously sneaky shit to sweet talk my old man into marrying her. She's landed herself a fucking whale for financing future campaigns. Not too shabby for a politico, right? Fuck, you'll go far if you're half as big a snake as mama. Maybe you can find yourself Prince Charming, some dude who's loaded to make it easier for you to stand around and lecture everybody else."

Wow. I come to a dead stop. I'm almost speechless.

Ass. Hole.

When the words come back, they come fast and hot. So do my fists. I fly forward and start hitting him over and over. He grabs me, stops me so easily, grabs my wrists and twists them like I'm a child. It's as infuriating as the laughter pouring out of his evil sexy lips.

"Knock it the fuck off, babe. Throw me a fucking bone and don't play stupid. You're a smart girl. We both know what this marriage's all about. Are you pissed because I opened your eyes, or because I threw something you already knew in your face?"

"I'm pissed because you're the most condescending, insulting jerkoff in the entire world!"

"Ah, the whole world," Ty muses, loosening his hold on my wrists and lowering them to my waist. "You must get around a lot for a Congresswoman's daughter. Shit, here I thought North Korea still had some bigger pricks than me."

I flap my limbs, arms and legs pumping, putting sorely needed distance between us. It's my turn to start walking. The beautiful daylight wanes fast, and not just because he's once again made a complete ass out of me. I stare at the thick clouds rolling in from the Pacific, doubling my steps to make it to the car before it starts to rain.

I don't dare look back. Ty doesn't even chase me or say anything until my old car comes into view, an ugly metal lump totally out of place on this gorgeous beach. It doesn't matter that the scenic value is about to plummet with a Washington rain coming ashore.

"Hey." Ty's voice hits me from behind, just as he grabs my shoulders. "I didn't know you were so sensitive. Never meant to make you this pissed. If you want me to walk home, I'm more than happy to –"

"Just get the fuck off me and get in the car!" I scream, spinning and slapping him away. "I don't understand you!"

"Feeling's mutual, babe."

"No, it's not. I didn't decide to zero-in the moment I first saw you and treat you like complete shit. I don't get why you're doing everything you can to get a fucking rise out of me. Is it just a sick game? Are you hitting on me? Playing me for kicks? You're supposed to be my fucking brother!"

He laughs, arrogant as ever. "Don't fucking flatter yourself, babe. You think I'm so desperate I'd fuck my own little Sis?"

Of course I do, even if I'm afraid to say it. He's proven he's Prince Asshole, with all the dangerous looks of Prince Charming. I can't rule out *anything* on his agenda.

"Bullshit!" he roars at last. "You really don't know me, do you? I'm Tyler fucking Sterner. Every goddamned day's a pussy buffet at my club. I can and *will* fuck everything in Seattle before I'd ever lay my hand on you. Even if you weren't little Sis, you're not the kinda chick I take to my bed unless I've got one or two hotter girls on the other arm. You're a side dish. Nothing more. Get the fuck over yourself, Little Miss Perfect – pussy like yours is a dime a dozen."

Tears sizzle in my eyes. I hate him so much.

He's stabbing me in the heart again and again, reminding me what a worm I am compared to the almighty billion dollar golden boy. He's a stain, a disease, and if I had any goddamned backbone, I'd leave him behind. I'd head back to Seattle and scrimp together whatever money I can for an apartment, exit this sideshow Mom's snuck into my life.

I should reach down and scoop up some sand to plug my ears so I don't have to hear his crap the rest of the drive home. Either that, or scoop up some dirt and throw it right in those perfect blue bastard eyes. I want to fucking blind him the same way he's doing to me.

Facing the ground, I put my hand over my brow, hiding the tears.

I've got to keep moving, while my legs still work, or I'll never escape this torture. I get in the car and slam my door before he can answer.

It takes everything to fight the tears back. It helps to know that I really *am* a better person than this pompous, indulgent shit who won't stop looking sexy as he wipes his feet all over me. And because I'm better than him, I'm not going to abandon his twisted ass out here in the middle of nowhere.

Ty lingers outside for about a minute, until I honk the horn, giving it a long, hard push. The sound blasts out to sea, now taking rain from the clouds overhead.

He looks at me, shuffles over, and gets in. His eyes are softer, more sober looking and less cruel. I can't resist revving the car, letting the engine voice the growl that's tearing me apart from the inside-out.

"Claire, look, shit got outta hand." Ty's voice sounds softer than I've ever heard it. "I didn't mean to insult your ma or your intelligence. You're a smart woman – bright enough to stay the fuck away from me. Nobody else does that. Normally, I'd have your panties as a souvenir by now, and I'm glad I don't. Not just because we're in this fucked up family arrangement, but because you stood up to me. It's all this poison talking, this shit I can't get over about the marriage. You understand? I was a kid when I lost my mother. When some strange woman walks into my dad's life without warning, what the hell am I supposed to think?"

I don't know the answer. I can't figure out whether there's some sick truth to what he's saying, or if my mom's truly gone head over heels for the first time in my life. And even if the bastard next to me is right, it stings even worse.

"Here's what I think," I say, slowly circling through the sandy parking strip, heading for the main road. "You don't like my mother. I'm not too fond of your dad. Hell, Ty, I'm not a fan of *you*."

His lip purse, just enough for me to notice. His gorgeous blue eyes flash icy dark for a second, and then he's glaring at me, angry like I just spat in his coffee.

I don't get it. It's not a big secret – we're enemies. Step-rivals. One big, dysfunctional family.

How can he be so damned oblivious?

"You really hate my ass, huh? After I just gave you an

honest apology?" Ty snorts. "So much for smoothing things over. I'm an open book, Claire. I won't hide a damned thing from you. Yeah, I've given plenty of shit, and I'm gonna keep giving you more because it's what I do. It's me. If you can't handle me the way I am, then we're gonna be strangers after all."

"Yep. Honestly, I'd rather keep my distance than be roped into more of your head games!" I snap. "We can't control what our parents do. For one very brief second, I thought maybe you were right, maybe we could find some common ground. But you've ruined that today. You proved it doesn't work. I think you're delusional to think anything else. I'm not your step-sister, Ty. I'm just another bitch who came along for the ride when my mom decided to crash your dad's wonderful life."

I try to keep my eyes fixed on the road. Still, there's no ignoring how his fists flex, making his huge biceps bow up. Jesus, what guns he's got strapped to his shoulders. If most fit young men are carrying rifles, then he's got cannons.

It's a joke when most men say it, flexing and prancing around like bulky peacocks. With Ty, it's God's truth, otherworldly perfection sculpted from head to toe.

Unfortunately, there's an asshole inside the body of this Greek god, and now I've laid all my cards out.

I'm barking at him here like a cornered animal. I'm not afraid to let him know how bad he's hurt me, pissed me off, but I can't let him see how my heart races a little bit faster every time I take a nice long look at him.

There's dead silence for the next mile, maybe more. He's done talking. Cautiously, I look over, staring at him while he's got his head turned to the window, aiming his deadly blue eyes out at the stormy Pacific.

"Ty..."

"Shut the fuck up." He spins his face around, and it's lined with anger. "Just get us home. I don't need any more of this horseshit before my big fight."

"Fight? For charity? I didn't know you had one coming up."

"None of your business. I thought about asking you to come, but there's no fucking way now. You can't stand me getting in a few words here in the open. There's no goddamned way you'd handle watching me pummel Fat Boy to the floor."

Oh my God. And he's the one who called me sensitive? I can't tell if he's really that stung, or if this is just one more mind game. If I give into the urge to smack him across the face, as hard as I possibly can, I'll probably wreck this car.

"You're right," I mutter. Every syllable threatens to lodge in my throat and choke me. "I've got my internship starting this week. I don't have time to watch you beat on some other big ape. Time's all I've really got, Ty. I need to make money and get my career going. I'm not a billionaire's kid like you."

My inner filter's officially crumbled. Gone.

I don't dare look at him as he shoots me one last death glare. For a second, I'm half scared he'll reach over and suffocate me with those monstrous hands.

Then my brain does it for me, turning against me, forcing me to imagine what those rough, huge paws would feel like all over my body.

Great. Being around Prince Asshole Sterner collides with my virgin insecurities.

It's sick. Taboo. Wrong.

It's also lodged in my head like a bad song on loop. All I can think about for the rest of the drive is how good it would feel to hate-fuck this savage sonofabitch, blowing off the smothering tension between us, and probably a lot more too.

So much for ever having a normal sex life.

I don't realize how hot my blood's pumping until we're past the guardhouse, heading for the garage. The oversized opener attached to my visor isn't working for some reason. The car idles as I awkwardly tap the big button several times.

Ty's arm jerks past. He pushes my hand down with a growl, rips the black box off my visor, and then punches a neon green square next to the big button.

"That one opens the garage. You're hitting the fucking panic button for the guards."

Hot, brutal red stains my cheeks. I'm too embarrassed to make another sarcastic comment. By the time I pull in and get ready to snap back, my door pops open, and Ty leaps out of my car.

He doesn't even stop to look back as he jogs to the house door, rips it open, and disappears inside.

I don't move for at least a solid half hour. I'll fucking die on the spot if I run into the prick in the halls. My entire body can't stop shaking, and the tears come, furious and blinding hot after their delay.

Is this what a panic attack feels like?

I'm clueless. The storm sweeps over me for the next ten minutes while my brain flashes through my parents, their sudden wedding, and this new home that'll never feel anything like *home* should.

This place is a fucking prison, no matter how many luxurious acres it is. And Ty's just another inmate here to taunt me, to toy with me right down to base biology. Why, why, *why* does my fucked up brain want to kiss the lips that won't stop telling me I'm worthless?

You know that old cliche about uptight good girls melting their panties and losing their minds for the worst badasses around? Yeah, I'm living it.

"Shut up! You better open those legs a fuck of a lot wider if you want what I've got pounding your pussy, babe. Don't you fucking scream 'til I say you can."

It's his voice.

At first, I think I'm having a sex dream. Not just any sex dream, but an honest-to-God pussy creaming wet dream about my evil step-brother.

"Oh, Ty!" A woman's voice bubbles through the darkness. "*Oh, my.* Fuck, that feels so –"

She gasps. I open my eyes, listening to Ty's rough growl. I can practically hear him throwing her skirt up and

72

burying his face against her skin.

I sit up in my bed. He's not in my room, but the voices are so close it sounds like it. More shifting, movement just outside my door. It takes me a few seconds to realize he's outside in the hallway with some random slut, and she's pressed up against my door.

Oh, hell no. *This* can't be happening.

The clock next to me glows 2:00 AM. Normally, I'd be furious to have someone wake me up in the middle of the night. I used to give my roomies hell about it back at the dorms.

But I turned in so early after our fight on the beach that I feel like I've slept for eight or nine hours.

"Ty, Ty!" her infuriating voice chirps again, hot and heavy, moaning his name like she's worshiping him.

Maybe she is. The wet smack of lips pressing and hands roaming around forbidden places tells me he's got another poor girl wrapped around his wicked finger.

I'm about to jump out of bed, fling the door open, and throw my slipper at him when the girl giggles. She sounds a little further away now. A second later, the door to Ty's room next door opens, and then clicks shut.

That's right. This house is bigger than half the hotels I've ever stayed at, and yet we're locked in close quarters like rats. Don't get me wrong – the rooms are huge, spacious, and totally private. But I'm still next to him – *him!*

I'd rather be sleeping next to Mom and her new billionaire boy toy, or whatever the hell he actually means to her. Hearing them fuck through the walls wouldn't be half as gross as what's about to happen.

A body slams against the wall behind mine. The woman keeps laughing and laughing, hissing pure pleasure through her teeth. An image of Ty holding her plush against the wall flashes in my mind, the perfect position for shoving his face between her legs.

I have an eerily good idea what they're doing. But what the hell's up with me?

I don't realize I'm against the wall on the other side, pressing my ear to it, until hot blood rushes through my temples. The stranger's high, soft feminine gasps are coming faster now. If I lean really close, I can hear the wet, steady slap of his mouth on her flesh, his growl stabbing through it every so often like he's starving for this.

There's no denying the way she starts to shriek and tries to cover it. He's eating her from the bottom up, holding her lips open and fucking her pussy with his tongue, refusing to let up for a single second until she explodes on his mouth.

"Jesus, Ty! Just a little more," she begs. "Oh. *Oh!* I think I'm going to –"

One second of pure silence. Then there's a hard, tense banging on the wall as the girl's fists flop on her sides, all she can do to keep from screaming so loud everyone in the house will hear it.

Gawh! It sounds like she's screaming through his fingers.

Everything below my waist gets hot and tight. A trembling hand goes to my chest. I'm panting, just as breathless as the bitch getting her brains fucked out one

74

wall away, listening as my arrogant, nasty, inked-up step-brother forces her to climax.

Obviously, I knew Prince Asshole could fuck like a pro, but hearing him do it is something else.

Her hips are rocking against the wall and she keeps making little sharp sounds. She's coming, dragging her clit on his tongue, grinding her pussy into his beautiful face. Maybe he has a mean hand clapped across her lips to make sure she doesn't scream too loud.

I'm not sure.

Shit, I'm not sure I'll ever be the same again with my hand sliding between my legs, listening as they both break for air. Spreading my fingers on my panties, I cup my mound, discover it's even wetter than I feared.

I hold it there and try to focus on my breathing. Every single breath hurts. It's jagged, hot, heavy and confused as everything swells and winds up inside me.

And they're not done yet. I'm not that lucky.

"Holy fuck balls, Ty." She's got a dirty mouth. It's not hard to see why my filthy step-brother chose her. "You've got a hell of a mouth. Do you want me to return the favor, baby? I can –"

"Shut the fuck up. You can suck my dick back to life after I come in you a couple times. Open your fucking legs."

God. Damn. It.

I don't know why it's a surprise, but he's an even bigger bastard in the bedroom. He's commanding, brash, ordering her around like she's a hired whore. I don't think a man like him ever needs to pay a woman for sex, though. She's probably drooling all over herself just for the privilege of running her fingers over the bloodthirsty tiger inked on his chest.

"But, Ty –"

She's silenced by the heavy plop of clothing dropping on the ground. It's probably Ty's – maybe what little he hasn't stripped away yet. Closing my eyes, I picture his magnificent body in front of me.

Naked. Throbbing. Tattooed. And all mine.

No, it's not mine tonight. It's hers. It shouldn't make me aqua green, shouldn't poison every drop of my blood with filthy jealousy.

But it does. I rub between my legs, playing with my clit, feeling the same agonizing shame I always do when I touch myself. Except tonight, there's a thousand times more emotion screaming through my blood.

I hate myself for listening to this piece of shit ravage her. I hate him for waking me up with his insatiable dick. And I *really* fucking hate him for making me stand here like a pervert, two fingers drawing the cream that drips out my pussy up to my clit, rubbing it like there's no tomorrow while I listen to them kiss.

"Get on the bed. I need to be inside you right the fuck now, woman."

Next thing I know, there's a sharp squeal of springs. The slut gasps as he eases inside her, picking up steam. His thrusts come faster than I expected.

They don't have slow, loving sex. I wonder if that's even

possible with a man like Ty. No, this is straight up fucking, using her to jack himself off and empty the tension in his body the same way a starving man devours a meal.

It's sick. It's emotionless. And for some lunatic reason, it's totally hot. I'm out of fucking control – even worse than the woman who sounds like she's got a pillow stuffed in her mouth as his hips pound hers into the mattress.

Thud-thud-thud.

It's the sound of the bed clattering and my own ruined heart. I hate him. I want him. I don't know whether to bang on the wall and tell him what an asshole he is, or just stand here and keep touching myself while he brings her off again.

Obviously, I make the easy choice.

Her gurgling, cooing mess reaches a sticky crescendo and the bed jerks harder. "Give it up for me, goddamn it. You better clench hard on this dick if you want me to come with you."

I can't believe his bed is any crappier than mine. But it sounds like a freaking antique with springs that have never been oiled as he pounds her ruthlessly, throws her into orgasm.

My fingers stroking desperately at my clit go wild. Leaning on the wall, I bring my free wrist up to my mouth and bite it, all I can do to save myself from the biggest embarrassment ever.

She's coming for the second time. Then I hear Prince Asshole roar, bury himself deep inside her, and growl like some feral creature. His bed screams so loudly with the sound of him fucking and coming, I swear it's shaking the entire house.

I bite my wrist hard, fall to my knees, and suffer the strongest orgasm of my life. Whimpering, screaming, and barely breathing, I come with them. I give into the fucked up degeneracy Ty's unlocked, obliterating my own ego for more than a minute as my body writhes, quakes, and sweats through the spasms.

My pussy's still throbbing when it's all over. I can't move until I hear the bed in the other room squeal one more time, probably from him flopping down next to her to rest.

When I can finally stand up, my own hot teeth marks are branded in my arm. Christ.

I'm probably going to need to wear long sleeves when I go to work tomorrow. Ty's talking softly to his sweetheart for the night. Meaningless small talk. I can't possibly believe she means anything to him.

She's – what did he call it? – pussy that's a dime a dozen? Just like me. Supposedly.

My stomach lurches when I come off the high. I've got to suppress the urge to vomit. I'll just die if I need to step out of my room and cross the small space in the hall to my private bathroom.

Why the hell can't it be built right into the room like a master bath?

I can't let him know I'm awake. Hell, both of them. If I get a good look at the fuck buddy who's been eating out of his hand tonight, I'll either cry or scratch her eyes out.

Then I'll wind up getting carried out of this house, kicking and screaming, and probably create a media scandal so bad the billionaire has me thrown into the nearest mental institution for life.

The urge to throw up passes, and I manage to crawl back into bed without making too much noise. Still can't tell if the walls are paper thin down here, or if Ty was just fucking her so hard I heard nearly everything.

I lay there, and roll over, trying to stifle the noises and go to sleep. It's quiet – but not for long.

About two seconds after I close my eyes, the bed squeaks again in the distance. Ty's rough voice filters through the wall, but I can't quite make out what he's saying being further away. It's probably something crude, some dark threat telling her all the despicable ways he's going to toy with her body tonight.

The low creak and pillow talk sharpens. He's fucking her again, grunting and cursing, pounding her so hard the headboard's slapping the wall.

Fuck. I'm never going to sleep tonight. If I'm lucky, I'll get up in time to clear my bloodshot eyes and wash the stink of sex and shame and desire off my skin.

His fuck-fest next door is completely indifferent to my suffering. There's nothing left to do tonight except reach for the nearest pillow and cover my head, drowning out the lewd noises behind the wall as much as I can.

"Rise and shine, honey!" There's a knock at the door, and my mother's voice sounding way more...motherly than

I've heard her for years. It's how she used to wake me up before spending half the year in DC.

Stumbling to the door, I straighten my clothes, hoping like hell Mom can't smell last night's sweat and lust steaming off me when I yank the door open.

"Claire! You haven't showered yet?" She cocks her head.

"Still getting used to the house, my new room here," I say with a smile. "It took me a long time to fall asleep. Thanks for the wakeup call!"

Mom rolls her eyes and pushes past me, giving the first-day-on-the-job outfit I've laid out a long look. She gives me an approving nod while I reach for my phone, then I hear her walking ahead of me into the bathroom, laying out the towels and things.

"Mom, I'm a big girl. I don't need you setting me up like this."

She turns around and barely lets me squeeze past her into the bathroom. "I'm just being helpful. I don't want you turning out like the boy who shares this basement. I saw him come in late last night, and that thing he brought home."

She twists her nose. My eyes go wide and I try not to laugh. "Wait, you *saw* her?"

"At the breakfast bar this morning. The little tramp was eating my yogurt in nothing but yoga pants and a tank top." She shakes her head, and I cough. "Ty left with her early. It's a good thing too – I'd hate to have seen Gary's reaction to his son's latest antics."

Gary. I start to open my mouth to ask my mom again if

she's *really* into him, but something stops me.

Who am I to judge her love – if that's what's really going on here? I don't dare follow Ty's twisted logic and assume the two tied the knot for pure self-interest.

"I'll be up in a little bit," I tell her. She gives me a friendly nod and heads upstairs.

I'm not sure how to feel about being babied like this either. Not gonna lie – after last night, it's kind of nice, seeing how I'm feeling like crap and I'm still a hot, sticky mess after listening to my step-brother and his girl.

The shower feels good. It's cool, rejuvenating. I scrub the fancy body wash and salts into my skin. For a few glorious seconds, I almost think it'll let me help wash away last night's shameful eavesdropping.

Upstairs, there's a nice spread of food left by the housekeeper, Joan. I eat a bagel and some fruit, making small talk with Mom. When it's time to go, I grab my keys, my purse, make sure I've got my phone, and then I'm out in the huge garage.

That's when I'm hit right between the eyes by another surprise. My car is gone.

I spin around and almost run smack into my mother. "Jesus, Mom, you're never going to believe this."

Mom gently pushes me back outside and follows me, setting a hand on my shoulder. "What? That you've got a hot new ride to go with the job?"

No fucking way.

The shiny new hybrid sedan sitting in the space where my beater was parked is worlds away from anything I

81

expected to drive in the next five or ten years. My knees don't want to work as I walk up to it and get a good look.

It's the sexy, polished kinda vehicle you'd expect a billionaire's daughter to drive. Bitter shock forms a lump in my throat. I think I'm going to be sick, keel over and hit the floor, if my goddamned heart won't stop racing.

"Well? Do you like it, Claire?" Mom's right behind me, whispering excitedly in my ear. "Gary sends his compliments."

I spin around and we lock eyes. Her smile melts a little when she sees the crazed expression no doubt plastered to my face. "Gary? This was him? You...you shouldn't have done this."

"Nonsense. I thought it was a wonderful idea. If you want people to respect you, dear, you need to go to work in something that says you've already taken a piece out of this world." She holds up a small Washington keychain with a couple keys and a remote attached. "Here's the keys. Catch!"

My hand darts out just in time to keep it from slamming on the hard cement. I'm still standing there in my best business blouse and pants, acting like an indecisive moron.

"Claire?"

"Mom, it's just...it's so fucking weird."

She gives me a stern look. "Language. You'd better watch that before you get to the office. Now, honey, we both meant to surprise you. That's part of the fun. But if it's going to interfere with your performance, I can drive you myself..."

"No. I'll take it. I just don't like the idea of owing this guy you married anything."

Mom belts out a sarcastic laugh. "Oh, Claire. He's not buying your loyalty. He's not buying anything except a better future for his new daughter. Baby, this is pocket change for him, no different than you or I buying a bottle of nice wine. He's done you a favor. Don't worry that it took a lot out of us or anything like that. If we can easily build a better life for ourselves, our *whole* family, why shouldn't we?"

I don't have a good answer.

That's it, then. This is the new normal. Staring me in the face with its shiny coat of paint and souped-up leather interior.

"Mom..." I don't even know what to say except the obvious. "Thanks."

"You're welcome, honey!" she leans in, giving me a tight squeeze. "Gary will be home tonight. You can thank him later. I want you to stop worrying or feeling guilty about this, baby. You drive down there and blow them all away. If you start to impress them today, you'll own anything you want tomorrow."

Wow. I haven't seen Mom in full "inspire me" campaign mode since her last re-election, but today, she's beaming. Full of wisdom I'd brush off as rhetoric if there were anyone here besides me she were trying to impress.

We exchange one more smile and then I'm in the unfamiliar car, backing down the driveway. The newness smells so amazing. It's clean, pure, a good match for everything else in this strange new life. Everything except the asshole I can't stop thinking about.

I crank the car's satellite radio high as soon as I'm past the guard shack. The station plays some of my favorite rock songs, a welcome distraction that helps keep Ty out of my brain on the forty minute drive to the Cascades Now! headquarters.

It's near Arlington, a little ways north of Everett and Seattle, south of Bellingham. It's nice not having to fight the city traffic driving up from our old place in Tacoma. Yet another reason to love the new house, as weird as it is.

The office doesn't look like anything special. It's simple, small, about what I'd expect for an environmental lobby. I step out of the car and fumble with the remote, making sure the new car's locked.

Maybe Mom is right. Today's mine. This life's mine.

I don't have to let anyone get in the way – not even some ginormous muscle head who keeps me up fucking with nothing but a wall between us.

That evening, there's a knock on my cubicle wall. I swing my chair to see a tall, lean guy in a nice gray suit holding several manila folders.

"First day on the job, and you're already showing us we've been stupid not to hire a girl who knows Congress sooner." He steps inside my space as I flash him a smile. "I'm Dan. Office manager while my dad's hobnobbing in DC."

"Oh, you're Mister Jacobsen's son?" I'd been wondering

where the older man who'd interviewed me had gone.

"Guilty as charged. Listen, Claire, I don't tell every new girl I'm impressed, but I really mean it here." He opens the folder in his hands and starts flipping through it while he's talking, obviously excited. "I mean, hell, if we can get half these groups on board, we'll double the funding we need to fight the new business center going up on fifteen hundred acres of prime Cascades wilderness."

I clear my throat and mumble an apology. Half the business project's financing is from none other than my brand spanking new step-father. Talk about a conflict of interest.

I don't even know how to approach the subject with my new boss. I'm in no hurry, either, despite the way I know it'll cause a collision sooner or later.

Dan adjusts his glasses and cocks his head at me. Damn it. I'm a terrible liar, and even worse at covering my tracks.

"You're not worried because your mother just re-married one of the corporate jackasses we're taking to task, right?" He gives me a knowing wink.

Fuck. I'm more than a little relieved he's being so nice about it, but I'm not sure my poor heart can handle any more excitement today. There's been plenty of that the last couple days, and I could really use a break.

"Oh, Mister Jacobsen, I'm sorry. I didn't know whether I should bring it to your attention or just —"

He holds up a hand. "Please, call me Dan. Claire, you've got nothing to worry about. Have you met your new neighbor, Eddy?"

I glance over the wall next to me toward his desk. Yes, the portly middle aged guy introduced himself as soon as I sat down. Seems nice enough.

"I'm sure old Eddy didn't tell you he's Governor Lambert's nephew, right?" I hear my neighbor laughing uncomfortably through the wall.

My eyes go wide. The former Governor leveled more Washington wilderness than anyone before him thanks to some special contracts with his corporate buddies, as I've learned from my research. My new employer is still reeling from the aftermath, trying to turn back the clock on the mess he created.

Dan steps close to me and leans in. I get a big whiff of the spicy cologne he's wearing like a second skin. "We keep that on the down low around here. Eddy's one of our best, and he's got nothing to be ashamed of. Just wanted to let you know, Claire. We care about your work, your ethics. Nobody else's. I don't care if your mom married a robber baron, and neither does Pops."

I sit up straight, trying not to beam. I've got to hand it to him – he's just lifted about a hundred pounds off my shoulders.

"I won't disappoint you, Dan. I'm here to learn everything I can from this organization. If that means going toe-to-toe with some family interests...well, I'm game."

"Keep it up, and you'll be on our permanent staff before you know it." He leaves the folder behind for me and starts to head out, giving me one last wink.

I turn back to my computer, head abuzz with all sorts of things.

Despite the thick glasses and the even thicker cologne, he's kinda cute in a trim, geeky way. He just doesn't make my heart race like –

Damn it. There you go again. This isn't healthy, I think, warning my rebellious brain. *You've got to stop thinking about him. Pick up some earplugs on the way home.*

I'm totally serious. I'll sleep with plugs in my ears and my phone curled up to me on vibrate rather than hear Ty fucking his latest conquest again.

I still can't believe how he took her. They were at it for hours, smacking lips and twining flesh, rocking the bed springs so hard I swore they'd break.

Jesus. I can't stop thinking about him. And yeah, I definitely can't believe my own filthy desperation, the way I was drawn to the wall like a magnet, rubbing myself to bliss while they fucked.

It's not just that he's crude, arrogant, and he's treated me like trash every time we're together. He's totally off limits. There's something horribly addictive about it that warms my blood.

If I can't control the heat surging through my veins every time I think about Ty Sterner, then I need to make sure I never, ever act on it.

One kiss almost unraveled everything. And if there's a second kiss, or – God forbid – we go further, I'll never live it down. I'll ruin myself and this whole screwed up family.

No man's worth my reputation, I keep telling myself.

Not even one who looks like a Prince and talks like a convict. *Especially* not a man with a brutal knack for invading my every waking second.

Later, at home, I eat a quick dinner with Mom and Gary. They ask me all about my internship.

Gary doesn't even mention the new car until I do, and then he brushes it off like it's nothing. I know he's a billionaire, but my brain has a hard time reconciling my strange new reality.

We talk about my job, Alaska, the times the Vice President made a drunken ass out of himself at the private parties Mom attended in DC. Anything light and positive, really.

Everything except Ty, who's conspicuously absent.

I'm digging at the last of my garlic potatoes when I get the stupid idea to ask about him. "So, uh, where's big brother?"

Mom freezes up and Gary's laughter over the VP's secret antics goes dead silent. His lips pull tight in what resembles the world's most uncomfortable smile.

"Forgive me. I'm afraid my son hasn't given up wasting his days on practice for those barbaric fights he loves. I doubt we'll see him until tomorrow."

Gary's obviously had a lot of practice making excuses for Ty. All the zen-like cool in the world doesn't keep me from noticing how hard he stabs his fork into his next bite of steak.

Mom saves the day by going back to DC, telling us all

88

how grateful she is to be taking some time away from that God forsaken place. I laugh along with my parents, but I'm not sure whether to believe her.

She never talks about her campaigns until they're imminent. For all I know, I'll be wearing a pretty dress and taking time off next year to stump for her Senate seat.

Ugh.

It's a joy when Joan comes in to clear away the plates and serve coffee. I take mine downstairs in a big mug, asking for decaf. I've got to be careful to allow myself more time tomorrow morning, before I'm due back at the office.

By eight o'clock, I've taken my shower, and there's no sign of Ty. I cuddle up in bed with a book, more tired than I realize. I slip into a sleep that doesn't break until my phone wakes me up at dawn.

I'm almost dressed and ready for breakfast when there's a knock on my door. I walk over and jerk it open. Standing in front of me is the Asshole-in-Chief. Shirtless, ripped, and heavily inked. The snarling tiger on his chest matches his expression.

"Here. You asked me about the shit I do, and I'm gonna give you a chance to find out. I've changed my mind about this crap between us – I want us to have an understanding." He pushes a little scrap of paper into my hands. It's a small envelope.

I'm at a loss for words. I always am, except when he's digging his fingers into all my buttons. It's hard not to stare at the towel around his waist, knowing he must be naked without it. Naked *and* standing in front of me like it's just another normal brother-sister visit.

Ha. Ha ha awkward ha.

"Ty," I say his name, and he cuts me off instantly.

"Just look at what I gave you and decide what you wanna do, Sis. I've already forgotten the shit that went down between us. It's ancient history."

He turns and starts walking to his room. I'm too stunned to talk until it's too late, and the magnificent view of his strong, grabbable ass moving beneath the towel doesn't help.

"Wait!" He slams his bedroom door shut.

There's no sign he heard me, or cares to listen if he did. I gently close my door and begin tearing at the envelope.

I see a date and time – Saturday night. The place – Club Zing. Also, something sensational about blood being spilled, a knock down drag out fight for a good cause, and all the gloves coming off. There's a small glittery ticket with the words VIP stamped on it.

Heaven help me.

IV: Knock Out (Ty)

I knew something was wrong when I fucked the hell out of Maggie and woke up feeling like I hadn't gotten pussy for a week.

No, adding a second or third chick to my debauchery wouldn't have done shit. Neither would heading down to the gym and knocking the shit outta my favorite punching bag 'til my arms go numb.

It's her, goddamn it. *Little Miss Perfect.*

Sister. Bitch. Stranger.

Addiction.

Maggie milked my dick dry, and I couldn't even focus on her. My balls wouldn't blow 'til I imagined Claire under me, biting her soft little lip and digging her nails into my back.

Fuck, that lip. I wanna sink my teeth in. I'd kill a man to bite that soft, rosy flap of flesh. And if I told you what I'd do to plant my cock between her legs and slap my balls off her ass, I'd probably be captured and tried for war crimes.

Shit, shit, shit.

My head pounds like a fucking junkie all day while I take a good, hard run along the family's shore. I run for miles, up and down the coast, letting it rain all the fuck over me.

Running's always been a good cure for a lotta shit. Just

not this. My knees burn and my heart pounds like it's gonna bust, but I still can't stop thinking about her.

Christ, I'm hard as granite even while I'm running. I don't think it's possible to see Claire in my mind and stay soft. Not unless I've fucked her, the only thing in the universe that'll put me outta this misery.

I hate losing control, and I *really* abhor being strung around by a wet daydream.

I lost my goddamned mind on that run. I lost it to her.

Sweat poured down every inch of me, my skin overheating despite the seaside coolness. By the end, I'd lost my clothes and I was completely naked. I had to strip to keep from self-combusting.

Yeah, running naked gives my old man one more scandal to sweat. By some miracle, none of the assholes out on their yachts noticed a nude guy with tats jogging like a maniac up and down the ten mile stretch of prime Pacific coast. And I kept running too, plowing the sandy beaches 'til my toes hurt like they were stepping on glass, watching the ocean devour the setting sun.

I must've been out all fucking night, feeling the chill wafting in from the sea. It wasn't good for me at all with a fight coming up this weekend, but I had to try something. My options are running *really* fucking thin since I told Little Miss Perfect to fuck off and keep her distance.

I was pissed at her, sure, and now I'm even more pissed at myself for trying to cut her out. I thought I could forget. Since our last fight, I've tried every damned thing I know to scrub the little Sis I never wanted from my crazy skull.

Predictably, nothing fucking works. Nothing that doesn't involve my raging dick getting a full rough introduction to her sopping wet slit.

By morning, a twisted sorta peace has fallen over me. I know what I need to do.

There's no choice but to fish the ticket outta my pocket I was gonna give Maggie. I made up my mind while I was taking the longest, hottest shower of my life, trying to blaze away the ocean cold and get my body's thermostat back to human range.

I stuffed it in an envelope and marched it to her door without looking back.

She stared at me like I had a second goddamned head growing outta my neck when I shoved the envelope in her hands. Her eyes were all over me, big and beautiful and disbelieving. I had to be careful to suppress a smile.

Wasn't easy keeping my eyes off that prissy office blouse on her either. Shit, even now, I can't stop thinking about lifting up her skirt, ripping off her top, and bending her over the nearest desk for a fuck that'll teach her a thing or two about my business end.

I'm haunted. I'm obsessed. I'm fucked.

Of course, she didn't say a word. Barely had time to stammer in that cute and infuriating way she does. I didn't wait for her to get anything out. I pushed what I came to deliver into her hands, then slammed my door shut and stewed 'til I was sure she was gone.

Now, I'm looking at the ruins of my life, and coming to

the grim conclusion I *need* to fuck this girl. I'm done without finding out how tight and hot she feels riding my cock. I can't fight, can't function, can't even settle into my own house with her one wall away. I can't be happy getting my dick wet in other chicks, not when I know the best piece of pussy I'll ever have in my life's right next door.

My bed's still a mess from the most unsatisfying sex of my life. Yeah, Maggie's got the looks and she took my hateful thrusts like a champ, but my balls haven't stopped aching because they know damned well what they want.

Who they want, I should say.

I fucked the last woman in my bed rough and loud. I fucked angry, fucked her with steam whistling through my blood, rutted her soft wet cunt so hard my frustration nearly ripped a few condoms.

I know damn well what I really wanted too while I was railing my club girl in a way she'll never forget. I *wanted* Claire to hear it all.

I'm such an asshole I wanted to keep her up, rob her of sleep, anything to make her wonder what it'd feel like to have my cock owning every inch of her fuckable silk.

How fucked is that? It's pretty far down the road to hell. And if there are a few demons circling like vultures, waiting to usher me in with their pointy pitchforks, I don't give a single fuck.

Everything I care about begins and ends with her holding onto that ticket.

I don't even know if Little Miss Perfect's gonna give me the time of day, much less show up to see me beat the guts out of another dude. My asshole father dropping a new car in her lap's just icing on the shit cake, the fucked up confection we've made with this rampant hate between us.

If she tells me to fuck off forever next time I see her, I won't be surprised. I'll understand.

But there's not a single chance my dick's gonna stop throbbing as long as she's in this house, one wall away, warm and wet and way too perfect.

There's only two choices here. Counting them on one hand just makes me wanna form a fist and smash it through the nearest wall. But I can't ignore it. I can't do shit with this fork in the road except roll the dice and choose a side.

It's simple. I'm either gonna fuck my own step-sister before the summer's out, demolish her high and mighty act forever on my dick, or else I'm gonna end up drooling in a straitjacket.

I keep a low profile for the next few days. Making the rounds at the club earlier in the evenings, then waking up early to train. I skip every bullshit family dinner.

There's no point in seeing Claire 'til she's ready to tell me what the fuck she's decided about my invitation. And there's definitely no reason to subject myself to more evil eyes from my old man, and more fake sympathetic looks from Congresswoman Golddigger.

I wash down my Gatorade with a few shots of thousand dollar bourbon snuck outta my old man's liquor cabinet. It's all I can do to get some shut eye during the day, or else keep myself from marching right through the wall and demanding an answer from Sis.

Sis. The word alone tells me she's untouchable. But I won't take no for a goddamned answer.

Hell, the taboo is half the reason my cock turns into steel every time I think about taking turns with my mouth, my hands, and my dick between her thighs. If she gets one taste of me, she'll never go back.

One kiss. One squeeze. One wet, growling fuck.

That's the goal here and it's all I need. I refuse to let myself wonder whether or not she's a virgin – thinking she is brings my balls dangerously close to rupturing. If she's ever fucked another man, then I'm gonna fuck every single trace of him away forever when I get my hands on her.

I'm not only gonna fuck her a few hundred times by autumn – I'm gonna hear her beg for it.

There's a gentle rap at my door early Friday morning. I hit the sheets after a late night at the club. Two drunken shitheads got themselves bloody over some girl, and I had to break it up personally, then hung out past four in the morning for the police report.

The grog instantly fades from my head as I shoot up. I readjust my shorts as I'm walking to hide the massive wood that's been rampaging through my dreams. Tearing the door open, I almost can't believe she's really there.

But she is.

Smart black skirt, baby blue business blouse, and a wavy top that gives her that hot nerdy school teacher look I love on my babes. My dick tries to do a fucking somersault in my boxers.

"You coming to find out when we're leaving, or what?" I try to hide the hopeful tone in my voice.

She lowers her pretty brown eyes right away and I know it's not good news.

"Ty...why do you have to make this so hard?"

Fucking don't, I want to say. *Don't let me. Don't breathe a goddamned word unless it's about how you're coming with me to the big match.*

"I've decided you're more of a hothead than a total asshole." She pauses, probably stunned by the rosy red blossoming on her cheeks.

"Hothead, huh? Fuck me sideways. That's good news, right?"

"It is," she says softly, digging her small teeth into that lip I want to rule with my tongue. "Look, you're probably not a bad guy. But if our last few encounters taught me anything, it's that we always end up pressing the wrong buttons. I don't want to piss you off again and cause another crazy argument. And the truth is, I don't know *how* to avoid pissing you off."

"Easy," I growl, grabbing at her hand and pulling her inside. The door slams shut behind her with a quick jerk. "You chill with me, look pretty, and laugh at my jokes. I'm not asking for the fucking world, especially when I'm just looking for some sisterly love and support."

She frowns, throws her hands up. There's a little flinch in her wrists as she comes dangerously close to touching my chest.

No, it's not my imagination, fueled by this raging hard-on I've got for the chick in front of me. She can't keep her hungry eyes off me. I watch as she takes her sweet time trying to regain control, find her words.

"Ty, I'm not saying we have to be enemies..."

"Then what the fuck are you saying? Talk straight. I don't like this dance." I fold my arms, all I can do to keep from throwing them around her and heading straight for the hot ass underneath that skirt.

"We can't be friends." She blinks slowly, finding the courage to look at me. "We both know there's too much tension between us. God, it's more than just the constant bickering. You know what I'm talking about too."

Her eyes are bright, searching, pleading to come much closer to mine. Know it? Fuck yeah, I do.

Unlike her, I'm way past ignoring it. I stop her right there, close the small space between us, and rip my t-shirt shirt off.

"Know what, babe? I know you're bullshitting me, pretending you don't want to see this shit in action." I flex my muscles, bowing up like a fucking peacock.

God help her, she smiles, lights up in the middle of all the confusion and anguish pulling at her face.

"Come the fuck on, *Sis*. We're family. We'll never be picture perfect, but we don't need to kid ourselves. Be straight – just for once in your life. Forget prim and proper." Fire shoots through my veins, and I push her to the wall, running one hand through her hair. "Be honest."

"I – I can't..."

My free hand goes straight to my dick. I wait 'til she looks down, and then I give all ten angry inches in my boxers a squeeze, letting her see it jerk in my fist, drool the pre-come I wanna gush inside her.

"You want me, babe. Admit it. After all the blowouts we've had, after all the times we've locked horns, you'd still be all over this unruly bastard in my pants if I wasn't your step-brother. This bullshit marriage is the only thing that's stopping us from breaking the bed."

"Ty! No, no." She shakes her head ferociously, trying to get away. "See, this is what I'm afraid of..."

"Don't be scared. Embrace it. We gotta talk about this shit out in the open if we ever wanna move past it. I'm no psychologist, but I know sticking our heads in the sand like goddamned ostriches won't fix shit. It's okay to want this body, Sis. It's okay to think about me fucking you. I've had the same thoughts – and I want more than fantasies."

Her face darts up and her mouth drops open. I smile, feeling like the millions in my trust fund just for getting that shit off my chest, out into the open. Doesn't do a damned thing to stop the blood roaring in my cock.

I try to focus on picking Claire's jaw off the floor so I don't get my hands on her skirt, giving into all the depraved shit I've been thinking about nonstop since she came into this house.

"Stop worrying, Claire. We're not gonna fuck. Not really."

Yeah, right. I can't believe the words coming outta my

99

mouth. I fully intend to mount her and find out if that sweet cunt's just as tight and hot as the rest of her. But I've gotta throw her a white lie, just a little one, before she runs off screaming, overheats, and blows herself to kingdom come.

"I don't understand where you're going with this, Ty. This...this is officially *too* fucking much."

Shit. Every f-bomb firing off her tongue ties my dick in knots. Her dirty mouth soils the prissy good girl, shows me there's more inside her than the flagpole up her ass.

I step up, place a brotherly hand on her shoulder, tightening my fingers in her soft flesh. Mostly so I don't head for the perky tits just inches south, or slide up underneath that skirt I want gone like nothing else.

She's gotta be soaked. Even with her face twisted and on the verge of tears, she's looking at me like every girl has before I carry her to bed for the night.

"No, it's not too much, Claire. This is what we both need. I *need* to see you watching me pop this bruiser's jaw outta alignment. You can run your eyes all over me. Go ahead. You don't gotta feel guilty about it. You need to take a good, long look, just like the sun, and let your eyes burn so you can't see me this way again."

She's trembling. I angle myself so my raging dick isn't right against her belly and wrap my arms around her, pulling her in. Jesus, she smells so sweet. Soft. Feminine.

"Is that really what it's going to take? How do you know it won't make things worse?" She looks like she's going to die just acknowledging I've uncloaked her feelings.

"It's all we've got. Who knows how fucking long this sham marriage will last – months? Maybe years? Hell, maybe the rest of our mom and pop's natural lives." I can't imagine it, but stranger things have happened. "Do you really wanna do this dance forever? Make these awkward faces across the dinner table and scream at each other on the beach because we can't fuck? What the hell do you think your hubby's gonna say some day when he sees you can't keep your eyes off your rowdy step-brother?"

She cracks. Claire's sniffling when she pushes her face into my chest. I feel her tears against my bare skin. Something about that gives me a tiny shred of guilt.

Shit. I'm a manipulative sonofabitch. But I'd never hurt her.

No fucking way.

I'd lift up the whole fucking world and body slam it cold if *anybody* ever hit her with a barbed tongue or a malicious fist. No, I don't know what'll happen after I end up snatching her panties like I think I will.

All I know is I won't break her heart, and I've never been so sure about something in my life. Shit, I can't even think of doing it, especially if she opens her legs and finally lets me in.

"Think on it for another day. Just one," I whisper. "When you come home this evening, let me know if you're coming to the fight. I'll drive you there myself. Hell, you can take a cab and leave a note if you want. Just be honest with yourself for once, babe. Open up and do exactly what you want."

She jerks, tearing herself away from me. This time, there's no stopping her. The conversation is done. Claire yanks my door open and stumbles out into the hall, tripping all over the heels she's got on.

I feel bad about that. But I also can't stop imagining those office shoes digging into my ass while her legs are wrapped around me, fucking her into sweet submission like the wild bull I am.

"I'm going to be late for work," she snaps. "I'll...I'll let you know. But I swear to God, Ty, if I decide I don't want any of this, then stay the hell away!"

Her finger darts out. Her eyes are watery, angry, and red. I'm standing there shirtless, with the worst boner of my life stretching my tight boxers, leaving no doubt about my true intentions.

I give her a nod. She turns around and heads for the stairs, and this time she doesn't miss a step.

At some primitive level, I think she realizes what I'm doing. I haven't just asked her to be my little Sis at an underground brawl she's got no interest in.

Moral support? I don't fucking need it. I'm used to doing everything myself. I know what the old man thinks of my shit, and I resigned myself to blazing my own path a long time ago.

This isn't about that. This is about an invitation to sort out our problems with raw, hard, frequent fucking. It's the best medicine – hell, the *only* medicine – I've ever known since my balls started pumping come.

I sink backward against the wall, so wound up I'm about

to explode. I'm gonna run and punch and swim myself into a goddamned coma before she comes home. We both know what's on the line.

And the idea I might actually get what I want makes my muscles tremble 'til I stop and clench everything from head to toe.

If Claire gives me a yes tonight, then she might as well sneak into my room, strip off everything except those bitching heels, and straddle my face.

If she says yes, it's only gonna feed the fire. It won't really resolve shit between us.

Yeah, I'm a bastard for lying, but she's a smart girl. We know damned well there's no extinguishing this shit once it gets going without us all over each other, every fucking hour.

I grab my dick one more time and lick my lips, heading for the gym. I've never wanted to know what a girl tastes like this bad while I'm warming her up to fuck.

Before the weekend's gone, I swear I'm gonna find out.

I don't hear shit. I shouldn't be surprised.

By evening, right before I'm supposed to head to Club Zing for the match, I'm going berserk. I'm scared for my opponent in the ring, and whatever skanks I find after it's done.

I'm gonna fucking kill somebody tonight, and it's all because of *her*.

Little Miss Perfect, the only woman who can't be bothered to give me the goddamned time of day. Little

Miss Perfect, chickenshit as she is hot, the most infuriating bitch on the face of the earth. Little Miss Perfect, who won't stop burning up my balls, even when she's leaving me high and dry.

I'm seething. I nearly rip my clothes dressing, feeling the lust and disappointment come raging into my knuckles.

There's a knock at my door, and for a second, I stop. Could it be?

I fling it the fuck open and my heart dives like a hawk. There's my old man standing there, a sour look on his face.

Goddamn. This isn't the night. If he wags his finger at me, I swear I'll break the fucking thing right off.

"What's up, Dad?" It's all I can manage without letting out my volcanic smoke.

"Message from Claire, relayed through Mandy. She asked me to come down here and tell you myself."

Now, my ears are up. I step aside, letting him into my room. He hardly ever comes into this space, and he can't hide his disdain either. He takes one look at my messy bed and the gloves I use for practice, and turns up his nose.

Fucking asshole. Messenger or not, some things never change.

"Your sister says she'll be at your club tonight. It's just taking her a little longer than usual to get home from work. She's doing overtime today for the internship." He says it like it's supposed to mean something to me.

"Whatever, Pops. So am I. You think these charity things aren't good for business? I'm all about giving as much as the next guy with a heart, but it's good for building the club's cred too."

"Ty, come on." He slowly blinks and rushes back toward the entrance, ready to leave just as suddenly as he arrived. "I know all about the PR value a little charity brings. Spree raised fifty million a few months ago for –"

"I know. You crowed about it all over the press while I was celebrating my last birthday."

He stops, turns, and sniffs. "Now, Son, you know I'm a very busy man. That's the price for lifting up our name and giving us this lifestyle. Someone's got to do it. There's no need to get angry."

Not you, the fuck's preaching between the lines, throwing it in my face like he always does. He doesn't think I'll ever match his lofty heights.

Well, fuck him, I don't need to. I'm gonna live my life as more than a slave to the shareholders, and I'm sure as shit never marrying a gold digger looking for a few more cash injections to fluff her political career.

"I wasn't getting pissy about it. I'm a big boy, Dad. It's not like I need you to light the candles on my cake. Don't need your help running my club either. I know what works."

"Of course you do, Ty. I'll be right behind you whenever you announce an expansion in the near future." He cocks his head slightly, knowing I've refused that shit a thousand times. "Try not to bring your sister home drunk or damaged. She's a good girl. Much too good for this family, I'm afraid."

There's no point to screaming in his face. I grab the

door and slam it so hard in his face it rattles the whole basement. I'm lucky it didn't break the frame or splinter the wood – wouldn't be the first time.

I wait 'til my old man's footsteps are on the stairs before I move. Shit, I haven't even had time to think about what he said.

She's gonna be there. She's accepted my invitation. That's something, yeah? Even if she's either too busy or chickenshit to say it to my face.

Fuck. It's happening.

I finish packing up my shit, polishing my little speech to the donors from a few notes I've scribbled on my desk, and then I'm gone. I'm not gonna blow tonight and squander this chance to get my lips all over the hottest chick I've ever met.

The weekend traffic going into Seattle slows me down. I'm roaring into my private parking space with less than ten minutes to spare. My boys meet me at the door and start ushering me to the back.

Ed, Mike, and Tommy keep this place in one piece when I'm away. They've been my brothers since high school, and the only thing that keeps this place from running on auto-pilot without me are their own egos butting heads. That's why I've put the big Swede over them as head manager, a guy named Karl.

It's like half a dozen people are trying to talk at once amid the endless clatter of their phones going off.

"Shut the fuck up, guys! One at a time, and nobody

speaks if it's not important," I finally say, coming to a dead stop in the middle of the hall, ripping off my shirt and pants. I strip down to nothing but the trunks I'm wearing into the ring.

Nobody says shit. Yeah, that's what I thought. Just a bunch of overeager friends jockeying for my attention. I'm used to it by now, but it still gets grating before I head into the ring.

"I'm ready to go. Karl!" I point to the muscular Swede with blonde hair and baby blue eyes just slightly duller than mine. "You're telling me what's what. Is everything out there set, without any problems?"

"Sure is, boss. The turnout's looking fantastic. Fat Boy wanted to say a few words before you climbed in together, but it doesn't look like there'll be time for that."

I nod, remembering my opponent's moniker. I don't study up on this shit beforehand because I like a surprise, a challenge. I don't use those silly fucking wrestling names either.

Maybe it's a good thing the guys on the receiving end of my fists do because it always seems to go over well with the crowd. As for me, I'm just Ty, undefeated owner who keeps bringing these hungry bastards in, trying to knock me out.

They always lose, and that's not changing tonight. I'm the one who wins, and so does my club and the charity we're raising cold hard cash for.

"What about the chick I texted you about?" He shakes his head like hasn't gotten the message. "Find her and make sure she's safe and sound in her VIP box. That's Claire Frost, my new step-sister. I gotta know she's safe and sound, without any hitches."

"I'm on it." He breaks and starts running down the hall.

A couple guys are at my side, and they walk with me toward the big door leading into the storage area behind the bar. It's the only place big enough to accommodate the ring and several hundred chairs. The back of the club's an old, heavily remodeled theater, and it could've seated twice the crowd in its prime.

My boys open up the big door and I walk through with my fists in the air. People flip the fuck out and come close to bursting their lungs, guys and their gals alike. There's lots of scanty clad sluts in low tops and even lower skirts lining my path. They all reach out and brush their drunken nails over my skin while I walk past. They must think I'm a lucky fucking charm, or else they've got some magic touch that'll make me climb into bed with 'em later tonight.

Most nights, they'd be right. Many times, I've simply gone down the ranks and chosen two or three girls for the night.

But if Claire's out there, just like she said, then...there's no fucking way. There's just one woman I'm interested in bedding tonight, and I'm focusing all my energy on her sweet ass like a goddamned laser.

I bound up the steps and swing through the ropes. Fat Boy's already in his corner.

He's about five years older than me and he's got a gut like a medicine ball. Chubby or not, the dude has arms and legs as big as mine with huge veins popping out. Reminds me of those gorilla-like Russians you used to see competing in weight lifting world championships.

The spotlights shine blinding bright. The crowd's screaming. Those lights are hot too, like miniature suns beating down on my skin in the desert. I start to sweat as I look around.

The referee comes out in an old timey striped shirt, shoving a microphone into my hand. He's more announcer than referee, but again, everything's about appearances here. Whatever it takes to rile up the crowd, keep the money flowing, and make *damned sure* the name Club Zing winds up burned in their frigging skulls is game.

"Yo, the air's humid as fuck up here," I growl, letting the reverberations sweep over the crowd and bring them to silence. "I said – it's thick. Swampy. Suffocating. Ladies and gentleman, I'm gonna give you a fight that'll blow your hair back, and I need each and every one of you to make it *rain* tonight. Let's cool this motherfucker down."

Laughter rings out. I've still got my money clip strategically placed on my trunks. I rip it off and walk over to an attendant, not far from the side that gives me a direct view of the VIP seating.

"You hear that shit?" I wait 'til he holds up the collection plate.

That's right. We use collection plates, just like in church, except ours are silver plated and managed by boys who'll start cracking the skulls of anybody who thinks about stealing one red cent.

"You hear that, ladies and gentleman?" I slam fifties and hundreds in, one after another. "That's the patter of rain, friends. Tink-tink-tink-tink-fucking-tink! But why the hell's it so lonely up here? Why the fuck am I the only bastard making noise? I'm not looking for a little sprinkle tonight. Fat Boy and I need a goddamned deluge! Stand up, open your wallets, crack your purses, and let it *fucking pour!*"

I scream the last line. The crowd goes wild. In the commotion of people standing up, milling around, and digging for their cash, I see her. My eyes lock.

Claire's there in her box, sitting next to Karl. She looks totally out of place in her professional blouse and skirt. She's dressed too smart for Club Zing, but just smart enough to set my dick on edge.

Fucking shit. Her soft pink lips pull up in a bashful smile. I wonder if she can see my dick springing to life, pressing against my trunks. Hell, if the crowd weren't going apeshit, they'd see it too.

I decide right then I don't give a fuck. Not one.

If the thousand people jammed in here want to see the hard-on I've got for my Sis, then they will. It only matters to Claire and me. We're the only ones who'll remember after the fight. The instant I get down to business with Fat Boy, they'll forget all about what's flexing below the belt.

"Keep it coming, you crazy motherfuckers!" I roar, listening to my voice break in the speakers. "I wanna hear your pockets turn inside out before this night's over! I wanna see moths flying outta your clothes!" They love the shit talk, so I pour it on.

110

Then I tear my eyes away from Claire. It's not easy because I can still feel her locked onto me, even when my back's turned. Unfortunately, business calls.

I walk up to Fat Boy and give him a shallow, respectful nod. He stares at me glumly.

Fine, jackoff. Be that way.

Some of these guys are like that. Charity events aren't supposed to be career builders, but some of these assholes treat it that way. Any man who punches out Ty Sterner, heir to daddy's billions, is guaranteed some wild media ass kissing.

"I hope you've brought your game, big ace. Club Zing doesn't quit rockin' 'til one us is flat and we've broken a few records with our money storm." I spin around, facing the crowd again. "Don't stop! Keep it the fuck coming! We've got some sick kids out there tonight who need that shit way more than any sorry fucks here do."

Tug at their conscience. Pluck their heartstrings. Bully them 'til I get the nod from Karl out in the boxes – the one that lets me know we've shattered our old record.

It's persuasion 101. And it's going to a good cause too. We're supporting the local children's hospitals tonight, and everything we raise gets split between research and boosting quality of life.

Fat Boy's still not talking. Usually, my rivals get in on the act and join me, but I don't think this fucker's here for charity. He's here to rumble for glory, and nothing else.

The referee crawls back in the center, waiting for me. I give everybody one more roar of thanks, push the mic into

111

the ref's hands, and watch as Fat Boy lumbers up to the center.

"It's the moment you've all been waiting for!" The old man in the pinstripes shouts. "If you've been here before, folks, then you already know the rules – there aren't any 'til a man goes down! Anything, and I mean *anything*, can happen tonight! Will we see our boss pull out another big win, or is this the first night Club Zing gains a new reigning champion?"

More explosions from the crowd. It's so loud my eardrums are about to break. Good, because that means more money flowing in too. There's a direct, no shit correlation between decibels and dollars. Judging by the noise, tonight's gonna be a bank buster.

I take one last quick look at Claire, surrounded by all the chaos. Her eyes are big, excited, pleading. I can't tell if she's getting into the fight, or if it's the hunger she showed me the other morning on steroids.

"No more talk! Keep those dollars flowing, folks, and pop your last few cents when it's all over." The ref pauses and looks at us carefully before he says the last important line. "Let's. Fucking. Go!"

Ref gives us both a nod and steps back, sinking toward the edge. He's really there for show, and to officially put an end to the fight when I've laid out another bastard.

There are no rules in this box short of killing a man.

Fat Boy looks like he wants to do exactly that. The big bastard lunges and swings, strong but slow. I dodge and get off a few good whacks at his side.

I can practically see the steam shooting out his ears. He hops up and charges me like a bull. This time, he's a little faster.

It's like a screaming meteor slamming into me. I hit the floor, and the next thing I feel are fists landing on my face. It's seriously like a three hundred pound bear squatting on my chest, holding me down, pounding me right in the fucking face, over and over and over.

Thinking about Claire all the time's put me off my game. I've left myself open.

I rock up with all my might, punch him right in his saggy gut. Fat Boy grunts and topples off. His weight works to my advantage while I'm struggling to get on my feet. The audience starts to scream when I stand up, and the whole damned world's spinning.

Something hot and thick trickles all the way down to my chest. I realize he's given me a bad nose bleed, something no other man in this ring has ever managed.

Fuck.

I can't let it stop me. I charge the asshole just as he's getting up, beaming his dark boar eyes at me. I should have a dead bullzeye on the back of his head.

I'm ready to pound him flat now if I have to, ending the fight early. It's not ideal for donations, but the crowd just cares about the excitement. They'll spend the rest of the night re-hashing a five minute fight and throwing down more money at the bar if it's exciting enough. Then I can throw a good portion at the children's fund.

The boulder in front of me moves. He rolls right into

me when I'm coming at him, and I go crashing on the floor, one inch away from smashing my tender face.

Mother-fuck. I should've seen it coming.

I also should've known Fat Boy isn't moving an inch further than he needs to. Before I can force my bruised elbows to get my ass up, he's on me again, throwing his fists into my abs. He hits me so hard I choke, knocking my wind out, holding his ass on my legs so my desperate attempts to break out are total failures.

Christ. He's gonna fucking do it, I realize, as soon as the blows I'm trying to block start getting through, smashing me in the face.

There's a ringing sound like the end of the world. Everything goes black.

I'm drowning. Falling into an empty, desolate, bottomless pit. For some reason, I'm not that concerned about being beaten or even dying.

What really, *really* pisses me off is the idea that I'm about to leave this world without ever having Claire. I need to taste her. Need to feel her. Need to fuck her.

I can't let it end like this. I can't go down. I can't humiliate myself and leave before I've done everything I mean to in this life – starting with *her.*

Is there more to this weird shit between us than lust? I need to think about it, and I mean seriously fucking think. But not 'til I gasp awake and find myself with my neck snapped to the side, drool and blood streaming out my mouth.

The referee's face is crooked, upside down. He's standing over me, giving Fat Boy an uneasy look, like he's about to call it so the fucker doesn't murder me.

These fights are rough, brutal, and borderline illegal because it brings us crowds like nobody else. Too bad my whole damned operation will be in hot water if anybody suffers a serious injury here tonight, much less a dead owner.

I think about my asshole father, standing over me in the hospital, gloating like the summer sun. Congresswoman wifey'll be at his side, giving me that fake sympathy she does so well. And she'll have all the confirmation that I'm scum underneath it, a fucking moron who couldn't stand flirting with danger.

All because I had to satisfy my ego against my billionaire father's.

I think about Claire. She'll never fuck me if I don't win this fight, and I can't blame her. It's not about being pounded to a pulp by a stronger man.

The only one beating me right now is my own fucked up lack of discipline and self-control. It's everything she scorns, and all because my dick's begging my brain to let him jackhammer between her legs twenty-four seven.

I can still move, so I'm not dead. I have to fight. I can't fucking give up.

Fat Boy's tiny eyes whirl with dark excitement. He's cold, stunned, frozen in disbelief. The bastard probably can't believe he's done it, beaten Ty Sterner on his own turf. The asshole has a few heavenly seconds where all the incredible possibilities of winning flash before his eyes.

That's all he gets before I bolt and uppercut the fucker's jaw with both fists, before the ref can call the win.

I hear the crack. It's loud and sharp as lightning. If I haven't broken his jaw, then it's splintered at the very least, and he's probably lost a few teeth.

The audience surrounds us in a deafening, chattering blanket as I jump, landing on top of him. Something primal rips through me. My senses are so overwhelmed I can barely see, but I don't need to as long as I can feel him underneath my fists.

I punch him in the guts and keep on going 'til I can't feel my own arms. It's a miracle I'm able to get up and fight like this after losing all my oxygen, but this fucker won't manage because he's not as lean and buff as I am. His bulk fucks him over.

The primal thing tears out my throat. I'm hollering like a chimp with rabies as I beat the bastard blind, holding back from killing him only because I think about the same scandal that'll erupt if I put his ass in a coffin. I have to protect this club.

My lungs won't work. My heart's about to crack my ribs with its damned thunder. My muscles are gone, and there's just stones fixed to my bones, hard and unyielding.

I fall down next to Fat Boy, face-to-face, staring into his barely conscious eyes. "What the fuck did you wanna say to me? Before the fight?"

He growls. I land one more punch and his head lolls back. "Just fucking tell me. Do it."

"Wanted to say it's me. I was gonna be the man to beat you. Ty...fucking...Sterner." The last part's like a whisper.

He stops trying to get me off him and goes flat, his huge body softening beneath me. The referee comes over and starts slapping the ground, doing the final countdown.

Shit, shit. I roll off him and struggle to get up. I manage to hold myself in a push-up position with my exhausted arms, anything to keep this from going to a draw.

Slap-slap-slap. The ref's palm keeps hitting the floor, and I lose count.

I barely realize it when he's standing up, speaking into the mic. "Ladiiiies and gentleman! It's been hella close, but we have our winner. It's Ty Sterner. *Always* undefeated." He pauses for a second, but adds one thing over the crowd's hurricane force scream. "Undefeatable."

V: Undeniable (Claire)

I've never seen anything so brutal in twenty-two years on this earth.

Just a second ago, Ty's beautiful blue eyes were fading, winking out like dead stars. His head was turned my way all through the commotion, even when the man was on top of him, beating him senseless. I can't believe he saw me through the pain and the blinding spotlights, but his eyes were searching.

Searching for me.

Karl, the Swede, was laughing before, chuckling and slipping me drinks when the match started. He went dead silent as soon as Ty went down. I never knew hundreds of people jammed into the same small place could be so deathly quiet.

Everybody forgot to breathe until Ty pounced and began punching the big man like something possessed him. I sat glued to my seat, watching my step-brother with a whole new worry.

His eyes were different. They flashed crazy, angry murder, alive with the same ruthless energy in his fists. I watched him smash the other boxer to bits, and it scared the hell out of me.

I'm still afraid he's going to kill this guy and wind up in jail.

Obviously, I didn't have a clue what I'd gotten myself into. When Ty said fight and slipped me those tickets, torturing me every hour, I came because I couldn't resist. I couldn't lie and brush off the attraction, the fire threatening to burn me alive whenever I'm in his arms.

I expected something rowdy, clean, and civilized. I didn't expect to see men bloodied and brought to the brink of death.

Guess the tough guy thing isn't just an act, a rich son slapping his richer asshole dad in the face. No, the crap happening in front of me is as real as it is dangerous.

It should disgust me, send me running, prove that everything I've feared is totally right. But it doesn't.

I can't help but swoon when I realize he's won the fight. Karl climbs the seat next to me, screaming his lungs out. When he's finally done, he reaches into the cooler at his side, and passes me another wine cooler. I'm screaming too, even as I twist off the cap, yelling like a mad woman until Ty's finally out of sight, the attendants helping him off the stage.

I normally don't drink this much. Hell, I'm normally not this violent. I don't know what I am anymore, and I'm not sure I'll figure it out before I give into this throbbing urge to feel my step-brother's lips on mine.

I'm confused. There's something in the air tonight, something thick and sultry and otherworldly. I can't even describe it better than that.

"Hang tight with me, Claire," Karl says. "We'll get into the bar much easier once we let the crowd clear out."

He grabs my hand and makes me settle back into my chair. Probably a good thing. As soon as I stood up, my body rocked. I'm seriously tipsy, drunk like I haven't been since drinking with Dana.

I'm glad Karl's here to help. With this many drinks flying around, amping the crowd up alongside the testosterone and adrenaline, it might be dangerous going out there alone without all my wits.

I take a good, long look at the blonde haired man at my side. I've got to admit, he's kinda cute in a rogue way. He doesn't have the body Ty does, and the buff arms sticking out his sleeves don't have a single stripe of ink.

My mind's screaming through all the excitement. The big Swede's looking better with every new sip I take. Good enough to be my escape from throwing myself at my own step-brother, if I really want him to be.

I'm drunk, dizzy, and burning like never before. Honestly, I'm terrified of what I'll do when I'm alone with Ty again.

I can't really give into these insane urges, right? Jesus, I'll never live it down if I let him fuck me, if I let myself give away my virginity and my body to a fucking relative. No, we're not blood related, but he's technically my brother. That makes it wrong enough.

I have to keep my mind off the taboo. I just need to focus on having fun, treat it like any other girl's night out, maybe invest a little more energy in the handsome man at my side.

Except he's looking more and more like a disappointment with every step we take. I don't know what I'm going to do with Ty, but I know I don't *really* want his co-worker. Getting my V-card punched by a total stranger's worse than the asshole I know.

Karl flashes me a thick smile and grabs my wrist, this time a little more forcefully. "There's more waiting for us in the VIP lounge. We'll catch up with your brother later. Come on. Looks like it's all clear."

I follow him down the winding path and then upstairs, evading a few drunken stragglers bobbing in the halls. We head back toward the closed room where I ran into Ty fucking those whores the first night we met. There's another door just before it, not far from the restrooms. Karl jerks me inside a smaller, darker room that feels like a grotto.

It's elegant, dimly lit, and the walls must be awfully thick. I can't hear a damned thing in here, not even the hundreds of people milling around in the lounge.

There's only one other couple in there with us. The look up, give us an uneasy look, and then return to their drinks and hushed conversation.

Karl holds out an arm so I can pass by and take my seat at the small VIP bar. "What'll it be, Claire?"

"Something stronger than the wine coolers. We've still got like four or five hours until closing time, right?" He smiles and nods.

Yeah, I really want to drink tonight. It's either that or

fuck my step-brother raw. Maybe a few drinks will help clear my head before I make the mother of all mistakes.

Karl lingers near the bottom shelf, as if he's showing off his backside. It's nice, but I've seen better. He comes up a minute later with a massive bottle of vodka and some pomegranate grenadine. He pours them together and shakes it up like a pro. His muscles ripple as he preps the drinks, and I'm all kinds of conflicted.

I grab mine a little too eagerly and knock it back. Karl laughs, pops the vodka bottle, and pours more into my glass straight. "Something tells me you don't need the sweet stuff."

Staring like an idiot, I lean back and smile, tossing my hair. "I know how to put it back. Most valuable skill I learned in college."

Actually, it's not far from the truth. I spent my last year drinking with friends just as hard as I studied, and I'm dangerously close to carrying the same habits into the grown up world.

It's been such a long week. Why not get a little plastered and spend some time here before I need to confront my damnably sexy step-brother?

Why not cut loose and stop worrying this confusion boiling my brain? God, why not find out if there's more to this blonde boy with the sexy accent besides a nice distraction from Ty?

I can't make up my mind. One minute, I wish he'd lay me down and fuck me before Ty does, and the next I'm steaming for nobody else but big brother.

God. What the *hell* is wrong with me?

I slam my empty glass on the counter. "Another."

Karl laughs louder. His eyes are on my tits and I don't even care. He stares, not even hiding it, and I give my body a nice long stretch. It's refreshing to cut away from all the family drama, plus the new job.

This night isn't going like I expected. My head's so warm, burning up with alcohol now. I'm about to add some more fuel to the fire.

Two more shots, and everything whirls, melting into a blurry puddle of drunken goodness. I'm starting to worry why I haven't seen him yet. Ty was supposed to greet me shortly after the fight – does he even know we're back here?

My diligent bartender holds the bottle up again when my glass empties, but I put my hand up. "Where's Ty? Is he really going to be okay?"

"He's being checked over. We always have a medic standing by for these events in case anyone ends up seriously hurt. I think you understand, Claire, what we're doing here is risky, but we do everything we can to minimize the chances of any lasting injuries."

He slams down his own drink. Grabbing the bottle, he steps out from behind the bar and takes the stool next to me – a little too close for comfort. Still, I give him a smile as he refills my glass. This time, he's not taking no for an answer, and neither is the pleasurable urge to drink more building in my head.

"Are the fights always so violent? I'm amazed he hasn't

broken bones by now." In fact, I'm wondering if an undiagnosed brain injury explains Ty's crude, impulsive behavior.

Karl tightens his lips and waves a hand, dashing my concerns. "*No.* The boss knows what he's doing. He's trained for years, and he doesn't slack on anything. I'm not sure why Fat Boy had the edge for a little while. That's never happened before. Tyler's mind has been somewhere else lately. He's not himself."

Not himself. The Swede's words stop me cold. I remember how my step-brother stared at me while he was in the ring, his eyes blazing with a determination even fiercer than I'd seen when he was right in my face the other morning.

We were so close. I touched his rock hard torso, and I didn't want to stop.

Closer than any real brother and sister have any business being. It's suddenly cold in the lounge, or maybe the vodka's heat overloads my stomach. A shiver rolls off my back.

Karl's big arm goes around me and pulls me close. I'm so shocked my face almost hits the bar.

Okay, it's been fun fantasizing about him. He's obviously a safe and sane choice stacked up against Ty. But with my mind drifting back to the asshole who's the entire reason why I'm here at Club Zing tonight, I don't think I really want to sleep with Ty's underling.

I gently reach out and give his arm a push while I pull away. My other hand reaches for the vodka, just what I need to cover up the awkwardness. *Ugh.*

Okay, scratch those crazy thoughts about getting closer to this guy. I don't trust him. I kinda want to get up and go out on my own.

"I think I need to take off soon, Karl," I say softly. "I need to find Ty."

"What's the matter, lovely?" There's venom in his voice. "Don't you ever want to do anything besides talk about your brother?"

"I...I don't know."

I really don't.

Karl laughs coldly. "Ah, you're quite a tease, aren't you? I've dealt with women like you before. I fucking know what you really want, princess. Let's go."

Snarling, he grabs my wrist and pulls me off the bench. I'm too blitzed by the latest vodka pouring into my veins to fight back. Shit, I barely realize what's happening, only that my knees are moving on auto. I can't stop as he leads me through a metal door next to the private bar, into a chilly room stacked high with liquor crates.

I thought we were isolated before, but now? *Not good.*

The door clicks shut and he pushes me against the wall. I'm about to scream when his hand covers my mouth. His breath stinks. We lock eyes.

What the fuck's going on? Why's he gone all Jekyll and Hyde? I remember all the drinks he knocked down during the fight. The only time he even paused was when it looked like Ty would lose.

I've heard of mean drunks before, but I've never really *seen* one until now. He called me a tease too. Surely, he can't

126

really believe I owe him something, much less sex?

I try to clear my mind and look at him, hoping I'm badly misjudging all this. But then he speaks, and the cruel tone in his voice confirms my nightmares.

"Don't bullshit me, girl. I know you're the reason he's losing it. Boss wants you bad. He can't focus. He's going to get us into trouble if this continues. Now, I see why you make him crazy. I see what a nasty little tease you are." His free hand reaches down, and I sense him fumbling with his belt, or maybe the zipper to his jeans. "Let's make this fun. I'm going to give you the fuck you've been begging me for with your pretty eyes all evening. I'm not just doing it for our pleasure, Claire. This is doing the whole club a favor, everything Tyler's worked to build."

He draws his hand off to finish dropping his jeans, and I'm too drunk to scream. My stomach rolls violently. I wonder if throwing up all over him will get me out of this, or if I've screwed up so bad my first time is going to be with this wasted maniac.

He shoves me against the wall again – this time harder. His hands go places. There's no pleasure, only sickness, pain when he squeezes my nipple. My mind tosses and churns between hate and horror.

I feel him everywhere – on my breasts, around my back, cupping my ass, between my legs. I moan, and he mistakes it for pleasure, but really I'm crying for help. I'm sick to death. Scared.

I'm about to black out when the door snaps open and a wild animal comes crashing into the room.

Or that's what I think, at first, in my fucked up state.

Next thing I know, I'm backed into a corner, watching the screaming men at my feet. The bigger one completely covers Karl and holds him on the ground, flattening him while his fists go at the Swede's face. I recognize the wavy tattoos flowing down his shirtless back instantly.

Ty.

"You sneaky sonofabitch!" My brother's voice explodes, and several wine bottles break in the commotion, falling onto the floor from the impact of his fists. "Did I fucking tell you to touch her? You were supposed to be the one asshole in this place I could trust not to make a move!"

His voice is slurred from the beating during the fight, but he takes Karl easily because he's sober. Ty doesn't give him a chance to answer. His fists keep coming down, this time without any gloves. There's nothing between the Swede's face and my step-brother's bloody knuckles.

Karl moans, tries to sit up and plead, tell him it's all a big misunderstanding. Ty pushes him right back down.

It's worse than watching the fight. There's no referee here, nothing to save the bastard who tried to force himself on me from Ty's righteous blows. My heart flips.

I'm drunk, but I know he did wrong. I want him to pay for it – suffer for what he would've done. But then I hear the sickening snap as his nose fractures, and I think I'm going to be sick.

"Ty..." I whimper meekly. It doesn't get through.

He grabs Karl by the collar and hoists him up, but only for a second before smashing him down on the hard floor again. "Pick your sorry ass up and get the fuck out! You're done here. Drag your fucking carcass back to Europe, and I won't press charges. It's not a choice. I'll make sure you never work in this goddamned city again!"

His voice rumbles low, booming, savage. Scarcely human. I don't try to squeak out another word, even if I want to.

"No, no, no, boss," Karl blubbers. "She's a tease. She brought me here. Boss, please! *Boss!*"

I cover my face with one hand. Fuck it. He deserves everything the mad dog protecting me wants to give him.

Karl never gets out another word. Ty picks him up and drags him across the room, through a narrow space formed by boxes stacked to the ceiling. A door I hadn't seen before swings open in the back. I catch a glimpse of some loading docks, and that's where Ty throws his manager.

Well, *former* manager. The door slams shut while the man is still screaming, and he whirls around.

Now, I'm face to face with the devil himself. But if he's a devil, then Satan has the coolest, most beautiful blue eyes anyone can imagine.

I feel like I'm facing a firing squad. Only, instead of catching a bullet, I'm going to catch nothing but pure hell, or else a twisted ache between my legs.

"I'm sorry as fuck about this, babe. He's never acted like this before – or at least I've never caught him. Shit, it's always the ones you trust." Ty shakes his head.

I see he's got a bandage on his temple, and his skin's

gone slightly dark in several patches on his face. Fresh bruises are blooming from the fight.

I can't believe what's just happened – what I've barely escaped. Rage floods my brain in one blast.

"I didn't need your help. I would've screamed." I ball my fingers into fists, amazed at the words coming out of my mouth. It's pure defense. "There was another couple out there who would've heard us, broken up what he was doing. Thanks, but no thanks, Ty. I appreciate your help, but I don't *need* it. You're *not* my knight in shining armor, and you're definitely not my prince."

God. I sound like a total lying bitch, and maybe I am.

But I *need* to be. I can't let myself actually fall for the six-foot-something lunatic standing in front of me, looking like he wants to either rip my head off or pick up where Karl left off.

"Shit, you're drunk. I never should've let you outta my fucking sight for one second." He grabs my wrist, and for about the fourth time that night, I'm led around by a man.

Fire explodes in my belly. I yell, try to fight. It doesn't do me any good. We burst out of the room and he marches me through the VIP lounge, toward another not-so-secret passage in the club.

"Ty! Ty! Let me fucking go! I *can* walk on my own, you know."

"I don't know shit when you're like this. The only fucking thing I know is that I'm never letting another man lay his hands on you, even if he's not a sinister little pissant like my dearly departed Swedish manager."

We're going down a short, dark hallway now. The EXIT sign glows red above a door. As soon as it's open, I smell exhaust fumes and hear rowdy laughter. We step out next to his car, perfectly parked in his reserved spot behind the club.

"No way! I'm not going home right now." I stand up on my heels and glare at him. "I'm going back inside. I'll shake this off so I'm good to drive in a few hours. I can't let our parents see me like this..."

His eyes narrow. I should be expecting him to grab me and throw me into the car, but it's something else when he really does it.

I'm a screaming, bawling mess, totally going to pieces. Too drunk to pop the lock and get out again too. *Mercy*.

Catching a quick flash of my reflection, seeing what I've become, is all that calms me the hell down while he slides into the driver's seat.

"We'll take our time. I'll sneak you in. Your ma's oblivious, and Dad's got his head too far up his own ass to notice anything. Stop worrying all the goddamned time. You're in good hands with me."

Am I? I feel like I've got a boa constrictor around my throat.

Before, I was just confused, drowning in all the storming emotions he ignites inside me. Now, I'm livid.

He's doing it. Again.

The ever-cocky asshole steering us through downtown Seattle's controlling my fucking life. Sure, he saved me tonight, but then he has the arrogance to tell me he'll

131

decide who gets to lay his hands on me?

Where does he get off? *Where?* Or does he just get off on bossing me around like I'm really this little-sister-wannabe-lover combo he can't decide what to do with?

I'm fuming, trying to focus on breathing without passing out. My stomach heaves every time the car lurches, and I fight just to avoid getting sick all over his fancy leather interior, which is even nicer than the one in my new car.

Shit. My car!

"Hey, dick, since you're taking me for a ride tonight – who's going to get my car home?"

He looks at me out of the corner of his eye and sneers. "I've got connections. I own a whole fucking nightclub, babe. My old man's the richest man for several hundred miles. You really think I haven't sorted out the logistics of that shit about a second before I decided to get your ass home?"

He makes me feel so small. If both my hands weren't tucked close to my angry belly, trying to hold everything inside, I'd slap him clean across his stupid smug face.

But I guess we've been there, done that, haven't we?

Nothing gets through to him. Nothing.

I can't make him respect me. I can't decide if I really deserve it. All I can do is settle into my seat and let him punch my ticket to another rung of hell. The only thing I know about my destination is that I'm bound to suffer, *guaranteed* to bottle up my emotions while they eat me from the inside out, this fucked up love-hate thing we've got going that smolders like slow moving acid.

"You always have all the answers, don't you?" The saner part of my brain's screaming *shut up,* and it wants me to bite my tongue. But it comes out anyway.

Ty stomps the accelerator a little harder.

"Yeah, I do. I know how my world works, as much as I fucking can. Shit, you saw what happened back there when I miscalculated. I almost got you literally fucked by some piece of shit who's not fit to stick his dick in the nearest blender!" His fist comes down on the steering wheel – hard.

I blink, trying to comprehend what I'm hearing. It's bitter and violent, even by his standards. There's something else too.

Is Ty Asshole Sterner actually feeling...*guilty?*

I didn't think it was possible. I didn't think he had a conscience. He seemed like a wild beast before, a force of nature, certainly not a man with thoughts and feelings and regrets behind his inked up muscle.

"Huh? Are you really saying you're...sorry?"

He just drives for a few seconds. Then he looks at me and narrows his eyes. The shadows dance with a few fresh bruises on his jaw.

"Yeah. Sorry some asshole I trusted turned out to be a piece of shit."

I snort. I should've known he wasn't *really* going to give me an honest, heartfelt apology. Still, he's gone quiet, serious, and the bright blue eagle eyes he's got fixed on me haven't moved a notch.

"But that's only half the issue. Claire, you're right. With you, I'm a controlling motherfucker. I'm jealous. Loose cannon doesn't begin to describe the way my damned heart beats whenever I feel another man's eyes on you. Let's be straight – any asshole who swoops in for a kiss would've gotten the treatment I gave Karl. That's what anybody with a swinging dick's gonna get as long as I'm around. You're making me fucking crazy. I won't let *any* man fuck you, even if he brings you roses, candy, and martinis for the privilege. We both know the only dick worth having between your legs is mine."

My ears start ringing. I'm still a little drunk, and my brain struggles to truly process what he's saying.

I'm not sure if I should be flattered or completely horrified.

The car jerks, and for a second all my worries are dashed by the fear that he's going to drive us right off one of the high ocean cliffs overlooking the coastline up to Bellingham.

By the time I remember to breathe, we're heading down a small service road, into a dense forest. He pulls over, kills the engine, and brings us to full stop.

"Ty...this is crazy." My voice sound so small. "We can't really do this, you know. We can't, our parents are married, we're practically brother and –"

"Sis?" He says it and sends needles dancing up my spine. "I don't give a fucking shit. It's not like we're blood related and we'll make mutant babies or something. I've been fighting this shit since the minute I laid eyes on you. I've never been so obsessed. I can't shake it. Absolutely fucking can't. And you know that? Pussy's easy come, easy go in my world. Only, for some crazy reason, yours is stuck on my mind, twenty-four-fucking-seven like a jackhammer drilling into my skull. Stop pretending you don't want this."

He unbuckles his seat belt and leans in close. My heart's swollen with all the bitter lies I keep trying to tell myself, trying to tell him. It hurts because they're not true.

I *do* want him, dammit. We both know it.

And now I remember how fucking good his lips feel against mine.

Ty's kiss crashes into my lips and swallows me up like a tsunami. His heat sweeps over me, and I can barely remember to kiss him back before he starts growling into my mouth.

God, that growl. He's a feral man, and that's what makes this so insane, but the heat in my body doesn't lie.

It shouts down the crap I've tried to tell myself. Lust is a thousand times louder. My nipples are like pebbles underneath my shirt, and everything beneath my waist coils tighter, tighter, ready to *snap* if he doesn't dig in and unwind the tension.

My mind races at light speed while his kiss quickens. Ty's got his hands around my back now, shoving me close, pulling me over the divider between us. I bend around him, as naturally as if we were always designed to fit.

"Fuck, babe," he snarls, fisting my hair. "You ready to admit you want this yet? Or do I have to prove how damned good it'll be?"

135

No. I'll deny it a hundred times if it makes him set me on fire like this. But eventually, kiss by fiery kiss, I'm going to give in.

The good girl inside me stomps her feet and whimpers as he kisses me again. I try to squirm back toward the steering wheel, but Ty's hands won't let me maneuver away, won't let me resist. He holds me down and pulls my soft locks again.

This time, he bites me. It's hot, unexpected, and just a little bit scary.

The scant kisses I've had with other boys can't even compare to this. They're not in the same universe.

He doesn't stop for air either. This man's lips don't quit. They're just driving deeper, harder, ruthlessly taking me over. His tongue pushes into my lips and holds me open. I'm shaking and I can't stop the moan from steaming into his mouth.

He growls back, sucks my bottom lip with his teeth, shoving his tongue against mine. I can't even imagine playing hard to get when he's already inside me, whirling his tongue against mine like he owns it.

Hot. Wet. Unapologetic.

His hands dip down and go below my waist. I moan for precious air when he cups my hips and squeezes. My ass jerks in his hands, and I swing up, accidentally grinding into his lap.

His lips quirk up in a smile against mine when I gasp, feeling how huge and hard he is. He must've planned this. He had to!

Nothing else explains why I'm going to pieces all over this thick, tattooed prince who talks like a street thug. When his thumbs hook just below the waistband to my skirt, catching my panties too, I jerk up and pull away.

I can't speak. I'm too stupefied, too alive with pleasure coursing through my system. My body doesn't want to do anything but *feel.* All my blood goes straight to making sure I'm burning and wet for him.

Ty's ocean eyes are brighter than ever, small worlds dancing in his sockets. He doesn't say anything as he shoves my bottom down in one rough push.

"Oh, God!" I practically come on the spot, and he hasn't even touched me yet. Not *there.*

If it didn't feel so good, I'd be embarrassed. He's fucked a small army of weekly concubines, and I'm just a pathetic virgin, one more reason to hate him for the gulf of sexual experience between us.

Yeah, that's right. I *still* hate this asshole with his hands on my bare ass, pouring his hot breath all over me, even if I happen to *love* what he's doing to me.

He lifts up a hand and aims it at the control panel beneath the window. I jump as the seat falls back, flattening itself low and nearly horizontal. Great, now my bare, slick pussy is practically pressed right against his dick, separated only by his jeans.

I try to edge up, but he grabs me, and pins me down on his waist with a growl. "Don't you fucking move, babe. That's my job."

"Ty, I don't know about –"

This? I think to myself, finishing it as his face goes between my legs. He drags me right where he wants me, making room for us, cutting off my words. One lick, and hell, I don't know about anything.

All the thoughts I have about wriggling away from him and saving face are obliterated the instant his tongue licks between my folds. He licks long, slow, and deep, making me feel how incredible this can be if I just shut up and go along with it.

He's controlling every fucking thing I do, even from the bottom. I want to slap him across the face, keep hitting him before the shame and confusion kills me. But this control, these orders gliding from his mouth on my tender skin...I don't mind it.

My trembling hands resist the urge to fight and clamp down on his shoulders. It's just as well, because his licks are speeding up, making my entire body rock with his hunger. He finds my clit, pulls it into his mouth, and starts dragging the ferocious tip of his tongue across it.

I think about those stupid superhero flicks Mom grew up watching, and insisted on sharing with me when I was a kid.

Bam! Pow! Hiss!

One thing's for sure – he's an honest-to-God ninja when his mouth covers my pussy – and he isn't going to stop until I either say it or blow the car's windows out with my screams.

It's an easy decision, and yet another one he makes for me. The wave pulsing through my body, shooting up my spine and exploding in my brain, doesn't stop for anything. It's like a runaway freight train, and I just realize my pussy's grinding eagerly back against his mouth before I lose it.

Stop fucking thinking so much, beautiful, I hear him growling in my head. *Shut the fuck up and come for me.*

His hands clench tighter on my ass and he drags me across his face, fucking me with his tongue, quickening the strokes like he's tonguing the last desperate crescendo on some instrument. Oh, except *I'm* that instrument, and my body can't hold anymore of the manic fire he's sending through my bones.

My blood boils a hundred degrees hotter and I dig my fingernails into his shoulders. My head snaps back and my neck stretches. The volcano in my lower belly goes off, firing upward, a full body eruption resonating from my pussy into every single extremity.

"Jesus! Fuck! Ty!"

I've never been a religious girl, but I think I've found a new holy trinity. I call out to it again and again and again as my body comes in waves.

And when I say my body, I mean *every* muscle.

It's so strong I almost can't stand it. But when the energy hits my fingers, my toes, curling them like burning bark, I stop just short of passing out. I rock and hitch and scream, gushing on his face, every muscle pleading for him to finish what he's started.

Ty reminds me once again how intimately he knows a woman's body as I'm coming down. His licks soften, growing gentler as I'm gasping and trying to focus my breath. The spasms lessen, and my first orgasm at the hands and lips of a man passes in one last flush of steam.

"Okay, you win," I ooze into his ear, resting my head on his shoulder. "Maybe I do want this. *Maybe.*"

He pulls me back and looks deep into my eyes. Then he kisses me again, making me taste the remnants of myself on his lips, forcing another hungry growl into my mouth.

"You'd better be fucking sure, babe," he says when he breaks the kiss. "There're no do overs here, Claire. No mulligans. This game goes all the way to the finish line. If you fuck with me, we'll both end up broken."

My fingers ache as I finally lift them off his shoulders, gliding them down his chest. Jesus, he's so ripped. I can't believe I'm freely touching him and loving it, admiring how chiseled his mountainous muscles really are.

"You think I don't know that?" My heart swells in perfect rhythm with other parts of me as he slips a hand underneath my blouse and runs it along with my spine. "I'm serious about this, Ty. I'm serious about you, especially because it almost sounds like you're looking for more than a quick and dirty thing."

His eyes go wide. I get a perfect, unobstructed view of those glacial eyes, now moving like they're melting under a high arctic sun. "Damned right I am. Just never found a chick worth trying that shit with 'til I met you."

He kisses me again. It's hard, long, hot, and furious. I don't think I can even find the words to describe this kiss.

My mind's spinning – fucking *whirling* – trying to comprehend the fact that I'm really about to let my brutal step-brother punch the V-card I've held onto for way too many years.

I don't know why I have to confess it. Maybe it'll do something to help me regain my footing, help me grab this thing by the horns before my pussy's wrapped around him the same way.

"Ty, wait." It takes all my energy to sever our lips. "There's something you need to know."

My lips shake. He looks at me when I pause for too long, then reaches up and brushes my hair back, tangling his strong fingers along the way.

"Tell me."

"Uh, I've never..."

Fuck. How the hell do I come clean about this?

"What?" He presses.

"I'm kinda new to sex. I'm...a virgin."

Something goes off in my head. There's a droning sound, something spinning, the entire world collapsing in on itself like someone's blowing a didgeridoo in both my ears.

"Babe?" There's a long pause in his voice. "Babe!"

I should've known it was too good to be true. A second later, the curtain falls across my eyes. I'm falling too deep into a thick, dark blackout to know anything at all.

VI: Long Fuse (Ty)

Fuck me.

A minute ago, I was two seconds away from tearing off my pants and burying my greedy dick deep in her heavenly cunt. Then she had to set off a nuke in my ear and pass the fuck out.

As if it's not a big enough shock to know I'm the first bastard who's gonna have her pussy, she goes dead cold. Out like a dude going down in the ring.

Shit. Fuck.

I lift Claire off me and roll her soft body 'til she's flattened in her seat, checking her pulse, wrestling to remember everything I know about first aid. I hold my face to her lips, measuring her breath.

I wouldn't have done this shit if I still thought she was drunk. I have a raging red flash of the Swede in my mind, and I silently vow I'm gonna put him in his fucking grave if he's slipped her something more than booze, even if I need to track his evil ass to Stockholm.

No, she's too stable to be drugged by more than alcohol. Her vitals are good. I'm no doctor, but I know when some poor woman's been fucked up. I've seen it before with girls in the club, and always end up beating the shit outta the rat sons of bitches who're responsible.

She's just on overload. Overwhelmed by what I did to her, what we were about to do.

Goddamn. I need to get her home. I pull her panties and skirt back up with a sigh, then readjust my dick so it doesn't rip outta my pants.

I drive like hell. My heart's still pounding as I go through the gate and pull into the garage. I never take my hand off Claire's, making sure her pulse stays steady and her temperature doesn't drop.

I should take the back entrance downstairs to sneak in. But I gotta carry her, and I'm not gonna risk tripping on some firewood or old gardening tools laying around side of the house.

I don't give a single fuck who sees us.

I'll take all the hell my dad or his Congresswoman wifey wanna lay on me. Getting her tucked into bed with some blood going to her brain's all that matters right now.

I move fast, holding her tight against my chest. We get downstairs without encountering any shit. Laying her out in her room, I draw a blanket over her, and then head to the wet bar a few rooms over for some water.

I don't know if I should wake her up to drink. She's out deep, mumbling to herself every time I brush her cheek. She's warm, like she's got a slight fever.

Fuck. This thing's got me twisted up. It's hell deciding what to do.

If I rush her off to the nearest doctor, the prick'll probably chide me for being a jumpy boyfriend, and there's always the risk our asshole parents will find out. That's sure to go over like lighting a bonfire inside my old man's yacht.

"Ty? Ty? Ty?" She keeps repeating my name, soft and sleepy. Hypnotic, almost.

I brush her face, but she doesn't move like she's fully conscious. She'll be okay. She's gotta be. There'll just be one fuck of a hangover waiting for her tomorrow.

I'm still imagining all the ways I'm gonna castrate the Swede if I'm dead wrong and something *does* happen to her. I have to stay here tonight. If I can't bring her in to the town clinic, then I sure as hell can't leave her alone.

I kick off my shoes and climb in next to her. Her bed's a good size, newer and bigger than mine, but it feels tiny with her pressed up against me. I wrap one arm around her waist and tug her close, using half my mental energy to make my dick behave.

It took having my hands and mouth all over her to make Claire admit she wanted this. Now, it's my turn to resist, and I've gotta strangle my own goddamned brain to keep my hands from wandering all over her.

It feels like hours pass before I finally drift to sleep. Right before I do, I make damned sure her heartbeat and breathing are steady.

So far, so good.

She'll get through this, and so will I. This shit's just one hurdle. There's still a lotta summer left to fuck the absolute hell outta this girl, rock her world 'til there's nothing left to stand on.

A virgin! No shit. I can't stop thinking about her dirty little secret while sleep tugs at my eyes. *How fucked up is it that I'm obsessed with boning a real, dyed in the wool, card carrying virgin girl who's never so much as touched a dick 'til tonight?*

I'm used to fucking sluts who've practiced sucking off half of Club Zing before they finally get their lips on my golden cock. But with her, I'm glad she's never had anybody else.

I'm fucking thrilled, calmed, tossed into Zen-mode by it. I wasn't bullshitting her earlier. One ugly thought of another man having his way with her, willing or not, is all it takes to twist the key in my chest and make me wanna go into full psycho murder mode.

It's nuts. I shouldn't be this possessive, this crazy obsessed with fucking and owning her every way a man can. Thing is, *shouldn't* doesn't really mean shit when I'm fully prepared to gut any ballsy motherfucker who comes within shouting distance of her panties.

I can't fuck her tonight. But I will. And I'll be the only one who *ever* does.

This sweet, innocent virgin girl wrapped up in my arms is gonna feel every inch of me, and she's gonna goddamned love it. She'll love me. She'll want me. She'll look right past all my flaws. And she's never, ever gonna get enough of this dick once it gets inside her, just like I'll never be able to think straight 'til I've had my fill of her.

Only problem is, I know that once I've had a taste, there's no fucking way I'll ever settle for less. I've got an eerie feeling the last woman I'm ever gonna fuck is hooked tight and warm around me right now, and it's fucking scary.

"Sleep tight, babe," I whisper in the darkness. "You'll need it. You were mine, mine, and only fucking *mine* the second you stepped into the club tonight. Once I get my hands on something good, I don't let go. They'll have to kill me and drag you outta my dead limp hands."

I wake up at the crack of dawn like always.

She's sitting up next to me, rubbing her eyes. Can't tell if it's disbelief that I'm next to her, or else if she's trying to shake off all the shit from last night.

"Ty?" Her voice is so soft.

I roll over, grab the water bottle I've got strategically placed on the night stand, and push it into her hands after unscrewing the cap. "Drink this and go back to sleep, babe. It's been a late night."

For a second, it looks like she's gonna pout. I give her a stern look and don't let up 'til she brings it to her lips. I'm secretly relieved she's not passed out or running into the bathroom to puke her guts out.

The fact that she's sitting up drinking means the exhaustion last night was all stress and hangover. Nothing more.

Claire looks at me, her big brown eyes flashing through the pre-dawn gloom. "What about last night? Did I disappoint you?"

I grab her, pull her close. Fuck, her warmth feels good. Dangerously tempting. I savor it as long as I can without my dick hounding me to fuck her.

"Nothing's changed, babe. Nothing. Listen to me and go back to sleep. We'll have all the time in the world to talk about it when you're well."

I'm a horny sonofabitch, but I'm not selfish or stupid. She's in no condition for the horizontal gymnastics I've got in mind. Fucking will have to wait – as much as I want to stab myself in the eye for thinking it.

She relaxes in my embrace. My words soothe her, and I help her lay down, pulling the sheets up tight for her. It doesn't take much more convincing 'til she closes her eyes. Soon as I see her chest slowing and her breath goes soft, I quietly slip out.

I grab a fresh change of clothes and wash up. Fat Boy left me with a few parting blows on the jaw, but nothing that won't heal with a little time. His sting reminds me the victory was hard won last night, making it all the sweeter.

So does the lingering taste of Claire's lips on mine. No shit, I can still taste everything. Her kiss, her pussy cream, everything I wanted to suck and bite and lick for hours.

God willing, I'll do it again. Soon. Just not soon enough to satisfy my utterly impatient fuck below the waist. There's only one remedy for blue balls that ever works.

I head down the long corridor toward the back door, itching for a morning swim. It's a cool summer morning. I've started many mornings like it – mostly the ones when I don't wake up with some easy broad in my bed, ready to empty my balls before I send her on her merry way.

A long, cold swim will have to do. Sure, I could head down to Club Zing right now and find a few stragglers who'd fall to their knees and suck me off in minutes.

But they're not *her*, and they'll never fuck with my head the way Claire does. They'll never make my dick hammer half as hard as she does, turn me into an aching mess before I've even been inside her.

I'm outside and the big glass door clicks shut behind me. That's when I get the shock of my life.

Dad's sitting in a lounge chair next to the pool, something he never does. He's got a cigar in his mouth. When he sees me, he stops smoking, and gingerly flicks a few ashes onto the tile.

"What the fuck are you doing out here?" I growl, stepping close to the very private space he's intruding in. The pool's always been an extension of *my* territory in this house.

Shit, he barely spends any time in his own house at all. Maybe a little more since he moved in his trophy girl from Congress.

"Why is it so hard to just say 'hello,' Son?" Dad stands, stubs out his smoke, and stops with just a few feet between us. "I know you came home late last night, carrying your sister, Ty. Is the poor girl still alive?"

He's got a sarcastic curl in his lips. He knows damned well she is, and the venom in his voice makes me see red.

"How the fuck did you know?" It hits me, and I run a hand across my face. "Joan. God damn it. You said you'd stop pulling that shit after I turned eighteen – I'm not a fucking kid anymore, old man! You don't need to threaten her to spy on me."

Dad doesn't flinch, even when I get up in his face. He's the only bastard on this planet who doesn't, probably because he can remember me when I was just some gawky kid a few inches shorter than him.

"And you assured me you wouldn't drag Mandy's daughter into your childish antics. She's a good kid. If she's come home too plastered to walk, then you're the reason, and I want to know why."

Okay, Dad, I think. *You want the truth?*

My fuckface of a former manager at the club tried to force himself on her in the backroom after my roughest fight in months. I broke his fucking nose and drove her home, but not before I shoved my face in her virgin pussy 'til she came her brains out.

Hey, maybe we've got something in common after all, assuming your new wife's pussy tastes half as good as little Sis'.

Fuck. That's everything I want to say, but obviously I don't.

It's bad enough the asshole in front of me threatened our poor housekeeper. He's done it before when he wants to pump her about my latest fuck ups, holding her job security over her. Joan cleans early and late, just doing her job, but she sees a helluva lot. She deserves better.

"This is all on *you*, Tyler." He narrows his eyes. "You know that, right? It's time for you to take responsibility, son. Our poor maid wouldn't need to have these unpleasant conversations with me if I didn't have to worry about what's happening in my own goddamned household."

"That's just it — there's *nothing* for you to worry about.

Claire's fine. She just had a late night out. I took care of everything. I stayed with her while she went to sleep. I know how to look after people, Dad, and I sure as shit don't need you to look after me."

I'm about to storm out before this shit gets much more explosive. It was a big mistake coming out here. I'll get in my car and drive to beach, swim in the choppy fucking Pacific to blow off steam. And I've got a lot more circulating in my system now that I'm once again wrangling with this dick I'm ashamed to share blood with.

"When are you ever going to grow up, Ty? When?"

My back's turned, but I can feel him shaking his head behind me. Something about that shit causes me to freeze, spin around, and lock onto his icy stare.

"When are you gonna stop being such a selfish jackass? You don't give two shits about Claire's health or what I'm doing with my life. You're just afraid we're gonna do something dumb in front of the media and rock your little empire, or maybe derail wifey's Senate campaign. You don't need to keep pretending you give a fuck about anything besides money and prestige."

He comes striding up fast, his cheeks flushing red hot. "Little empire? Little?"

Oh, fuck. I can feel the volcano preparing to blow.

"It's that *little* empire that gives you a standard of living ninety-nine percent of the people on this planet will never dream of, Tyler. It's everything I've built with my bare hands! Hell, I would've *loved* to go gallivanting around with women and muscle men in my twenties like you. You know

151

what I was doing?"

Fucking shit. Here it comes. I can't roll my eyes fast enough. Too bad it doesn't shut him up. I tune out for half his rant.

"Living like a monk at the goddamned library...ass in chair, coding like a monkey, building Spree line by line and struggling to earn a thousand dollars a month...I swear, son, you just don't get it...you'd blow your stack and run the minute you stepped a single foot into a room full of fucking angel investors!"

It all washes over me. We both know it. Hearing him drop a rare F-bomb snaps me back to attention. I take a few steps backward and start laughing.

Dad looks like a damned grenade about to blow up and shower me in shrapnel. His fists are pressed tight to his gray slacks and they're trembling. He's not man enough to punch me – sometimes I wish he would, just so we'd finally have it out at a level I can actually understand.

But no, I'm not intellectual enough for him. I'm not a suit-wearing workaholic. I'm not rich enough. I haven't pissed away the best years of my life licking other rich dudes' assholes, and shitting my pants every goddamned week over some new lawsuit or fresh regulation or profits for the shareholders.

"And what would you do if another guy walked up and smashed you right in the face, right fucking now?" He's looking at me like I just threatened him.

Well, fuck it, maybe I did. I'm not gonna be the one to break my old man's jaw – even though he's begging for it.

Somebody else out there is bound to do it for me one day. I can practically hear the old karma train chugging away in the background, hungry to chew pricks like Dad up and shit them back out.

"I'd walk away before that ever happens," he stutters. "I'd...I'd call the police."

The crap coming outta his mouth makes me laugh all over again. I can't help it. If this weren't deadly serious, I'd be rolling on the goddamned ground.

"What, are you a hyena now? This is why I've got to treat you like a child, Ty. You haven't grown up yet. It looks like you never will."

"At least I've grown a fucking backbone." I can't stop growling, and the droning in my throat only quickens when I see the disgust rippling in his eyes.

"You've wasted half your damned life stacking up coin and never doing shit with it. I know I'm gonna get a call one day from some asshole underling who's found you slumped over at your desk." I pause. "As much as you piss me off, I don't want that to happen. I wish you'd let go and pull the stick outta your ass just once. The world doesn't need us to be the perfect model billionaire family. It just needs us to be real."

"Real?" He throws his hands up and paces a lap around me. "What is it with you and that word? What the hell do you know about the real world, anyway? I've given you everything, Ty, and you've taken it all for granted. The six-figure prep school you flunked out of, the summer jobs at my company you blew off, the club I helped you land for a bargain in Seattle...I gave you *too* much."

That makes me snort like I'm fucking drowning. It's just as well, seeing how I need to eyeball the water, or else I might end up punching him in his arrogant shit face after all.

"You didn't give me crap after ma died. Not anything that matters. You gave me food, shelter, clothing, the trust fund. You gave me tutors who tried to ram shit down my throat I wasn't interested in. You gave me all the tools I'd need to become a carbon copy of you. And that's *all* you ever wanted me to be."

Hatred flickers in his eyes like smoke. The fact that he doesn't have an instant comeback says it all.

I've hit the spike and driven it deep. Too damned far to deny because it's true.

"One thing we'll both agree on," I say. "You're more stubborn than I am. You won't stop trying to carve the perfect fucking family and make me into the golden boy you always wanted, even when you ought to know it's too late for all that. You want everybody in this damned house being your props for the perfect PR campaign. You won't just chill and accept this shit for what it is. You're too big an asshole, Dad. Hell, if you'd shut the fuck up and accept I'm never gonna be standing in line to take over Spree when you're gone, maybe I'd give you a pass for picking up your DC gold digger and pissing on Mom's grave!"

Near the end, the filter connecting my brain and my mouth snaps. It's too much, even for the bastard giving me the evil eye. I don't expect him to seriously do it – but he fucking does.

For the first time in a long while, Dad surprises me. He moves real fast, and something hard smashes me right in my bruised jaw.

I tumble back. It's all shock and awe. I've been hit by bigger, badder guys hundreds of times. But the fact that I've actually moved my old man to physically strike for the first time in his damned life is like the sky coming down.

I reach up, touch my lip, and I'm bleeding. He's hit pretty fucking hard for a guy who spends all day at meetings. I wipe the blood away and grin, making damned sure he sees what he's done.

Dad jerks his finger out and stabs me in the chest. "You want it this way, buddy, then you got it. You'll never call her Mom. You'll never respect her. Fine. But you will *not* insult my wife to my face. Understand?"

I'm almost sorry if he weren't such a giant cock. Still, I manage to nod, and he jerks away.

I listen to his footsteps fading behind me and don't turn around 'til they stop. I'm wondering why I haven't heard the door close, and it's because he's still standing there, looking at me like I just stomped mud across his precious Turkish rugs flown in from Istanbul.

"I've been wrong about you. Everything I've given you...it's only held you back. It's poisoned you, Son." His voice is low, cold, robotic. "You've got until the end of summer to pack up your things and leave the state. Make some tough decisions, and do it without me and my dirty money, Ty. I'm selling your club. I'm setting you free. And

155

if I find out you've done *anything* to upset Mandy, Claire, or – God help you – my company, I *will* have you prosecuted and locked away. I don't care if you're my own flesh and blood. You're a sick animal, son, and there's nothing more I can do for you."

I'm fucking stunned. Gutted. I can't believe it's taken me so long to see the fighter instinct is genetic.

Except, unlike the combo punches and gut busters I use to take down my opponents, my old man rips hearts out and pops them in his withered hands.

It's all over quickly, so freakishly fast I can't decide whether to rush him and choke him 'til he passes out, or else fall to the ground and puke my guts out.

He's gone before I can do jack shit. The door pops open and slams shut behind him, rattling the heavy glass.

I've got half a mind to pick up the deck furniture and start throwing it through every hand-crafted window pane lining the back of the house. But fucking up my old man's castle won't really do shit. It'll satisfy my monkey brain and nothing else.

It won't take back what just happened, it won't fix anything, and it sure as shit won't extinguish the firestorm he just hurled on my head.

I'm fucked.

Shit, I'm past wanting the asshole to change his mind. He whipped his dick out and swung it, forever reminding me that I'm a goddamned worm without him and these riches I'm supposed to worship.

Forget it. Damn it. *Fuck it.*

There's nothing left to do except what I came out here for in the first place. I tear my shirt off and drop my pants. Then I run to the pool and dive in buck naked.

I swim fast, furious, and hard as I can, splashing water all over the place. When my limbs are full of fire and my lungs don't wanna pump anymore, my mind's clear enough to start thinking about all the decisions I should've made years ago.

Nothing but the swim keeps me from burning myself alive.

I've got a hundred questions and no good answers. First thing on the list – where the fuck can I go that'll still have waters as clear and crisp as this to clear my head in?

VII: Everything to Lose (Claire)

I wake up more rested than I've felt for years. Guess there's something about having the weight of this insane attraction to my step-brother lifted that makes all kinds of things easier.

And no, after last night, he's not just my cocky, foul mouthed step-brother. He's become my lover.

He's stopped just short of claiming me the deepest way a man can. More importantly, he stopped when he could've taken me, leashed his desire because he cares.

Nobody else ever helped me when I'm sick or drunk except a few close friends like Dana.

Sure, Mom used to do it, but it was always somebody else's job like the housekeeper she hired during her long sessions in DC.

I wake up feeling like a billion dollars for the first time since I moved into this mansion. All the pieces are in place, and that makes me smile. It doesn't fade when I'm in the shower and freshening up. It's so nice to throw on a t-shirt and shorts after my first week wearing all business attire.

Breakfast is next on my list, but first I want some fresh air to help feed the cozy afterglow heating up my brain. I head down the hall to the big glass panels leading outside, hoping the morning chill has faded by the pool.

It's a lovely place to sit and I really haven't enjoyed it enough this summer. Lucky for me, there's still time to enjoy lots of things before the Washington's infamous rainy season creeps in.

I'm almost to the door when I see someone moving in the pool. One quick glance at the smooth, shapely muscles delving through the water like it's nothing tells me who.

It's Ty. And he's – holy shit – completely *naked*.

My body heats with the same delicious energy running through my veins last night. I was buzzed, pretty fucked up really, but I remember perfectly how amazing he felt. Actually, I'm relieved to find out it wasn't just the alcohol and the close call with the Swede that made everything so intense.

No, I'm feeling it again. Something's changed.

I fold my fingers in front of me and clasp them tight, all I can do to relieve the tension building in my muscles.

Jesus. I didn't think it was possible to want another human being so bad, but I do.

The thick glass between us muffles sound, but I swear I can hear his lungs chugging, hot and heavy like a grizzly bear running down a rival. He moves the waves aside like he's Moses, plowing through the waters effortlessly.

Damn, if only Moses had bulging biceps and savage ink on his skin. I'd have paid more attention in church when I was little during Mom's half-hearted, short lived attempts at passing on my grandmother's faith.

I study him, admiring the raw power and grace in his body. It's hard to believe this is normal for him. He's always out there, always training for the next match, a born fighter who won't hesitate to use all that muscle to protect what's his. And apparently, that now includes me too.

It makes me giddy.

Somewhere in the excitement, I notice his face. It's scrunched up in a furious, painful looking way. Fear sparks my heartbeats faster.

At first, I want to run out and yell, ask him if he's all right. But his laps are steady, and I don't believe he'd stay in the pool if something were really wrong. He certainly wouldn't be circling round and round like a shark.

No, it's not his body that's hurting. It's something inside him.

Ty proves me right a second later when he stops, slicks back his messy brown hair, wiping the excess water away. Then he tips his face to the rising sun and screams, fists in the air, bobbing in the water. He's roaring the same way I imagine a man does when he's shipwrecked and knows he's totally adrift, hopelessly severed from civilization.

Alone.

I need to help him. I reach for the door, put my hand on the knob, and freeze just before I open it.

The war cry ripping through the glass is over, and it's quiet again. But something about this new silence *scares* me.

I've seen him upset. I've seen him act like a total ass, watched him wreck a man for putting his hands on me. This rage pouring out of him is somewhere else on Ty's

161

anger spectrum, some dark, evil place I can't comprehend.

No, this is different, and it scares the hell out of me.

I bite my lip and step back, too afraid to go out there. What will he think if I'm intruding on him like this? It might startle him just when he was opening up, destroy the wonderful thing we had last night when it's barely begun to flourish.

I'll find out what's going on. Just not until he's out of that pool.

Scurrying away from the door, I head upstairs and get another surprise. There's no breakfast laid out for me like most mornings. Strange because Joan's been so good about it, and so has my mom. I'm about to head into the kitchen to see if the billionaire might have an emergency Pop-Tart or two when I hear voices.

They're hushed. Angry. Serious.

"Are you sure about this, Gary? It's rough out there for a young man. I can't imagine doing this to my Claire."

"Damned right. I've made up my mind. The boy's had his hand held too much. He's twenty-three years old, for Christ's sake! Sure, he works hard at that club, but he's never learned to work smart. He's used it as a personal playground with his women, his drinks, and those ugly charity fights. It's an embarrassment. Frankly, I'm surprised we haven't all been shamed by the media spotlight by now. It's a nothing short of a miracle."

I stiffen up against the wall. They're talking about Ty, and I've got a sickly feeling it has everything to do with why he's swimming himself ragged and cursing the sky.

"Gary...I don't know. Maybe he just needs some time away. A different job could do him good, something away from the alcohol and testosterone. I could land him something. Lord knows I've pulled enough strings for Claire, and it won't hurt me to get back into touch with some of the folks I'm going to need on my side for the race next year."

My heart sinks like an elevator. God. I don't want to believe that I'm just as privileged as poor Ty and my own work's just as worthless in my mom's eyes, but there it is. It hurts.

"No," Gary snaps. "My mind's made up. Your compassion is a virtue, Mandy, and I love it. But mercy isn't going to get him anywhere. He's had his chances. Honestly, I'm surprised you're not more upset. Your daughter came home stinking drunk last night – that's totally out of character, isn't it?"

"Claire's a young woman," I can hear my mother shrug. "I trust her. She's got a lot to learn, sure, but she'll work through it the same way I did. Trust me, Gary, there are far bigger mistakes a girl can be making at her age than having a little too much fun at the bar."

Fuck. How do they know? Did Joan see Ty bring me in? I can't believe the housekeeper would willingly rat on us, even if she did see something she shouldn't have.

Some seriously bad stuff went down, and I've got a feeling it has everything to do with Gary making threats. Hell, if he's ready to turn his own son out, why wouldn't he threaten the older woman's livelihood?

I didn't like the man Mom married before, but this seals the deal. I fucking hate him.

And he's still droning on about how it's all Ty's fault. Something about how he couldn't get over losing his mother, despite the billionaire's best efforts. He makes himself out to be such a martyr.

I can't seriously believe Gary ever gave a shit. Not with this tone.

"It's a good thing our kids are grown. Well, yours is, anyway," Gary adds, fueling the angry heat simmering in my blood. "I think we'll have to agree to disagree about our parenting styles. Ty's my son, Mandy, and having him out of our hair really is the best thing for everybody. Claire doesn't need his bad influence. Neither does your campaign, and you'd better believe I sure as hell *don't*. I've put up with it for more than twenty years, and I'm done."

That's it then. Exile.

Christ. How long do I have left with him? He could be gone by the end of the week for all I know. Gary's crazy and cruel enough to do it.

I can't take it anymore. I walk into the kitchen and rip the huge stainless steel fridge open, making sure Mom's kefir and kombucha bottles clang together.

Their voices stop. I pretend I'm looking for my breakfast as Mom trots in, concern lining her face.

"Oh, Claire. I didn't know you were awake. I would've had Joan set something up for you..."

"I'm good with cereal, Mom. Hey, are we out of milk?" I'm so flustered I don't see it.

A large hand reaches past me, deep into the second shelf, and pulls out a tall glass bottle. Creamy white and all organic. What else? Everything in this house has to perfect, especially when it's run by the asshole staring at me.

"Here you go, Claire." Gary's smile is so fucking fake it makes me want to spit in his face.

We lock eyes. I can't hide the dark anger undoubtedly swirling in mine, and I'm sure he can see it. He gives me a sharp look, like he's on the verge of chiding me, but then he purses his lips and scurries out between us.

"Sorry, everyone, I should've left for Seattle half an hour ago. I'm going to be exceptionally late if I don't get out the door now."

Mom takes a long step after him like he's forgotten something. Probably her kiss goodbye. Gary keeps going, and doesn't look back before he's out the door.

I feel bad for her. But I'm not sorry I missed seeing their gross morning kiss under these circumstances. She turns back to me, brushing away the worry pulling at her features with a big, politically correct smile. Diplomacy's in her blood.

"You'd better rest up today, honey. I'm surprised you were out so late after losing your first Saturday to overtime."

I shrug and bite my tongue as cereal crashes into my bowl, followed by a generous splash of milk. I've got to admit, the food in this household isn't bad, even if it's as guarded and selectively picked as everything else here.

"There's got to be some time for fun in the career world, right?"

My mom belts out an anxious laugh, and then quickly catches herself. "Oh, of course! Don't let work consume you, Claire. Seriously. It's okay to let loose a little."

She gives me a stern look. I give her nothing more than a shallow nod. I still can't believe the utter shit I overheard.

I'm not in the mood for taking any motherly advice. Not today. Sure, she offered a little resistance to Gary, but nothing that would put teeth into him for screwing over Ty.

Why do the assholes always have to get away with it? *Why?*

Funny, I realize I used to think of Ty as Prince Asshole less than twenty-four hours ago. But I guess I've been wrong all along. There's more of Prince Charming than I thought in him, and I've been overlooking King Dick the entire time.

Mom mutters a few more bits of small talk my way. I mostly shrug and don't respond.

She finally gets the message and heads somewhere else. I eat my breakfast slowly, nursing my stomach after the rough night.

It's a miracle my body didn't collapse after the drunken bender. Not to mention what went down in his car later that night.

God damn it.

Just thinking about it makes me tingle. I remember how hard his hands squeezed my ass, how he pushed his face between my legs with such reckless abandon. We were so close to going all the way too, if only my exhaustion hadn't ruined it.

His mouth was amazing. How incredible would his dick feel inside me? Would he fuck me hard and fast, or would he fill my pussy with deep, long strokes?

My legs shift uncomfortably under the breakfast bar just thinking about it. I have to help my cereal down with some jasmine tea I quickly brewed up on the Keurig. Thinking about sex with Ty scorches me, robs the air from my lungs without him even being in the same room.

I don't know very much about sex, eager student that I am, but I know it's got to be rare for a man to live up to his wild reputation.

So fucking rare.

And the idea that I might never feel how good those lips feel on mine, much less anywhere else, ever again really pissed me off. I can't let this crap with his dad get in the way of *us*.

I wrap up my breakfast and set my dishes in the sink, then take a long walk through the mansion before heading downstairs. I should go shopping or something to lighten the load on my mind, but I can't, knowing he's here.

I head down to my room and read for a while, keeping my ears perked up for any movement in the basement. I'm deep into this article for work about grizzly bear restoration in the Cascades when Ty's door swings open and slams shut. I hear him stirring through the wall, making quick, angry movements.

It's hard to believe he can move after taking so many vicious laps in the pool.

It takes me a minute to gather my courage. I get up and step outside, slowly closing my door behind me so he can't hear. I hesitate when I walk the few steps to his door and hold my hand over it, ready to knock.

Too slow.

Before I can make a single tap, Ty rips the door open with a *woosh*. It's so sudden and rough I jump, holding one hand over my chest like a startled old granny.

Ty snorts with amusement. "What the hell do you want?"

"Can I come in?"

He nods, steps aside, and slams the door behind me. I walk deeper into his room for the first time, trying not to lose my mind. His scent is everywhere, masculine and sexy and overwhelming.

Crap. It takes me a second to remember I'm actually here to talk to him.

"Hey, I heard some things this morning," I say softly, meeting his furious eyes. "I saw you swimming when I got up. You were so angry. I didn't understand why until I went upstairs and heard our parents talking. Gary's got it in for you bad, he's —"

Ty holds a hand up and storms past me, crashing his butt down on the bed. "I don't wanna talk about that fucking jackass. I know what's he got planned. It's no loss. The swim helped me make up my mind."

Why the hell is he so hard to talk to? I'm getting

frustrated, mostly at myself for being so flustered. I step forward and sit next to him on the bed, gingerly laying a hand on his shoulder.

"What are you going to do? I'm here for you. Talk to me."

He gives me a stark, half-skeptical look. But after a few seconds, his eyes soften. I have to suppress a smile, stunned that I've really worked my way into him. He's going to let me in – *right?*

"I'm leaving Washington, Claire. I'm going somewhere I can leave this shit behind and start over. And I mean really, truly start the fuck over. I don't need his billions to make a man outta myself. Just a little coin I've earned in my own damned club, plus my own bare hands." He pauses, looks at me, and delivers the death blow. "I'm going to Alaska."

It slams into my heart like a knife. Jesus Christ. *Alaska.*

It's so foreign. It's the place Mom visits once every so many years when she needs to run off to the wild and escape civilization. Much as I love nature, I've never had the guts to follow her. The stories about thumb-sized mosquitoes and villages with more bears than people are too much.

"Why Alaska? What's there?"

He cocks his head when he hears how defensive I sound. But I can see the determination in his eyes, and that hurts even more, knowing there's absolutely nothing I can say or do that'll change his mind.

"Hard work. Virgin land, babe. Mining. Fishing. Badass motherfuckers who are probably in need of some serious entertainment. But you know, I'm probably not gonna start another club up there – at least not right away. I'm gonna go out to sea, try my hand at fishing. I don't care if the money sucks. I know a thing or two about how to turn a couple bucks into hundreds, and then thousands. I'll clear my damned head for a year by working myself raw, and then I'll figure out the rest. I want the complete fucking opposite of the mold my old man tried to force me through. I'm heading down a different path, and I might as well go all the way. My gut tells me Alaska's the place to find it."

He stops. It feels like my lungs are collapsing in on themselves. I'm starting to wonder if last night was a mistake. It's a cataclysm, a riddle I can't figure out, and it's tying my heart in so many knots I'm not sure I'll ever smooth them out.

I can't regret anything about our night together. If it's all I'll have with him, then I'll cherish it forever. But I can't stand thinking it might be my only taste of this savage, beautiful, tyrannical bastard next to me.

"You're shaking your head again, babe. What's going through your brain?"

Guilty as charged. It takes everything I've got to push down the bitter lump forming in my throat, before I spit out the question suffocating me.

"If you're sure about this, then where do *we* go from here, Ty? What about us?"

"Us?" He rolls it around on his tongue. "Babe, we both made a big fucking mistake last night. I think we both realize that, and it's my fault. I shouldn't have sucked your sweet clit on the side road last night. Listen, if I had any clue my old man was gonna go all mad dog this morning, I'd have never done that shit. Hell, I shouldn't have done it anyway, but you looked so fucking good."

A mistake? A fucking boo-boo?

That's it. This brutal, heart wrenching confession overloads everything in my system. I need to get away from him, and I have to do it now.

I jump off his bed and go marching to the door, but Ty runs after me. He grabs me, whirls me around, slams me effortlessly against the wall. Somehow he does it without hurting me, which is always amazing.

Of course, the glaciers he's formed across my body start melting the instant I'm under him, completely covered by his rock hard muscle. His heart's beating much faster than it was just a few seconds ago. My palms lay flush against his chest, wondering if he's always been so hard through and through.

Maybe last night was a big fat mistake. Maybe I saw something that wasn't really there – an honest-to-God heart behind his steel.

"You're teasing me like a motherfucker, Claire. I'm trying to let you down easy – and you're just making me crazier. Getting my mouth all over a virgin, all over my own goddamned sister...that's where I fucked up. We both know it." He stops growling just long enough to run his tongue across his lips. "What the fuck's going on with you? For real? Why do you make me stupid? I try to back away, try to do the right thing, and you pull me right back. You can't stop teasing every fucking inch of me, begging me to shovel my grave deeper, hounding me to fuck you."

"So do it!" An electric jolt runs through me. "Stop being scared. Don't talk about mistakes. You're all about living on the fly and figuring things out, right? Why don't you just shut up, fuck me, and find out what happens after that?"

The low, breathy rumble in his throat builds. I swear to God there's a pit bull somewhere inside him, and he lunges for me a second later just like a starving dog.

Ty crushes me against the wall. His lips collide with mine so hard my breath vanishes in a single second. I'm not just going to lay down and take it, collapse against him.

I can't decide if I love him or hate him, and that's making me insane. It's making me hate myself for being so mixed up, just as unable to let him go as he is with me.

I give him everything in my kiss. I kiss him, bite him, shove my tongue against his, moaning like a total whore into his mouth when his huge hand squeezes my thigh.

"Tell me you fucking want this," he snarls, breaking the kiss. "Beg me to fuck you again."

"Do it, you bastard. I don't care anymore. Nothing makes sense when I'm just staring at you, feeling you. I need you inside me. I need it *now.*"

He lets out a low laugh and shoves his chest to mine, flattening my hard nipples on his shield-like torso. "That's what I need to hear. I know it's real when you say that shit. I can almost believe we're not making a huge mistake, almost believe it's meant to be. You're lucky you got it out now, Claire. I wouldn't have fucking stopped, even if you told me."

He thrusts between my legs, hard as ever, stroking the massive erection popping out his shorts against my pussy. Jesus, we're closer to joining than ever, separated by only a couple thin layers of fabric.

And his lips don't stop. They keep coming, burying mine in waves. I'm a sucking, biting, sopping wet mess by the time he breaks to run his fingers through my hair. Ty growls, fists my brunette locks, and pulls my head taut to give his next few kisses an even better landing.

His tongue's hypnotic. No joke. No lie.

Time loses all meaning as long as mine's wrapped around his, led in a dizzying clockwork dance that stirs every ounce of my blood.

Neither of us know what the next hour, day, or week's going to bring. Right now, I'm content to live in the moment, as long as it means being pressed to his granite flesh.

The saner part of me keeps screaming *no, no, no.*

You can't do this, she howls. *You can't seriously push down your panties and fuck your own step-brother.*

It's weird. It's wrong, so terribly twisted on so many levels I don't even —

Moaning louder into his mouth, I shut the good girl up. My body knows exactly what it wants. My heart's just as confused as ever, but my pussy's humming with delight, wet and blooming open for him to take me any second.

Ty swoops away from my lips and begins stamping fresh kisses down my neck. I gasp pure delight at the sensation, wondering how low he's going to go. He shows me an instant later, shoving my blouse aside, sucking deep into my neck while his hands wander up and squeeze my breasts.

My knees drop out. I'd seriously hit the floor if it wasn't for his strong arms holding me up, and the pressure of that seriously mean dick grinding between my legs.

I don't know how I'll die first if he doesn't give it to me soon. Will I burst into flames, or just drown from the bottom up?

I want him. I fucking need him. And I never, ever want him to let go, no matter how harsh and crazy things get with our messed up family.

"Ty, Ty, Ty..." His name hisses out like a mantra, all I can do to keep myself grounded.

I'll never live it down if I pass out again while we're this close. I'm not drunk this time – not on liquor – but I'm definitely intoxicated by his touch, his taste, his divine scent.

Ty steps back, points to my shirt, and then grabs my hips. "Take that thing off for me now. I'm gonna work your pussy twice as hard while you strip."

Holy shit. Before, his orders just made me see red, but now I'm tugging at my shirt like it's made of poison ivy, desperate to drop it on the floor.

Ty's falls to his knees and jerks down my jean shorts. When he spots the wetness on my panties, he stops and

174

smiles, then lowers his face to the wet spot like a target and grabs my black lace with his teeth.

Typical virgin. I practically orgasm right on the spot before he's even licked me. I don't know how I can possibly be more sensitive than yesterday, but I am, maybe more so this time because there's not a trace of anything from a bottle scrambling my system.

My boobs fall out and catch his hungry eyes. I'm about to work off the bra when loud, wooden thunder claps next to us.

Oh, no. Oh, Jesus Christ.

"Claire? Ty? Are you two both in there?" Mom's voice calls out less than a second after knocking at the door.

Ty gives me one quick glance and then he's off, grabbing at my clothes with one hand, and carrying me over his shoulder with the other. Ripping open his closet door, he points to a narrow space between a couple boxes and an old guitar with his eyes.

"Cover your nose and mouth. It's not too dusty, babe, but you've gotta stay quiet."

He pushes the door shut just as Mom calls my name again.

"Coming. Give me a damned second." It's all he needs to throw on a shirt and straighten his shorts.

I cringe when I think about my mother seeing that huge dick peeking out of his pants. That's right – the same one that was about to fuck me, if only the fates hadn't conspired to keep it away from me *again*.

"Ty!" Mom sounds oddly surprised. "Have you seen

your sister anywhere?"

"She went out for a long walk. That's all I know."

There's a long pause. I can practically see Mom's eyes studying him, checking for truth. I keep my hand pressed tight over my mouth, anything to avoid breathing a little too loudly or coughing when I shouldn't and blowing my hiding place.

"Hm. I suppose I'll wait until she returns. Listen, I'm really sorry for everything your father's putting you through. I tried to change his mind."

"I don't need your fucking sympathy. My old man's an asshole, plain and simple. You'll figure it out too with a little time, Mandy."

"We'll have to agree to disagree about that, young man." Mom says smartly, mustering her sharp Congress tone. "You know, whatever life has in store for you, it'll go so much smoother if you just find a way to relax. You don't need to be so angry and on edge all the time. *Chill.*"

I almost laugh. I've never heard her use that word, and it's so fucking out of place while I'm standing here half-naked and wet, every part of me still pleading to fuck my step-brother when it's the most reckless thing I can possibly do.

"Whatever, Congresswoman. I'll work on that. Now, if you'll kindly go pester some lobbyists or something, I've got shit to do."

The door slams shut a second later. I listen closely for Mom's footsteps, feeling them synched to my thudding heartbeat. There's a new bitter lump lodged deep in my throat, and I'm choking on the cold realization of just how fucked up things really are.

God damn it. It won't let up – will it?

If I needed a sign from the heavens that I'm about to screw the pooch even harder, it's this. I'm not meant to fuck him. I'm supposed to sit quietly until he mopes away from the house and I never see him again. Maybe if I'm lucky, I'll end up getting my pussy stamped by some nice, clean boy with a six figure salary and one lonely, carefully concealed bunny tattoo.

Ty marches over and rips the closet open a second later. I'm pulling at my clothes, trying to cover up my nakedness, feeling the heat rush out of me.

"Fuck, that was close. You okay, babe?" His shirt's off again.

I stop and gawk at his chest, but this time I feel my lust melting. It's like a cruel reminder of everything I can't have.

"No. Not anymore, I mean." I can't lie to him.

I'll disappoint him, I'll get under his skin, but I'll always give him the truth. That's something I can offer that no one else in his life does.

"Claire? What the fuck!" He jumps when he sees me heading for the door, blocking its path with his huge, tattooed body.

The wildcat on his chest looks extra angry today – mad enough to leap off his skin and tear me to shreds. It's the last violent straw I need to feel hot tears stinging at my eyes.

"Goddamn it, babe, talk to me!" Ty jerks me into his arms and closes them tight, smashing my face into his chest. "What the fuck happened in there? I thought we were gonna fuck?"

"Oh, come on!" I need to pause and catch my breath, suppress the shameful shudder sweeping through me. "Don't you get it yet? We're not meant to do this, Ty. We really aren't. You were right earlier – this thing between us is just a big ugly mistake – and we were about to make it bigger. Just let me go. Forget about me. You'll have plenty of girls when you get to Alaska. They'll be easier, hotter, and not related by marriage."

I try to make another run for the door, but he jerks me back, flattens me against his chest. I'm crying and acting like a total idiot, but it doesn't stop me from feeling a wicked pleasure when he brings his face close.

I don't know what the hell I want anymore. I just want him to decide for me.

Rough stubble on his jaw scrapes my cheek. He's winding his way to my ear, and his lips stop, hot and heavy with breath.

"I don't buy that superstitious bullshit, babe, and neither should you. The only thing stopping us from hitting the sheets and fucking right now is what's in your head. Now, you gonna forget about it on your own so we can get down to it? Or do I have to make you by slamming your pussy so hard you won't think about anything except how good you feel?"

My spine's tingling. I don't resist as he brings his lips to my throat, hot and possessive, sucking in flesh that's becoming tender again alarmingly fast. Several sucks and love bites like that and he grabs me, whips me around, pushes me up to the wall where we left off.

He drops to his knees and fists my panties, tearing them away in one jerk. I have to bite my tongue to keep from screaming out loud.

I don't know what to think or feel anymore. All I can do is hold on to the pleasure rushing through my veins. It's like standing next to a freight train whistling by me at full speed, especially when he pushes his mouth between my legs and finds my clit with his tongue.

"Oh...*fuck!*"

My ass bobs against the wall and I fight to keep my balance. My hands go to his shoulders, and I dig my nails into his perfect skin, feeling a dozen curses light up my brain at once as his licks across my pussy deepen.

Ty sucks me. He needles me. He bites me.

I thought I understood what it's like to come all over his marvelous lips after last night in the car. But this is different. It's rougher, it's raw, and it's so fucking real my skin sizzles with every jolt he sends through my nerves.

Mostly, he spins me around and around by the clit with his devilish tongue strokes. I can't get enough air into my lungs the closer I get to going over the edge, and he's forcing me there lightning fast, dragging me to the precipice by my smothered, throbbing clit.

When he feels me tighten up and my knees start to wobble, he grabs the backs of my thighs and pushes me closer, catching me before the climax brings me to the floor.

Fucking hold on and let it all out, babe, I hear him telling me through his lips. *Come on my goddamned face. Come like you've always wanted to.*

I don't know if I'm really reading him. I don't care. I do it.

My body tenses up and the fireball in my belly explodes outward. For the next few glorious minutes, I'm running on autopilot, a breathless, gushing, blinded mess who can't stop grinding on his chin.

My hips drag my pussy straight into fresh licks, and he doesn't stop, even when I'm collapsing on top of him, begging through the explosion. He's fucking killing me with this white hot pleasure, and I'm ready for my heart to stop.

I wish everything could stay obliterated the way it is when I'm locked in climax. There's no worries here. Nothing holding me back from just enjoying our skin fused together. No complications or family dramas to smolder the fires in our hearts and minds.

When I'm finally coming down, I feel him take his face away and wipe it, but only for a second before he lifts me up. Ty holds me while he drops the rest of his clothes with his free hand, guiding me over to the bed, that magical forbidden place where I've imagined him fucking me too many times to count.

It's cool against my bare ass, or maybe it's just the furnace still roaring in my bones. "Fucking shit. You taste so goddamned good, babe. You know I've been thinking about how tight this gets since the day you moved in?"

He cups my wet pussy with his hand, laying two stiff fingers against my clit. He circles it just hard enough to make me squirm. I'm amazed my body recovers so quickly. It's like I'm addicted to him, and rest is totally out of the question whenever he's touching me.

I manage to open my eyes and shake my head. It's seriously hard to believe he wants me as bad as I do him, but his words say otherwise. Hell, so does his touch.

It's also hard to believe how fucking huge he really is.

I'm getting a good look at his dick for the first time, pulsing away in his fist. I'm not sure how the hell he'll fit inside me, but damn if I'm not going to try to take every inch.

He's long, swollen, angry. A bead of pearly sap forms on its little slit and dribbles down to the bed, his pre-come marking the sheets, which are about to get a whole lot wetter.

"Fuck. I can't stand it anymore. You need me to wear a rubber or what?" He reaches for my thighs and pushes them apart, blue eyes glowing like a hungry wolf's as he stares at my pussy.

My cheeks are so red. Some of it's the pleasure, but I'm scared as hell of disappointing him.

Do the words ever come easy when two people are staring at each other buck naked, ready to fuck the way they've imagined for weeks?

"No, no," I shake my head and whisper. "As long as

you're clean...I've been on the pill for a while. Just never had a good reason for taking it until now."

His eyes glow even brighter. "Thank fuck. I'd be scared of fucking right through the condom anyway. Once I'm in this pussy, babe, it's mine. I won't stop 'til long after you're screaming my name. There's no off switch, no refunds, no reverse. Understand?"

I don't. But I want to.

My knees are shaking as I spread my legs wider, reaching for his hand. He clasps my fingers and takes it as a cue to crawl forward. He covers me, an immense beast as big and feral as the tiger tattooed to his chest.

"You're wet as fuck, but I'm gonna make you cascade. Come on, baby. Push that clit against my dick. I wanna hear you moan. Beg me for this dick with every breath."

He drags his full length up and down my pussy several times. My folds push snug around him, so fucking close to swallowing him up, feeling him inside me, everything I want with an intensity that completely devours every hunger I've ever known.

Our flesh steams, pressed together. It's hard to believe he's there, right up against me, ready to dig in and fuck me skin-to-skin. But I can't deny *this* pleasure, so deep and dark and much more primal than having his mouth teasing me a minute ago.

With a growl, his mouth slips down to my nipple. I'm shocked for about the hundredth time today, and let out a whimper as my back arches into his bite.

God, it's good. His hands catch mine and pin them

down above my head. That's when I realize he isn't screwing around – he seriously wants me to beg him for it.

Not just with my words, but with my body.

And – believe me – I'm a hot, pleading mess half a minute later. My fingers flex against his, scratching his skin. My words barely come through the teasing friction of his tongue flicking my bud, and his rock hard cock sliding against my clit.

"Please, Ty. *Please*. Fuck me. Give me what I want."

No, that can't be right. This is *way* beyond wanting. I fucking *need* him inside me in the next five minutes, or I'm going to die of a stroke right here in this bed.

"Ty..."

He cuts me off by tightening his teeth around my nipple. He holds it there, slashing his tongue against it in circles, making me feel the same shock he gave my pussy all over again.

"Come on! I know you want it too. You need it, Ty, just like me...don't you?" I roll my hips as hard as I can into his dick. He needs to want me too.

He growls pleasure through my breast. It works. He lifts his face a second later, beaming those bright blue headlights in his handsome face straight through me.

"Fucking-A. You're a goddamned whore when you're pussy's on my dick – you know that? I fucking love it."

So do I. I should be offended, but his filthy talk turns me on. Prince Charming has a tongue like a whip, and I bare myself for every strike.

I grind my soaked slit against his length again, showing

my teeth, hissing out my wanton need that's all slut.

Never doubt a virgin girl who's been clinging to her purity for far too long. Ty pulls back and gives my wrists a rough shove, holding them in place. His dick takes aim and starts to push inside me when he thrusts forward.

My eyes go wide. I'm struggling to count inside my head so I don't forget to breathe. But my brain can't even comprehend numbers when he's halfway inside me, pushing his way in, filling me with that mad, masculine fullness that's Ty to the core.

"Fuck, you're tight." He sounds amazed, and it comes out in a whisper.

Apparently, I'm not the only one going breathless here. He's much more experienced than I am, and he shows it a second later when he increases his force, plunging his cock into me until it can't go any farther.

My pussy stretches around him. The tingle's hot, precariously positioned between pain and pleasure, but I know I want more of it.

I shove my lips up to his and we kiss. It's all the signal he needs to roll back and pound into me again, this time a little faster. I moan into his mouth and twine my tongue with his. His tongue pumps in and out, rhythmically matching the tempo of his dick, fucking me in both holes at once.

My hands keep flexing, struggling to grab onto something, but he won't let them up. I'm being buried by this animal all over me, my filthy step-brother, the last man on earth who should be slamming his giant cock against the entrance to my womb.

I don't care anymore. I swear I fucking don't.

I can't bring myself to care about anything except how good it feels, and how incredibly quick he's making me come my brains out.

"Just keep fucking me back, babe," he growls. "It's about to get a whole lot faster."

He isn't lying. My pussy struggles to accommodate him as he tilts his hips and starts pumping me two, three, four times as fast. I manage to get one hand on top of his hand and hold on for dear life.

A scream comes belting out of my mouth. There's no time to muffle it, but Ty does it for me, shifting up so he can fuck without needing to hold the other hand on the bed. He grabs my legs, pulls them around him, and keeps on going, clapping his palm tight over my mouth.

The insane pressure sets me off.

I fucking bite him as everything below my waist coils up and explodes. The firestorm hits my brain a second later, and I'm bathed in mind-bending pleasure, a current of animal pleasure that takes me into a whole new zone.

When I'm here, I don't care about Gary or Mom or even the fact that Ty's leaving. I don't care about bursting a lung and telling everyone in this house that I'm fucking my own step-brother.

Jesus, I don't even care about how I'm going to sit straight at work tomorrow.

Ty snarls, quickening his thrusts, slamming between my legs like a human jackhammer. The bed's slapping the floor and squealing. I swear it's louder than the way it rocked when he was fucking his club slut.

It's a big mistake thinking about that bitch halfway through my orgasm. Her memory makes me want to suck every last drop of come from his balls, make him unload everything inside me, all the seed he'll ever have.

If he's my first fuck, then I want to be his last. I want to keep coming on this cock forever, depriving every other woman on earth from experiencing his glory.

I'm finally starting to breathe again, coming down from the high, and realizing what a jealous bitch I am. Ty looks at me and slows his strokes, just enough to bring his lips to my ear.

"You'd better get used to this feeling, Claire. You're gonna spend every spare second you've got glued to my cock when we're both in this house. I'm fucked when I come inside you. Straight up fuckin' doomed. I'll be thinking about how good this sweet cunt feels wrapped around me the same way I think about drawing my next breath." He pauses, slams his cock into me harder, rocking my whole body. "I fucking need this, dammit. I need what's mine."

There's that M-word again. Hearing it a few more times doesn't lessen the impact. When he says it, my toes curl, and not just because his cock's plunging deeper, harder, faster.

What the hell does it mean to truly belong to Ty Sterner? To be *his*?

I come a little closer to understanding when he picks up

his hips and fucks into me again. The hot, feral voice in my ear fades into a sucking kiss just below my ear. His teeth graze my tender skin, and then he sinks them in rougher.

He's biting me. Marking me the same way a wild animal claims a mate.

As if this couldn't get any more wrong...

Fuck, why does it feel so good to be bad?

He finally releases the death grip he's got on my hands. I wrap my fingers over his strong neck and hold on tight, pulling myself up tighter to meet his deep strokes, fucking him back.

Ty's words come in slower, heavier bursts when he releases his teeth. Or maybe I'm just losing my sense of time. The superhuman pleasure crashing in this bed blurs everything.

"Oh, fuck...baby...fucking shit...fuck, fuck, *fuck!*"

The last few F-bombs drop in a steady beat, perfectly synchronized with the thud of his hips on mine. He's fucking me so hard and deep his pubic bone grinds against my clit, introducing me to yet another delicious sensation.

I can feel the music in our bodies. My veins sing, lungs full of fire, begging him to fill me. I want to overflow with his seed.

My pussy starts clenching on his dick just as a lower, rougher growl pours from his throat. The next few thrusts are dynamite. Explosions pick my muscles up and slam me down – or else it's just the incredible clap of his skin on mine as he slams himself into me at breakneck speed.

I can't feel my fingers. I'm probably scratching raw lines

down his muscular back, but there's no sign he cares. If anything, it's edging him on.

I'm coming before he grabs my ass, pulls me up onto his cock, and impales me on his fullness. That's when I feel him swelling, holding himself against my womb as his tip balloons.

"Fuck, Claire – fucking come with me!"

I have to bury my face in his shoulder before orgasm beats me blind and stupid. It's all I can do not to scream so loud it'll echo through the house. Ty's shaft throbs deep inside me, and he holds me down while thick magma jets burst inside me, deeper than ever, completely flooding my depths.

We're fucking and rocking and coming for a small eternity. I swear our bodies match the rolling Pacific behind the house.

Hungry. Roaring. Insatiable.

His muscles flex around me like never before. It would take a bomb to break us apart. We're glued together as molten come pumps into me, pumps deep, pumps for what feels like forever.

He doesn't stop growling. It's a steady hum, a mantra rooted in his ecstasy, a sound I'll remember on my deathbed. I'll never get tired of hearing this thunder.

I'm already missing it when the pleasurable hurricane washing over us fades. Baser sensations return to the numbness pooling in my toes, and it rolls up my body. I'm going to hurt like hell tomorrow.

I'll probably be sore, inside and out, but it's not like it

stops me from wanting more. I bring my lips to his and bury myself in a long, wet kiss.

His lips taste sweet, full, and addictive. Okay, now I'm in really big trouble.

What the hell are we going to do? The deed's done, and I hope to God it's not the last time. But if he really has to leave before the end of the summer, that means I'll lose these monstrous muscles wrapped around me.

His hands help me settle on the bed. Slowly, he pulls out, climbs over my legs, and flops down. I lay on his chest, just savoring his heartbeat, trying to quiet all the hateful worries flooding my head.

"That was so good, Ty. Better than anything I imagined." My voice purrs faintly, robbed of its energy by our sex. I like it.

"Good. We'd both be in trouble if I disappointed a fucking virgin." He smiles. "You rocked my world too, in case you're wondering. It doesn't take mad skills to get me off. Long as you look half as pretty as you do now, I'm gonna need to rub balm on my dick or some shit before the summer's out."

The joke's so crude and ridiculous it makes me laugh. I roll my fingers down his chest, fixing them around the tiger's black eyes staring out through his muscle.

"Okay, what's the deal with the cat? Did you eat too many Frosted Flakes as a kid, or what?"

He slaps me on the ass. I yelp, shocked, but quickly return his soft smile when I hear him chuckling.

"That's my latest and greatest, babe. Probably got room

for a few more, but this one will be hard to beat." He stares at the ceiling, as if he's taking a long journey through time and space. "I had it done a couple years ago, right after I got back from India. I pretended to give a shit about Spree's new market so I could tag along. Soon as I was off the plane, I slipped out and explored. Ended up having tea with this shaman, who did some mystic reading and told me this was my spirit animal. I thought he was full of shit 'til I saw the cat staring at us out his window."

"No way!" I slap his chest, wondering if he's just jerking me around. Then again, I guess we already did plenty of that.

"No bullshit. That big, beautiful bastard came right up to the window and showed his teeth. Man eating tiger, stripes and all. He looked right at me. The old guru just shrugged like he was expecting the thing to come in and drop off a package. The sly smile on that fucker's face trumped my doubts."

Flashing him a mischievous smile, I slide my hand lower, resting on his tight packed abs. "Oh? I thought you told me you weren't the superstitious type?"

"No, not really. Shit, I'll leave the door open to anything, even a little crack. This world's a strange place. Besides, I'll say anything if it gets me more of this pussy, babe." He preempts my slow, plodding circuit to his dick by pushing his hand between my legs and finding my clit. "I'm not just saying that to be an ass. I'm hooked. I dunno about nirvana beyond this world, but the pink between your legs is as close to heaven as I'm gonna get."

He rubs just enough to bring me into the zone. Then, without warning, he pulls his hand away, bringing his fingers to his lips. I watch in stunned silence as he licks my cream into his mouth.

His hand darts out and slaps my ass again, this time a little more playfully. "Now, stand up and get dressed," he orders.

What the hell? We can't be done here!

"Huh? Why?" I stutter.

"Because somebody needs to go upstairs and make sure the coast is clear. If you don't see your ma or Joan putzing around, we'll go right back to fucking, and I won't even have to gag you this time."

Asshole.

I'm smiling, trying to fix my screwed up sex hair as I quickly dress. Asshole or not, I want to hurry up and return to this bed as soon as I can. Anything to have him inside me again.

"How the hell am I going to survive the rest of the summer?" I ask him, pulling my shirt down over my belly.

Ty folds his hands behind his head and shrugs. "Fucked if I know. Good thing we've got about seven or eight weeks before my old man has me arrested for hanging here. That's plenty of time, and I'm gonna do more than break you in. Your pussy's gonna fit my dick like a goddamned glove by the time I ship off for Alaska. That's a fucking promise."

I wish I could make him promise not to leave.

Tomorrow's a complete mystery to me, and so is next

week. It doesn't bother me as much as it will later. Today, all I want to do is fuck my step-brother a few more times until I can't move.

Is that so wrong? And if it is, I've got a bad feeling I won't know what's right ever again.

I'm dragging on Monday morning.

Every time I stand up, walk, or even just sit with my legs stretched out, my body reminds me of the filthy fuckfest we had all through the night.

Ty on top of me. Ty thrusting into me from behind, pinching my ass cheeks tight in his hands, shoving my face into the pillows. Screaming my pleasure to the steady clap of his balls against my skin. Ty all around me, burying me, owning me, fucking me, growling threats into my ear about all the ways he's going to make me crave him forever.

God. I think I know how a freshly fired pistol feels.

The worst part? He's absolutely right.

I'm on day two since getting my v-card punched, and I'm already hooked to this man and his savage bedroom ride. And if that's not incredible enough, Ty got up early to drive me into work. It's hard to be around him all dressed up, thinking about the ways he can mess up my neat business outfit all over again.

I can barely concentrate during the team meeting this morning, much less this list building exercise Dan Jacobsen wants done by the week's end.

The names wash over me. I see nothing but vulgar, sweaty, tattooed fucking in every name and email I click through. The gutter has officially pulled my mind in deep.

Of course, none of it changes the fact that we're going to face a terrible reckoning when Ty really has to leave. I'm not sure what'll happen. It hurts just to think about it.

This crazy thing can't last, can it? But I don't want it to be over. Not when it's barely begun.

I bite my lip, working as well as I can, imagining all the insane possibilities. I'm seriously considering joining him in Alaska after my internship ends. It's starting to sound a lot better than struggling to move into a high priced apartment in Seattle for whatever political gig I can wrangle up next.

No, I *don't* want anything to do with Mom's Senate campaign. I'm still pissed she's decided to march to Gary's brutal drum. If she can rationalize him kicking Ty out and leaving him cold, what else will she cave in to?

And I definitely don't want a cent more from the billionaire prick who wipes his shoes on his own son the same way he does to the rest of the world. I don't care if he bought me a car. He's a total bastard who puts appearances over everything else.

"Claire." There's a knock at my cubicle.

I spin around and see Dan standing there, tall and genteel in his dark brown suit. "What's up?"

"I'd like to see you in my office at the end of the day. There's a special project we need to discuss." He pauses and winks. "Don't worry. Nothing about the quality of your work. That's been fantastic, and I can see the lists are going splendidly."

"I'll be there."

Dan doesn't wait another second. He takes off and leaves me staring, wondering what the hell he's got in mind.

Ugh. I guess there's such a thing as working *too* well.

I don't exactly want more responsibilities dumped on me with Ty tempting me to follow him to the ends of planet earth. Having a quiet, lazy summer is starting to sound really good, especially if it's the only way I'll get to be alone with him. Well, before I have to make another fateful decision about uprooting my life.

Am I really willing to chase this tattooed bad boy's cock all the way to Alaska?

The good girl inside me stares at me like I should be wearing a straitjacket. The rest of me knows damned well what she wants. She sneaks up and starts choking the hell out of the perfect princess, my conscience, screaming for me to follow my heart into the wild.

At least there's a few more weeks to decide what I'm going to do. Who knows, maybe I'll find out once and for all if Ty's heart really matches the oversized flesh hanging between his legs.

"Mister Jacobsen? Dan?" I knock on his office door and it swings open.

He's never got it totally shut. Guess he subscribes to the new Zen of office openness all the managers are preaching these days, especially in the relaxed, progressive work environment Cascades Now! represents.

"It's beautiful out there, Claire. Too good to waste." He's standing by the window, and turns to face me when I'm inside. "How about we get out of the office and talk over drinks? There's a little Irish place I know up the street. Killer happy hour."

My heart stops. Mother of God.

My boss isn't seriously hitting on me – is he? If he is, I'm more worried about how the hell I'm supposed to let him down.

I can't say I have a boyfriend. Somehow, I don't think telling him I'm secretly starting to love my foul tempered step-brother and his massive fucking cock will go over well either. Dan's a traditional man, however radical his environmental views.

I freeze up and try to think through it, letting the rational side take over.

It's just a drink. It's innocent. He won't force anything on you unless he wants a harassment suit. Just go with it.

I shrug and give him a small, friendly smile. "Sure. It's been a long day. I guess I can use a beer or a glass of wine. Um, a friend drove me in today, so I'll need a few minutes to call a cab."

"Nonsense!" Dan pounds his fist on his desk. "We'll go together. Just let me know when you're friend's coming to pick you up later. I'll drop you back here at the office and you can go home from there."

Jesus. His eyes are wide and hopeful like a puppy's staring through a pet show window. I feel awful about leading him on. Even worse that Ty's the one who'll be picking me up. He snuck a few more grabs at my thighs and ass before I slid out the door this morning.

He can't keep his hands off me, and I don't want him to. I start to wonder what'll happen if he pins me down and smothers me with his lips right in front of my boss. I shouldn't let him, but I can't promise I'll keep a grip on anything the instant his hands are on me.

For a crazy asshole, my prince has got *charming* nailed down.

I need to be careful. Jacobsen can't see the badass in the fancy car picking me up – and no fucking way can he see the look Ty gives me when his eyes are glued to my body. It'll be a dead giveaway for everything.

I have to get out of this, and I need to let my boss down easy. I want to be polite and professional, no matter how good it feels to let Ty wreck everything civilized with his kiss.

"Okay," I say smartly. "Just let me grab my purse and we'll go!"

I'm trying to stay upbeat all the way to the bar. It's a little further than Dan says – just the kinda cruising distance a man in full courtship mode plans for small talk. I go along with it, always steering the topic back to work and wildlife preservation when he starts to get too personal.

The bar is really pretty decent. Thank God for small favors.

It's been way too long since I've had a nice, tall, bitter Guinness. It's a welcome distraction from the awkward scarecrow sitting across from me. Yeah, even if I didn't have step-brother on the brain, I wouldn't date a man as lean and soft as Dan.

"Tell me, where do you see yourself in five years, Claire?" Dan asks, staring down at his half-empty lager.

"Kicking ass and taking names."

He laughs like a fool at my lame cliché and I want to shoot myself. My mind's still drifting back to Ty. My pores open up and sweat when I think about how good it'll feel to sink down on his cock later.

I'm sore, but I'll take it. Every damned inch. I want to ride him tonight, bury my face in his slab of a chest and lick his tiger right on its roaring mouth.

He likes it rough. Apparently, so do I.

I'm going to bite Ty while I'm dragging my nails across his skin. Hell, I'm going to make him bite *me*. I never knew I was part pain slut until I came the hardest with his teeth clamped down around my nipples, or sucking at my throat, leaving his hot, vicious impressions all over my body, inside and out.

Dan slams his heavy glass down with a clink. I blink. Shit. Is he still talking?

"What's that, boss?" I smile sweetly, hoping all these dirty thoughts aren't painting my cheeks bright red.

"I said, isn't it a bit warm for that thing?" He points to my turtleneck. "Summers are short in these parts, Claire. I thought you were born and raised in Washington like me?"

Nodding, I pull on my sweater, adjusting it uncomfortably. "Totally. Lucky me that I get cold *real*

197

easily. The only place I ever enjoyed wearing skirts and flip flops was DC in the summer. Can't imagine living there, though!"

I've always been quick on the draw when I need to be. The sweater's a big, fat lie hiding the aftermath of our fucking. It's unpleasantly warm when I'm wearing it outside, but it beats the alternative, having nosy pricks like my boss see the hickeys stamping my neck.

Then again, maybe I should've let him see them. Then I wouldn't be sharing this insufferable happy hour with a guy who has zero chance of going anywhere further than a friendly conversation.

He relaxes, an understanding smile tugging at his lips. "Ah, I'll drink to that. Everything about DC's stifling, and I don't just mean the politics."

I give him a pathetic, fake smile for about the dozenth time since we sat down at the bar. Jesus, I'm fidgety. I need to pay him some tiny morsel of respect, I know.

But it's hard to give my boss the time of day when I've got a bad boy waiting to pick me up. It's hard to do anything except think about how he's going to rail me tonight, beat the worries out of my head with those piston hips slamming me into the mattress.

"So, you're set on staying in Cascadia, then? No big ambitions to move somewhere else and follow in your mother's illustrious footsteps?" Dan smiles shyly.

"Ew, none at all. I *love* helping out on causes I believe in. But I fucking hate politics."

Dan cocks his head when I drop the F-bomb. Great.

Ty's dirty mouth is really rubbing off on me in more ways than one.

"Sorry. Didn't get much sleep last night and I hit it pretty hard at the office today. I really shouldn't use that kind of –"

"Hey, it's nothing to apologize for. You're more political than you think." There's that awkward wink again. Dan licks his lips and continues. "I mean, that's how it looks to me. You've got the right mouth on you to intimidate some of those bastards in Washington for sure."

"Thanks."

"No, I really mean it, Claire. In fact...I'm hoping you'll consider a full time position with our organization by August. We've got one coming up, and with the quality work you've been doing, well, you're first in line to fill it."

Talk about desperate. I haven't even put in ten days, and he's already kissing my feet. It's awkward, uncomfortable, and kinda disappointing.

Is this really how things work out here in the real world?

I take several long pulls from my dark beer before answering. Cascadia Now! is fine for an intern gig, sure. But my life's totally up in the air with Ty in the picture. I'm not exactly looking forward to spending more time than necessary with Dan Jacobsen and his puppy dog eyes.

I'm also wondering how he'll react when I finally shoot him down. Some guys take it badly. How awkward will it be if he keep his distance after, or decides to retaliate for showing him I'm not interested?

"Can I think about this?" I look up into his hopeful

face.

His smile slowly fades, and then twists into a frown. "Of course."

He shakes his head and straightens his close. "How silly of me. You must have other offers coming in."

"No, no, it's nothing like that." I cradle my beer close to my chest. "I'm just mulling my options, wondering if I should go further afield for some good experience before I settle in any one place for the long haul."

Of course, what I'm really mulling is how many times I'm going to feel my pussy clenched on Ty's cock as he fills me tonight, driving his molten seed hard and deep. I bite my lip right in front of my wilting boss, squeezing my legs together.

"Sure, I can respect that." He pulls out his phone and taps the screen. "Hm, what time did you say your friend would be by?"

"I can text him right now."

Thank God. It looks like he wants to kill this thing just as much as I do. Ten more minutes of hell, and I should be closer than ever to the heaven in my new step-lover's massive tattooed arms.

I feel like I've just dodged a bullet. All I need to do is get back to the office and climb in Ty's car.

Dan looks about ten years older than me. Maybe he's gotten the message. Maybe he won't hold anything against me.

That's what I think until we're in his car for the short drive down the road. Then I hear the words that turn my blood cold.

"Listen, Claire, I appreciate your honesty this evening. I really do. I think our little discussion clarifies a lot of things. My father handed me the job of finding a new full time employee, and I think I finally know exactly what we're looking for. Cascades Now! needs someone who's interested in long-term solutions. I'm looking for someone a little more enthusiastic, someone who wants to *leap* at the opportunities our organization presents. Unfortunately, I'm sorry to say it looks like we'll have to part ways sooner than I anticipated."

VIII: Closing In (Ty)

I'm taking a seaside run somewhere halfway along Bellingham and Claire's office when my phone dings. She's ready for me.

About fucking time too. I've been waiting to pick her up and haul her back to my cave since I sent her off to work with a kiss and a slap on the ass.

Fuck, Claire's ass. Just thinking about it gets me hard. Running like a dog who's been cooped up all winter pulls energy from every part of my body except the steel hammering in my pants.

I've been on edge all day. It's not like the feeling's new. Before, I always went gunning for some new slut to drain my nuts at the club.

Now, I just go in to take care of business, thinking about bringing Claire home the whole time. Losing the place doesn't upset me as much as it did a day ago. It's like this chick's an antidote to the poison my fuck of an old man injected.

I'm Zen to the point of freaking everybody else out. Shit, half the chicks I've had my dick in tear up when they hear the rumors I'm leaving. They fall all over themselves, begging me for one last sympathy fuck, but I smile and push right past 'em.

They don't fucking get it. Olympus has fallen. Me, Ty Sterner, the badass billionaire fighter with a dick that never quits is about to go exclusive.

I've finally found the only pussy I wanna bury my dick in for the rest of my life – and it's a goddamned good one. Just thinking about Claire wrapped around me, moaning her little heart out the way she did last night, makes my cock ready to do the rumba.

I get sex off the brain long enough to climb into my car and finish the drive south. A little later, I pull up to the office and wait. Place doesn't look like much, especially if these fuckers are hellbent on giving my old man and lots of other tycoons hell.

My eyes start scanning. I'm expecting to find Claire waiting for me on the curb, or maybe behind the sleek glass door leading inside.

I sure as shit don't expect to see her sitting in some asshole's car, wiping tears outta her eyes.

"What the fuck?" My heart spits rage into my blood, and it goes straight to my fists.

I gun it and drive forward. The car screams to a stop next to the mystery man's car. She's looking up at me and waving her hands, but I'm already outta the driver's seat like a dog off the chain, heading for her door.

This motherfucker with a piss sucking look on his face steps out and glares at me. He's tall, but I'm taller and wider than his gawky ass. I push past him – jab my hand on his chest and fling him against the car – working my way around to where Claire's climbing out.

"Baby, what's wrong?"

She runs into my arms and buries her face. "Let's go home, Ty. Please. I don't want to cause more of a scene than I already —"

"What the fuck did you do!" I look at the shithead standing across from us.

It's not a question.

I'm ready to walk my girl to the car and then run back over, grab him by the throat, and put the motherfucker through his own windshield. He's got about ten seconds to explain why the fuck my woman's in tears, and the countdown's already begun.

"That's work business. You heard the lady. We're done here." He holds his hands up and gives me an uneasy grin. "Look, I don't want any trouble. I'll make sure someone packs up her things and gets them over to her, *sir*."

The last word comes out full of venom, like he's chewing mud. He looks at me like some shit he just found stuck to his shoe. I bare my teeth and lean down to Claire, whispering in her ear.

"Car's unlocked. Go get in, babe. I'll do the rest."

"Ty, no. This is embarrassing. Please, please don't —"

"Babe!" I hold up a finger and press it to her pretty lips. "You heard me. Now listen."

Her eyes fill with horror, but she casts one more hateful glance at the pretty boy scarecrow kicking at the pavement like a goddamned turkey. She peels herself away from me and heads to my car. I don't move 'til I hear the car door shut.

I'm off like lightning.

The asshole's eyes go wide and he reaches for his door, trying to scramble back into his car. It's too fucking late.

I get him by the shoulders and slam him down on the pavement. A satisfied growl rumbles in my throat when I hear his jaw crack.

He's moaning, stuttering with pain, probably shocked that I'm doing everything my warning gaze promised. Some of these fucks think they're so high and mighty they're above it all. Truth is, nobody's above pain, and my barbaric fists are just a reminder.

"Hey! Heeeey! Jesus fucking Christ, what're you doing? Do you want me to call the cops?" He's slurring his words like I've cracked the jawbone or a few teeth are busted out.

Good.

I rip his head up by the hair and give his head a jerk, making damned sure he realizes how easy it'll be to fuck his face up a whole lot more. I'll bounce his melon on the hard ground like a damned basketball if he doesn't start talking.

"You went down easy-peasy, so I'm gonna give you ten more seconds to explain what the fuck's going on here before I break your damned nose too. Start talking, asshole. *One...*"

"Jesus, you're Gary Sterner's son, aren't you?" The fucker tries to shake his head in disbelief. I jerk it still, making him spit blood.

"*Two.*"

"Ow! Fuck. Okay, okay! I didn't think she'd freak out like that. I decided she wasn't a good fit for our firm on the way back from a drink, and she agreed. Come on, Tyler, you've got to understand this is all just business and I didn't mean any –"

"You don't get to use my fucking name!" I rip his head backward and punch him in the temple with my other fist. "You wanna talk about respect? Start by apologizing for the shit you did!"

Fuckface howls his pain. I always keep my promises.

"Ty! No, no, no! Tyyyy!" I hear a faint sound behind me.

It's Claire, beating on the window with her palms, begging me to spare this piece of shit. Hell, I wasn't gonna kill him, just rough him the fuck up 'til I know he's *really* sorry for making her cry.

Whatever, I get it. The interrogation's over. It doesn't take a damned FBI file to piece together what's going on here.

The fuck made a move on her, she turned him down, and he threw a tantrum like the little boy he is. I've known enough overly sensitive trust fund kids in my time, and I've fought like hell all my life not to end up the same way thanks to the family wealth.

"Here's what's gonna happen – you'll pick your sorry ass up, walk into the office, and come back with a box of her stuff. Then I'm gonna watch you get in your car and drive off. Whatever the fuck you owe her, it'll be in her account tomorrow. And I'm talking about the *full* eight weeks she was supposed to be working for you assholes." I pause.

"Wait, nah, better make it *double*. I know she did good work for your sorry ass. Consider it severance pay."

"Are you nuts? I can't do it! We're a non-profit, man, don't you get what that means!"

"Yeah, I know. Except you're raking in enough in donations for your old man to take months off at a time golfing the same swanky greens my dad wishes he had time for. Don't feed me that bullshit. I'll tell you what, having plastic surgery on your whole fuckin' face is gonna cost a whole lot more than I'm asking for Claire. You're getting off with a drop in the bucket." I bring my lips to his ear, so close he feels the lava I'm steaming outta my mouth. "Don't let me change my mind."

I tighten my hold on the bastard's head 'til he nods. Slowly, I let him up, and stand by his car while he runs inside. I don't give a shit if he calls security or drags his feet cleaning up the pile he laid in his damned boxers.

I'll bust his fucking windows out and wring his fucking neck if there's any funny business. If I'm going away in handcuffs for flipping my shit and protecting my girl, then I'll leave his ass with some shit that'll last a whole lot longer than any jail time for my sorry ass.

Turkey boy comes trotting out about four minutes later. He's got Claire's photos, some papers, and the little bonsai tree she kept on her desk stacked neatly in a box. He shoves it into my arms and gives me another sour look.

I point it at him while I start walking backwards toward the car, never letting the fuck outta my sight. "You keep your goddamned mouth shut, you hear? If I find out you go to the press, or try to pin this on my family, I'm gonna come back. If I find out you send Claire a dime less than she's owed, or you fuck with her in any way, you'll see me again. We'll finish what we started today, believe me. And next time there won't be any ten second grace period. Now, go the fuck home and get that jaw wired shut."

The fucker actually sniffs. He's got hot tears in his eyes, the kind a man makes when he's shamed and beaten. Asshole doesn't realize he's lucky that's all I let him off with. A little ego stroke and an adjustment or two at the chiropractor will have him good as new.

Whatever, him and I are done. All that matters is that it's easy for Claire to say goodbye.

I throw her stuff in the trunk and then hop in the driver's seat, buckling my belt and waiting 'til her fuck of a boss drives out ahead of us.

We hit the road. She's got her face glued to the passenger window, refusing to look at me. She doesn't turn around and say a damned thing 'til we're halfway home.

"Goddamn it, Ty. I'm never going to live it down. *Never.* What you did back there..."

"What I did?" I shoot her a stern look. "Sounds to me like we outta talk about what your fucked up boss did before we get on my behavior."

She purses her lips, but doesn't say anything. I keep pressing her.

"Just tell me what the fuck happened. I've got a pretty good idea, but I wanna hear it from you. Your text sounded happy. How did things turn to hell in ten minutes?"

"He made a move on me, Ty," she says softly. "I turned him down. I didn't want to date him, and I wasn't interested in the long-term position he offered neither. I said no, and I guess he couldn't take it."

Christ. The steering wheel blazes like hot iron on my hands. It takes everything I've got not to whip this car around, head to the motherfucker's house, and put him in a body bag.

"Fuck," I growl. "I knew I should've busted his nose after all."

Nobody fucks with my girl, and he sure as shit doesn't make a move on her. An image flashes in my mind. I pick that skinny fucker up and snap his spine across my thigh like a junk branch.

But I can't do that. We're in too damned deep. I've done my damage to the little cocksucker in the suit, and now I've gotta figure the rest out for *her*. Meanwhile, I'm still trying to comprehend *us*.

Claire scrunches her eyebrows, but I can tell she's suppressing a smile. "Let's just call this done. God, now I need to worry about what I'm going to do with the rest of the summer. And explain to Mom why I've blown my first real job."

"Don't bother. You don't need to tell anybody shit about today, babe."

"What? Why? We can sneak into the house tonight and hide it, sure, but it'll come out by morning. She'll ask me why I'm staying home, assuming your asshole dad doesn't notice first."

"He won't. Neither of them will. They'll have a lot more to worry about when they realize we're not home."

I stomp the gas harder and we pick up steam. I've fucking had it. Me and this girl aren't gonna sort out shit while we're bogged down in Bellingham, pinned down by the weight of our parent's disappointment. We need to forge our own path, and I'll do anything to find it.

We're just a few more minutes from home. Claire keeps staring in stunned silence, her beautiful eyes flickering like the high summer moon.

"Ty...I'm afraid to ask what you're talking about. I can't run away with you to Canada or something. You know that?"

I snort. "You bullshitting me? I'm not a big fan of Vancouver myself. Besides, it's summer. I've got somewhere warmer in mind."

She shakes her head again, but she doesn't protest. I watch her hands move tensely in the darkness as I push the car onward. She doesn't open her mouth 'til we drive right past the gate and keep going down our private drive. There's another gate at the end of the road, but this one has an automatic opener.

I reach up, tap it, and start humming softly to myself.

I can't believe I've let almost June slip by without a cruising the Pacific. The night lamps illuminate the family boathouse like spotlights. Pulling the car to the curb, I hit the lock and order Claire out.

"Let's go. There's already some supplies on board. We

can worry about our clothes and shit later."

"On board *what*?" She looks at me pointedly, but I'm moving. "Hey, wait up!"

I don't slow down 'til we're inside the boathouse, and I hit the automatic door opener on the way inside. The place lights up like a huge garage and the *Stingray* wakes to the light. The big white boat can easily handle ten or twenty people. For us, it's a moving palace.

My old man always hired a pro to take the wheel half the time for our outings, but I've learned to steer it myself over the years. Nothing but the best tech and several upgrades means it only takes one man to captain this sucker.

I climb up the stairs leading to the deck and look down at her with a big grin on my face.

"Come on! This thing's not gonna wait all night. We need to get a start if we wanna make some progress toward the Oregon coast by morning."

She freezes. Her eyes go dark. For a second, I think she's gonna turn tail and run, fleeing back into the safe, fucked up world she knows.

Then she shakes her head, flipping that sugary sweet chestnut hair over her shoulder. She gives a little shrug and takes the stairs after me. I can't help but throw my arms around her once she's on the deck, smashing my lips to hers.

My hands slide down her waist, cup her ass, and squeeze. Her moan joins the thunder gushing from my throat, a voice to the demon need to take her here and now.

"Thought you said you couldn't run away?" I growl, pressing my forehead to hers, giving her one last chance to run.

"Maybe for just a little while," she whispers. "I trust you. You're the *only* one I trust anymore."

Just a little bit longer, I think, eyeballing the massive erection tenting in my pants.

Next time we fuck, it'll be on the open waves. And something tells me we're gonna be doing a lot of that for the next few weeks, 'til we decide to abandon ship or else my old man has the Coast Guard drag us home.

Fuck it. A man only lives and loves once. Claiming this girl's the only thing that matters.

We're really not so different, her and me. Don't know why the hell it's taken me this long to figure that out, but it's true. Take away the money, and we've both lived our lives suspended above the coals by some other asshole who's gonna make us bend, or burn us alive.

No more. No fucking way, ever again.

"Let's move, babe. Bet you never knew how easy it is to handle something so big."

She giggles sweetly and wags her eyebrows, staring at the dick pressing up against her thigh. "Something tells me you never do small."

"Baby, you've got no idea."

Later, I give her every fucking inch.

It takes a few hours to put some distance between us

and Bellingham. I'm careful to take us into the night, cruising for several hours 'til we pull into a marina a good way down.

She's at my side looking happily into the darkness. The huge, dark waves chop around the ship. Thankfully, it's a calm night, and the GPS and radio chatter helps me steer well away from any big rigs in the shipping lanes.

She stands up a couple times to get a better look. I pretend to stay focused on my instruments, but really, I'm sneaking every peak I can at her ass.

Fuck, *that ass*.

I'll never quit saying it. Those two supple globes crowning her thighs are the alpha and the omega for me.

That ass makes my dick throb like nothing else in the known universe. That ass is what drew me in, and the firecracker she calls a tongue did the rest. I'm heading for the flames like a goddamned bug, and I don't give a shit. Just as long as I die with my hands squeezing that ass, jerking it while she fucks my dick numb, I'm a very happy man.

Yeah, I like a challenge in a chick. That's the reason I've got her at my side while I'm stealing my old man's yacht and heading for God knows where. But I *really* like that ass, and I'm gonna keep loving it with all I've got 'til I'm a pile of dust.

She comes back to the passenger seat later and snoozes gently at my side. Sometime after we're anchored, I give her a gentle shove, just enough to wake her up. She rubs her eyes, sees the lights all around us, and sits up straight.

"Ty? Where are we?"

"Past the Pudget Sound, babe. That's all you need to know. We'll be staying here for the night and taking off late in the morning. You hungry?"

She shakes her head and yawns. "No. Maybe I'll have a sandwich or something later."

"Fuck, that sounds good. Unfortunately, we've got nothing but champagne and caviar coming out our ears. My old man's never been the type to just pack some cold cuts and bread. We'll have to pick up our groceries next time we park this boat."

She laughs, and I take her hand. I walk her down the long hall, heading for the master quarters. When we get inside, I can practically hear her sweet jaw clapping the floor.

It's a sweet room, no doubt about it. King sized plush bed with silk sheets, all the storage you could want, a jacuzzi in the adjacent bathroom, a mechanical wine cellar, and a helluva view outside.

For a second, I wonder if it'll be a problem that there aren't any curtains. No, scratch that shit. Anybody nearby will hear us fucking way before they think to look through the big windows near the top of the ship.

I'm gonna make her scream that loud. Gotta do something to get the shock outta her system. I wanna make her feel so good she forgets all about Dan the Boss Man, leaving home, and everything else that's been dumped on her since my asshole dad shacked up with her ma.

215

"You wanna know something? I've been dreaming about something like this since you landed in my house and got underneath my skin. We're finally alone, babe. Really, truly alone. You ready for this, *Sis?* I don't even have to gag you while we fuck to keep our fucking parents from hearing."

A shudder rolls up her back. She wiggles into me deliciously, pursing her lips for a kiss, answering me with her body instead of words.

She's a natural. She knows what I like. Of course, I know how to work her in spades, and I'm not gonna waste another precious second.

I grab on tight and whip her around. We crash down on the bed together, my teeth pulling at her bottom lip, starving for her taste. Her tongue hits mine in shy, desperate sweeps. I twine mine in good and start dancing circles, giving her the love she needs, but holding just enough back so she's fucking begging me for more.

Her tits press into my chest like they were made for my tiger tat. I can feel her hard nipples scraping through her shirt, so puckered they dig into me through several layers of fabric. I reach for her right tit and squeeze.

Goddamn.

Hot breath explodes in my mouth, and I swallow it, warming my mouth up for the fiery licks I'm gonna level down her curves and between her legs. My fingers pinch her nip tight, making her jerk with pleasure. Her hips roll up and down, grinding on my dick, breaking the thin cage still left around the beast inside me.

Right now, that beast wants to fuck all night. Harder,

rougher, and deeper than any girl I've ever been with. But she needs to know it's more than just animal need too.

I'm really into this woman. I haven't said the L-word yet because it's too soon, and it freaks me the fuck out. Fuck if I don't feel it, though. It turns the lava in my blood into plasma. Makes my damned heartbeat a hundred miles an hour.

I don't know when the fuck to drop it on her. All I know is I'm gonna combust if I don't get her under me this second and suffocate myself between her thighs.

Fuck, fuck, and mother-fuck.

I start tearing at her clothes, tugging off big handfuls. Never once do my lips leave hers. I keep her sweet mouth open, dragging my tongue in and out, fucking her lips the same way I'm gonna do to her pussy real soon.

When she's down to her panties, my fingers push down her waistband, find the wetness, and stroke her slit Two fingers slide in and she claws my back. I'm fucking owning her with pleasure, drowning her without even touching the mighty Pacific outside the glass.

"*Oh my God,*" she whines. "Ty."

It's so good to hear my name on her lips. Everybody else always says it like a curse, or else as a plea when they think I'm gonna wring their necks over some business initiative gone bad at my club.

Soon, Club Zing's going into my boys' hands. This woman in my hands, though, she's staying mine forever.

Mine.

I start sliding my fingers deep in her hot cunt, slow and

teasing. I don't stop 'til she's bucking her hips and I hear her breath getting shallow. Her kisses come sloppy now. She can't keep up, digging at my lips with her teeth a little more desperately as I find her clit and give it a good pinch.

"Oh! Oh, fuck!" Claire sputters. "Don't. Stop."

"I'm gonna." That makes her eyes snap open and beam pure hate, all while I pull my fingers up and grab her panties. "Who the fuck do you think you're dealing with, babe? Did you really think I'd let you come without tasting you first? I don't let good pussy go to waste. This is a fucking warm up. Now, spread your legs."

She moans loudly as I rip her panties down in one jerk. I can't even get 'em off her ankles before I'm sliding down her body, stamping my lips between her breasts and on her soft belly, down to the wet wonder I'm gonna fuck every way possible tonight, and then a few more I haven't invented yet tomorrow.

My chin hits the bed and I slide up. Her legs are shaking uncontrollably, so I hold her thighs and spread them wider, giving me all the room I need to wedge my tongue over her clit.

I don't hold nothing back. Her taste, her scent, her everything drives me fucking wild.

I feel the sheets beneath us getting pulled and tangled. She's trying like hell to wrap 'em around her fingers, digging her fingernails in like she's gonna leave this earth if there's nothing to keep her anchored.

Fuck it. I lick her pussy harder. I want her to hit the ceiling and bounce like she's on a goddamned trampoline.

My mouth goes wild. I'm sucking, fucking, strumming her cunt every way I know how. I growl as I drag her clit deep into my mouth, lashing it in long strokes. Her thighs turn to warm rocks in my hands, and that's my cue to lick faster, sending her over the edge.

Her breathless scream's the most jagged, inhuman thing I've ever fucking heard since I started bedding women. And I love every damned octave pouring outta her mouth.

Claire's thighs pinch tight, covering my ears, but damn if I can't hear her screaming, whimpering, wondering how the hell I can make her pussy feel this good. I don't let her ask too many questions.

I fucking show her.

My tongue's a machine all through her explosion. I follow her hips up and down, rocking on the bed, holding her down onto the mattress 'til her little ass sinks deep. Hot, sweet cream keeps pouring into my mouth. I lap it up like the champagne stored in the room with us, but no liquor I ever tasted compares to this.

Her pussy gets me drunk like nothing coming outta a bottle.

She's not the only thing soaking wet. I'll be surprised if my pants haven't melted from all the pre-come drooling outta my dick, and I'm sure that slick coating's the only thing that keeps the pike from drilling its way out.

"Ty, Ty, Ty, Ty...please don't stop. Please don't fucking stop." Her words come slow and desperate.

She's cooing like she's got a hit off my tongue, and my dick jerks for the hundredth time that night.

Shit, for all intents and purposes, she has. Her brain's pumping the same kinda fire junkies get when they hit a new high. I've been to kink clubs before and seen fuckers reach a whole new plane of existence from really good sex.

I don't know about the science, but I'm gonna make her feel so fucking good she can't feel anything except my ecstasy. Tonight's not one where she gets to worry about losing her job, what's gonna happen with me, or how hard our asshole parents are gonna hit the ceiling when they realize I've stolen the yacht and taken her with me.

No, goddamn it. She's devoting every minute we've got on this ship to me. I won't let her think or feel anything except how good my tongue, hands, and cock feel between her legs.

I'm not holding a damned thing back. I'll fuck her straight into a coma, and then ride her ass some more if I need to.

I don't give a fuck. I'm beyond it. I'm a mad dog tonight, and I'm foaming at the mouth – or since my mouth's too busy with her pussy, I guess my dick's doing the foaming for me.

Her lungs must be ready to explode by the time I'm done. I can't even feel my jaw when I break away, sucking in a badly needed breath myself. My dick's hammering so hard it fucking hurts.

I stand up while she's knocked the fuck out, trying to unscramble her brain after I short-circuited her clit. I stand up and stretch, eager to get the hell outta my clothes. They're gone a second later, so quickly I wonder if I've set a new record for stripping down to skin.

"You need a few more seconds to catch your breath, or what?" I fix my eyes on her naked body and growl, impatiently fisting my dick in one hand. "Think carefully before you answer, babe. Once I'm inside you, I'm not fucking stopping 'til we both pass out."

She smiles – only for a second. It fades just as fast when she realizes I'm not fucking around here.

Time's up.

"I'm ready," she moans, spreading her legs for me again.

It's all I need to hear. I'm already climbing on the bed, wondering if we'll make several tons of luxurious metal rock from how hard I'm gonna give it to her.

Shit! If she didn't make my heart flip, I'd break this girl by fucking. Hell, I'd break my own sorry ass in her sweet cunt, just fuck her and fuck her and fuck her 'til my balls pop.

Luckily, we're beyond breaking shit tonight. That shit's in the past. For the next few hours, she's all mine, and I'm gonna commandeer her body in the darkness the same way I took over the *Stingray* and pointed her where I want. I'm cruising my girl's body.

Hard. Steady. Without regret.

My dick's pulsing so hard I can barely breathe, giddy as all hell to slide inside her, to fuck her, to fill her. I haven't had nearly enough of this woman.

Claire arches her back when I get between her legs, reaching for my shaft. Her fingers wrap around it perfectly and she squeezes me tight. I grunt and roll my hips.

Her hand feels amazing, and it's only a tiny fraction of how mind numbingly good that hot wet slit in front of me is about to feel. I put my fingers over hers and give them a squeeze, then lift her palm away.

"New rule – hands over your head, or anywhere I tell you when you're underneath me like this."

"Oh? Just underneath you?" She swings her legs over the backs of mine, giving them a long, silky stroke with her feet. I almost blow my load on her belly like a fucking high school kid. "I didn't know you wanted to fuck missionary all the time."

"Babe, missionary's just a classic warmup. You're gonna feel your brains coming out your ears before you stop and try to make sense of all the ways we're fucking." My eyes narrow and I reach underneath her, grabbing her ass, aiming my cock perfectly for her entrance. "I need this like I've never needed anything else my whole damned life. I need *you*. You're mine, girl, all fucking mine and then some. Hold on tight while I make you feel it."

She opens her mouth to say something, but I cut her dead off by pushing into her. Fuck, she's wet, hot, and tight as the first time. I push good and deep, loving the fact that there's no reason to ease her in slow this time.

The shy, sweet virgin girl's fading. I'll miss her, but I love the woman I'm about to meet. Fuck by fuck, I vow to turn her into the hottest ball buster I've ever buried myself in.

I was the one to break her in, and I'm not done yet. Not 'til I've brought her into the world of raw, sweaty, unrepentant fucking. I swear I'm not stopping 'til she's stamped with my cock from the inside out.

I slide balls deep and then jerk back, ramming it home harder this time. She gasps, tenses, squirms beneath me. Her fingers are doing that adorable curling thing against the brutal hand I've got holding her wrists, and damn if I don't love it.

Holding on for leverage, I fuck her hard. I thrust 'til she opens her mouth and struggles to get oxygen into her lungs, shaking her sweet body, moving my mouth down against her throat. Her nipples brush me as I fuck faster, and I sink my teeth into the soft spot along her neck with a growl.

I marked her once, and I do it harder now. She moans loud, sharp, but doesn't stop. On the contrary, my girl pushes her neck harder into my teeth, and I gotta hold myself back from drawing blood.

We both come up for air and lock lips. I time my tongue to match the strokes of my cock, totally throttling her now. It's sloppy and imperfect, but fuck it feels good, the only kinda bliss that really matters.

My heart's chugging – not from the exertion either. I can't fight it. I can't pretend. There's truly something here when I'm rampaging between her legs, the same thing that's there when she's lying next to me steaming after a good fuck, running her pretty brown eyes over my body.

I think it's love. But her pussy won't let me think too hard about anything at all, and neither will my dick. That greedy motherfucker jerks me deeper into her body, faster, sending pure hellfire into my balls. He pulls me in to the hilt, and won't stop 'til I spit fire up her womb.

We're fucking so fast and hard the room thumps again and again with our flesh, smacking together in waves. She's screaming when I finally grab her wrists, throw her hands over my shoulders, and then fall back on my calves, pulling her up with me. My fingers dig into her round ass so hard it hurts – not that it slows me down for a single beat.

Her legs pinch tight around my waist and her ass rises off the mattress, suspended in my raging hands. She's right where I want her – wide open and totally wanting.

I slam her deep. I turn into a human piston. She tenses up and digs her ankles into my back, throbbing with the fury that lets me know she's on the cliff.

I send her right over it a second later. Claire comes on my dick; a convulsing, screaming, bucking mess. My balls are gonna burst if I don't shoot inside her soon, but it's too fucking good making her come undone like this.

Holding her hips, I slam deep and strong, raking my pubic bone across her clit. The added friction makes her shriller, and then she completely loses her voice.

Fuck! Everything around my dick gets hotter, wetter, tighter, stretched to its very limit. I think I've just taught her to squirt, and it's so fucking hot I almost lose my load then and there.

Somehow, I keep fucking through her climax, slowing my strokes a little as her limbs uncouple from their death hold on me and she starts to breathe.

"God, Ty. How do you do it? *How* did you ever learn to do half the things you do to me?" Her curiosity's real cute.

I pull out, settle her on the bed, and nudge her to roll over. "I'm showing you right now. Fucking's just like making music, babe. Practice makes perfect – except the practice is pretty damned sweet too."

She doesn't need to know about the dozens of women I've had before her, the hundreds of times I've rocked beds rough. All she needs to care about is that it's all hers now, my gift and my sacrifice for making her mine.

Her laugh turns into a sharp gasp when I clap my palm on her ass. I'm almost looking forward to another lashing from her tongue someday, giving me all the excuse I need to throw this ass across my lap and give it a proper spanking.

For now, I'm too fucking hard and eager to stop. I jerk her up on all fours and reach for her clit, holding onto her fine ass with my other hand. Her legs go wide like a good girl, and I sink right in, picking up where I left off before.

I'm gonna fuck her molten before I come. I watch her hands go out and claw at the sheets and pillows above her head. It's not enough with the way we're fucking. Every thrust slowly moves us closer to the headboard, where she steadies when she finally smooths her palms on the wood.

Shit, maybe this full body practice we're making today *is* perfect.

Claire's legs start trembling closed after another minute of bullet fucking. Growling, I grab them, pull them apart, and hold her by the thighs while I ram into her.

"Jesus," she whimpers, her fingers going white as she presses them flat against the headboard. "Oh, Ty. Ty!

Fuck!"

The last word shoots out like a gunshot. I'm off to the races.

My hips go insane, slamming into hers so hard her tits swing like soft pendulums. My dick throbs, and the lava churning in my balls won't hold back any longer. I'm gonna explode.

Soon as her pussy locks around my cock, sucking as she comes, I'm toast. I throw my head back and add my roar to her screams.

"Fucking shit, babe – don't quit on me now! We're not done 'til you're dripping my come."

I don't know how true it is 'til I bust a second later. I pump hot, thick ropes straight into her. It feels like I'm fucking melting.

All my energy runs straight into my balls, and then they shoot. I fill her deep and hard. I scorch her from the inside out as my nuts pump like foundries. Seed flies straight up my dick, last stop before I'm hurling it into her.

Coming was never like this before. This is something else. This shit squeezes my whole body and twists my muscles in knots, as if some giant picked me up and wrung me out like a rag.

I pour everything into her. I'm growling, spitting, swearing. She's turned me into a feral fucking animal grinding my hips into hers, pulling her back and forth against my dick, jerking myself off with her killer body.

That's when it hits me. Every year of sex I've had before her's fucking ruined. I thought I did good, rutting wild oats into the harem I collected over the years, right before Little Miss Perfect came along and dropped me to my knees.

Now, there's no going back. That shit I did before in bed with other girls? Absolutely fucking nothing.

What's right here in front of me, twitching and moaning as spastic aftershocks run through us, this is heaven. This is nothing *but* fucking nirvana in its purest form.

I root my dick inside her like a madman and don't stop 'til my balls are drained. Thank fuck she's the hottest thing I've ever seen, or else I'd have a hard time getting up again for the minimum four or five romps I've got planned for tonight.

Claire's slumped beneath me, her head on one pillow, trying to replenish the air in her empty lungs. I pull out and hop off the bed to grab a towel. It's gonna take a massive cleanup for anyone else to ever fuck in this bed again after the mess we just left, and we're only getting started.

She's still leaking my seed when I return. Something primal inside me wants to growl, push it back inside her, knock her the fuck up. The beast in my skull doesn't care if she's on the pill or not.

That's crazy talk, right? I've never imagined letting my seed take in any girl before. I wonder who the fuck I'm becoming. Fuck, who the hell is *she?*

I take a good long look.

This baby girl looking at me like I just handed her the goddamned moon's my lover, my confidant, my partner in crime. And yeah, she's still my fucking step-sister too, which is a big problem now that we're *fucking*.

My dick doesn't care. The greedy SOB is already getting hard before I climb into bed with her. Guess I'm not the only one who's got lust fever today.

Claire reaches for my cock and starts stroking it, slowly guiding her soft sweet lips to mine. I'm about to dive in when I feel something hot and wet splash my cheek.

What the fuck? Reaching up, I brush away a tear. I gently pull her head back and see there's a few more brimming at the corners of her eyes.

"Shit. What the hell's the matter, baby?"

"My life's a fucking mess, but I don't think I've ever been this happy. Why's it have to be like this? I wish we didn't have to go home, Ty."

I wrap my arms around her, pull her close. "We don't have to. We'll stay out here as long as we can. I've got the coin to keep this big bastard gassed up and supplied for at least a month. Maybe longer if my old man drags his feet with freezing my trust fund."

She looks up at me, her eyes narrow and hurt. "Then what? Something this good can't last forever, can it?"

"We'll make it," I promise.

And I mean it too, even if I don't know how. I bring my lips to her forehead and stamp them there tight. This closeness is nice, even though my dick's thudding impatiently against her thigh.

I hold her for a few more minutes 'til she moves her head. Then she shifts her lips into mine, and that's the kiss that leads me to savoring her hot warm heat all over again in the most carnal ways imaginable.

IX: Somewhere Between Heaven (Claire)

I wake up to my phone ringing off the hook. Ty's left the bed. By the time my feet are on the cool floor, I realize we're moving again.

Big Pacific waves slosh outside the windows, broken only by the outline of the shore beyond. We're probably making good progress to southern Washington by now, and we'll be in Oregon's waters in a matter of days.

I can't wait. The beaches are warmer, brighter and more beautiful than the gloomy sands of Washington's shores ever will be.

My phone dings again and I snatch it off the floor. I already know who's calling before I hit the button.

"Claire? Claire!? Oh my God." Mom's voice goes from panicked to relieved when she hears me breathe.

"Where the hell are you?" She snaps. "You've got to give us something so Gary can send someone to come get you. Jesus, I hope they drag Ty home too. I'm going to murder that boy myself if I find out he's hurt you."

"No, no, no. *Mom*." I let out a heavy sigh. "There's nothing to worry about. I left with him by choice. It's voluntary."

There's a long pause. Then she explodes.

"What! Jesus Christ, Claire!" I hear her take a sharp, steadying breath. "Have you lost your mind?"

"No. Dan Jacobsen made a rude advance on me yesterday, and he decided to let me go when I turned him down. There's nothing else there for me this summer. Ty had something in mind that sounded a lot more exciting than sitting around trying to find a new job, so away we went."

I swear I can hear her teeth grinding on the other end of the line. I can't blame her completely – it's a lot to take in – but nothing I say will ever justify it in her mind. I can't make sense of what she'll never understand.

"Claire, listen to me. I don't know what he told you, but that's not his boat. He *stole* it from the house, just broke in and sailed it right out into the open sea!"

"Mom, please. He didn't break into anything at all – it's not like the thing was even locked up. We both promise to bring it back in one piece. He knows how to handle it. And don't worry, we're not heading anywhere crazy. I'm looking at the coast right now. It's never out of sight."

I count ten seconds of nothing. I'm starting to believe maybe Mom won't have a shitfit over it, maybe she's more open minded than I ever believed.

"*God damn it*, Claire!" Her voice is so loud I need to jerk the phone away from my aching ear. "Don't do this to me. Just *don't*."

"I'm not doing this to you. It's all for me. I need the time and space to clear my head, Mom. Stop worrying. I know it's sudden, but nothing crazy's going to happen."

Another slow building explosion. I wait for it, seriously tempted to open one of the windows and chuck my phone into the water.

"You're ruining everything, honey! Everything! And you're wrecking yourself too," she adds hastily.

You're ruining my Senate bid is all I hear. My lips tighten.

"You've got to come home, Claire. *Please*. Just tell him to turn the ship around and come home now. I'll talk to Gary, make sure the consequences aren't too serious. I'll do it for *both* of you."

Oh. So we're going to be treated like common thieves? Christ. Maybe what Ty said about the Coast Guard barging in and dragging us home in handcuffs wasn't so far off.

"The only one ruining anything is you and your controlling, greedy freak of a husband. You two deserve each other. Goodbye, Mom."

I swipe the call angrily to end it and then shut the damned thing down. I probably won't be needing it where we're going.

I dress and wash up, then head outside, racing toward the bridge. Ty mans everything with rock music piping through the satellite radio, humming along with it. I walk up quietly behind him and throw my arms around his rock hard waist.

God, those muscles are tight. I'll never get tired of holding them. He's like my own personal mountain, *mine* as much as he calls me his.

He doesn't even flinch. It's like he's been expecting it. He smiles, gives me a good morning kiss, and pulls me closer.

"Everything all right, babe?"

"Yeah," I tell him, and I'm not exaggerating. I feel it. "Everything's just fine."

The next few weeks are heaven. Ten days zip by in a blur, and then a few more. Before I know it, we're docked in Lincoln City for the Fourth, watching as the fireworks explode above the little seaside resort town I've always loved.

It's like coming home. It's one of the few places where Mom and I went on trips before she went Congress crazy.

She's tried to call about a thousand times since I shut her off. I only check my phone once a day, and I don't listen to the voicemails anymore.

There's nothing new in them after the first ten. Nothing but threats and stern warnings, pleas and selfish whimpering. She isn't worried about me coming home safe. It's all about her career, and it hurts to see how deep she's been bitten by the same greedy bug perched on Gary's shoulder.

The woman who raised me and bought us ice cream in the town we're spending our holiday in is all gone. I barely recognize the woman I call *Mom* now, the woman who married a bastard of a billionaire for convenience.

She's not my youthful, vibrant, Lincoln City loving Mom anymore. I can't be her pawn.

Now, I'm hoping I can build some new memories here with Ty. Luckily, Independence Day has gotten things off to a good start.

Before the fireworks, we walked along the warm, sleepy beach. The sun glowed high and we ran barefoot, hand in hand, finding a few nice private spots not touched by the holiday throngs. Money and GPS can go a long way.

We hit a restaurant with an amazing wine bar for dinner, and then I insisted on buying him ice cream. Ty snuck away for a few minutes while we were at the ice cream shop. I swear I saw him run across the street to one of the little boutiques, and now I'm wondering what he's got up his sleeve.

The only thing we didn't like were all the tourist cameras. One sneaky photo with the right tag online could blow our identities wide open. Then Gary and Mom will really have a good reason to come after us if we hand them a real scandal, wrapped up in a pretty neat bow.

We're sitting out on the boat's main deck. Bright, orange contrails rocket up and explode magnificently into red, white, and blue, plus a sprinkling of almost every other color too.

It's beautiful.

"I've got good news and bad news, babe," he says, squeezing the arm he's got around my shoulder tight. "Take your pick."

My face scrunches. "Give me the good first."

"I'm gonna make sure this paradise we've found isn't just temporary. I know that's what you're worried about, and you don't fucking need to. Yeah, it's gonna take work. It won't be easy. But I'm gonna make it. I swear to you,

Claire, deeper and more seriously than anything I've promised in my whole damned life."

He doesn't wait. Ty swoops in for a kiss, and I lock my lips on his long and hard, just as another fireball goes off above our heads, splashing our faces with a brilliant orange glow.

I don't even want to ask about the bad. Unfortunately, I have to. Breaking the kiss, we stare at each other, and he slowly opens his lips.

"My asshole old man's frozen my trust fund account. I've got plenty of my own money to haul this beast home and figure out the rest, but not much more. It takes a couple thousand a day to operate this boat. Sorry, babe, but we've gotta cut our trip short."

I'm not shocked. I expected it. I push my face into his rock hard chest, unable to resist dragging my fingers down his abs.

Jesus, those abs, they're like small hills beneath my fingertips. I'll never stop being awed by his body. *Never.*

"Say something," he growls.

"Ty, it's okay." I look up and run my hand across his cheek. "Really. The whole point of this trip was to get away and figure things out. I think we've done that. If we can survive through all this turmoil without wanting to kill each other, then I think we can do anything."

He smiles. "You shitting me? Who's got time for murder when I'm too busy fucking your brains out?"

My eyebrow quirks and my pussy heats. "Oh? Is that all we do?"

He gives me another growl and lifts me up from my chair, walking to the edge of the deck and laying me down on the hard wood. A bright blue firework goes off in the sky, dancing its light across our skin and the ship's white hull.

"Don't play dumb, woman, or I'll have to show you what we do." He's got his hands on his belt, and I reach forward eagerly, helping him take down his pants.

His cock springs out, hard and alive, pulsing with a need that won't stop until it's satisfied. I lick my lips and roll my hand over his shaft, marveling at his size. He groans, and everything below my waist goes hot and wet and tight with satisfaction.

Well, satisfaction and flaming lust.

I take him into my mouth and shudder when his head swings back. He tastes amazing.

"*Goddamn*," Ty rumbles. "You're learning to suck better every fucking night. You're gonna kill me one of these days, girl."

I can't smile with my mouth full of his dick, but you'd better believe I'm happy. Pleasing him makes me light up just like the sky. I moan, tightening my hand on his base, and slide down his length. My tongue flicks up at the ridge underneath his head, twirling, begging to bring him off.

Ty groans. "Fuck. Shit. God. Damn."

Everything coming out of his mouth is vile to the core, and I love it. I can't imagine sex any other way except crude and hard and absolutely filthy.

For a second, I can't believe what I've become. There I

am, shy virgin girl turned wanton runaway, kneeling on the deck of a billionaire's yacht with my mouth stuffed full of my step-brother's cock. I'm sucking off the most arrogant man in the world, an utter bastard I never expected to fuck, much less fall for.

But the facts don't lie. Neither do the last few weeks.

Ty Sterner isn't such a soulless bastard after all. And I'm not such a good, plain girl anymore.

"Ah, damn. Holy *fuck*." His growls deepen. His rough fingers move through my hair, grab several locks, and pull.

My head automatically follows his motion. I sink down on his cock and just keep sucking him, tonguing his ridge, feeling his balls tighten in my palm. I'm ready for him to explode in my mouth.

Hell, I'm ready for him to take me anywhere, any way. I'm not shy anymore. I love this man as bad as I want him, even if saying the L-word out loud still scares the crap out of me.

His calloused palm feels hot, bobbing my head in quick strokes, holding me on his magnificent cock. I take another breath, pull him against my tongue, and wait, wiggling my cheeks and waiting for the explosion.

He pulls out at the last second, rips my head back, and stares at me. A bright red rocket explodes and reflects its fire in his glistening blue eyes. It's an incredible contrast, rare and frightening as everything about this relationship with my step-brother.

"What's wrong?" I ask softly.

He drops to his knees, grabs me, and pushes me to the

floor, tearing at my clothes. I hear his pants kicking off behind him. Before I know it, the tank top I'm wearing is disappearing over my head, and so is my bra. He grabs my breasts in both hands and squeezes them tight. My nipples bloom between his fingers and he pinches them harder, working to roll me over.

"What's wrong is you trying to make it too easy, babe. It's the Fourth of July for fuck's sake."

"Oh?" One hand slides down, shoves its way beneath my shorts, under my panties, and catches my clit.

Okay, forget *oh?* It's all *ohhh* now.

"You thought I wouldn't strip you bare and fuck you right here on the deck of the ship with fireworks exploding above us? You think I'd waste my load down your throat instead of making you leak my come for hours?"

Both hands zip down to my shorts and pull. In one jerk, everything is gone, and I'm completely naked. He centers himself between my legs and I get a perfect view of him rolling his shirt off his head.

Jesus, he's always so tightly wound, no matter what I do. I'd give him crap about it if it didn't always lead to such mind blowing sex.

His cock presses hard against my belly, throbbing with raw need. His lips are all over me, kissing mine into submission and then sliding down my throat, where he stops and sucks so hard I know he'll leave another mark.

My body screams. I can't help him. Call me sick in the head, or slap me across the face, but I've finally accepted

I'm addicted to every depraved thing he wants to do to me.

His hips glide low and hook to mine a second later. One perfect push and he's up inside me, thrusting slow, but hard. These strokes cut deep, his trim hair grinding on my clit, and I'm glued to the floor by the shock alone.

"Ty!"

It's all I think, all I feel, all I say. My entire universe is wrapped up in that single two letter word. It's a short, staccato curse for this Greek god with the mind of a demon, not to mention a massive dick and a pair of balls that leave me in a coma.

Finding my reserve energy, I wrap my arms and legs around him, dragging my hips to his. We *bang* ourselves together, hot and wet and desperate, as if we're human mirrors for the fire erupting in the sky.

A huge white firework bursts at just the right time to drown out my first climax.

It's a rush like it always is. I hold on tight and drag my nails down his neck, trying to hang on, trying to keep my sanity as my body feels like it's imploding. Lightning pulses through me. Orgasm hits my brain and buries me. The spasms pick me up like a rough tide, clenching all around his length and pulling him deeper, harder, greedier.

Ty grunts and pulls out when I've finally stopped coming. I look up, wondering if he came too, but I usually feel his molten heat.

He reaches for my hips with a wild urgency that says *fuck no*. He flops back on the wood and positions me on top of him, working my sopping wet slit back down on his length. I spread my legs wide, devouring him from above, watching as he sinks into me and fills me whole.

Ty's hands cup my ass and he gives both cheeks a sharp slap. I jump, and it's just the kick I need to get moving on his cock.

"Ride me, baby. Ride me so fucking hard I forget to breathe."

Oh, God. "You know I want to," I mutter. It's hard to form words when he's owning every inch of my pussy.

My hands go down his chest and spread out on his warm, impossibly muscular surface. His thrusts start rising to meet my hips. His thrusts pick me up and down like it's nothing.

We fuck hard and long. The fireworks keep coming, faster now, adding a thousand new colorful stars to the dark summer sky.

My hips rock furiously. The sea isn't doing much to cool us down, and I don't care. I'm dripping sweat all over him, and still we keep going, slippery and wet, starving for release. His fingers pinch deep into my ass cheeks, hauling up and down his dick. He slams me against him over and over, bouncing me like the fuck toy I've become.

And I'm okay with that. Hell, I'm *happy*. My sole purpose for living tonight is to blow his mind.

Tonight, something's different. Maybe we realize we're about to go home and face the very bleak music, or maybe love is in the air. Whatever it is, we've *never* fucked like this.

I didn't dare think it could get even better than all the nights he's rocked my body, but it does. He pounds into me with his whole body, his soul, sending crazed energy through every curve sticking to my bones.

My breasts flop so hard I can't even feel my nipples. My pussy's never been so wet, leaking all over him, pinching his cock tighter each time I come to pull him deeper still.

The grand finale starts, on the ship and in the sky.

Ty's strokes hit deep, growling like the beast he is, fucking me so hard my knees bang on the ship's deck each time I come down. I can't imagine how hard he's being rattled too, but we're both too far in the pleasure zone to care.

I swear to God the ship's bobbing from our sex, and it's not just the ocean. A huge, blinding flash lights up everything, and he pulls me close, shoving his lips to my ear and sinking his cock womb deep.

"I'm fucking coming, Claire. Give the fuck up."

His cock swells inside me a second later and I feel the first thick rope of his seed. I come on the spot, pinching my teeth together so hard I think they're going to break.

My eyes roll back and I jerk my body up, throwing my head back, grinding my hips into his as his cock pumps lava into my depths. His balls keep heaving it up into me, pulsing and shooting, filling me until I completely overflow. New screaming fireworks hit the sky, drowning out our love screams.

The same merciless fire bathes everything.

Above and below, inside and out, all over the fucking place.

I can't even take it all in as ecstasy pulls me in deeper,

drowning me for what feels like an hour. We keep rutting on each other for a small eternity. When I finally come down from it, I'm gasping for air, and only the last reverberations above us hit my ears.

A minute later, he's holding me, gently stroking my hair. It's quiet, and deeply satisfying.

Ty pulls out of me and keeps his hard-on nestled against my thigh. I swear he doesn't go soft. It's just as well, because I know we'll be right back at it soon.

It doesn't seem to matter how much we fuck. It's never enough for me, never enough to completely scratch the itch that's always there when my flesh touches his.

He reaches up, brushes my messy hair away from my face, and plants a kiss on my forehead. "You know how fucking much I love you, babe?"

My eyes snap open. We lock eyes for a moment, and then my gaze softens. I can't help but smile. I also can't believe that he's beaten me to saying it, and my heart swells faster than the rest of me.

I lean in, give him a long, salty kiss. "Of course I do. I love you too, Ty."

It's the perfect beginning to a flawless night. This is one of those nights where time breaks apart and blurs, losing itself in the darkness and passion.

The night cools around us as we lay and fuck, stopping only for snacks and drinks conveniently waiting around the corner. Caviar and champagne make our evening more decadent than ever, and I take my fill of everything.

We're still fucking by the time there's light on the

horizon. Ty has me on all fours, hammering into me from behind, fisting my hair in one hand so fierce it promises to leave me sore tomorrow.

I'm going to be a mess tomorrow, and I don't care, damn it. The sun coming up doesn't even bother me.

Tomorrow isn't official until we're back in Bellingham, plotting the rest of our lives, and that won't be for several days. After a night like this, I believe we can do anything.

We're unstoppable – aren't we? I can't imagine anything that'll come between us, even if our parents try to destroy this beautiful thing we've tasted.

One thing's for sure – his thrusts don't stop until my mouth forms an O and I'm completely breathless, bent over, and coming my heart out to the sound of the day's first seagulls squawking their way to shore.

We take our sweet time getting back home, almost a full week. The dream lasts as long as it possibly can, and I squeeze it for dear life. Unfortunately, there's no way to keep dreaming forever until you hit reality face first.

When we start to feel the cooler bite of Washington's mid-July waters, my heart sinks. It's two more days to home. My mind runs wild with all the grim possibilities we're going to find back at Gary's estate.

I tell myself I'm ready for anything, and I hope to God I mean it. I know I don't care what happens, just as long as I get to stay with Ty.

I swear I'm prepared for anything. They can try to put Ty in handcuffs or send me away from him, but we'll always find our way together again. We have to.

Mom and Gary can't control me. I'm twenty-two, for fuck's sake.

Sure, my first job was a bust and money's dwindling, but there's got to be a way to make this work. I'm smart, I'm motivated, and I'm in love.

That's got to count for more than all the hell our parents can throw at us.

Ty feels it too. He looks more serious when he's steering the ship into familiar waters, and he's not quite as playful when we stop in the marinas for drinks and dinner each night.

Thankfully, the sex is just as explosive as ever. I've got to set an extra reminder to take my pill with all the craziness going on. One night with this animal and no protection is plenty to leave any girl knocked up – probably with triplets.

I'm at his side when the dark day finally arrives. It looks like nothing's changed at the huge estate on the hill, surrounded by the dark forest. The tall castle looms over the horizon, just as cold and imposing as ever, and Ty navigates the ship carefully toward the boathouse.

We're coming in after midnight, and I'm grateful for the darkness. Maybe it means we'll have a chance to camp out and rest before dealing with some serious crap tomorrow.

"Come on, babe. We're here," he says, as soon as the ship's engine stops droning.

He takes my hand and leads me out, extending the stairs so we can walk down to the dock. It's a warm night, dark as thick mud, and it's like we never left.

I try not to freak out or worry as we exit the boathouse and head toward the house. There's no car waiting for us, of course. I don't know what's happened to either of our cars since we left.

Ty leads me on the long, slow walk, carefully passing along a few points off the main path so we don't alert security. We're coming through the gate near the back, right next to the huge pool, when we see a light on behind the massive glass panes.

"Shit! Stay the fuck down."

I duck, but it's too late.

Joan gazes right at us, frozen behind the huge glass door, a small squeegee for cleaning windows in her hand. Ty growls, shakes his head, and curses again.

"Come on, babe. Let's get this the hell over with. She saw us."

My heart starts pounding with every step we take. Tension lines the older woman's face as we draw closer, but she pops the door and holds it out for us.

I don't have a fucking clue what I'm going to say. Jesus, I don't know what Ty's going to say or do either. It's dangerous. If we have to confront our parents now, someone might end up getting killed.

We're not ready. *I'm* not ready for this. We haven't rehearsed or planned anything.

Joan speaks first. "Welcome home."

Ty cocks his head. I stand next to him, nervous and tight lipped as a guilty kid next to teacher.

"Thanks. You gonna tell my old man we're back, or

what?"

Joan's face softens. "I won't do that, Tyler. I don't care what he threatens this time. I've been ready to walk out the door for weeks without looking back now that I've seen somebody who has the courage to do it."

That makes me grin. I step forward, give her a hug on impulse. It's too hard to contain the relief humming through my veins.

Ty seems a little more uneasy, but he's not fighting mad.

"We're leaving soon," he says. Then he does something that almost drops me to the floor.

He steps forward and throws his arms around the woman, pulling her tight, the way a man hugs his mother after a long time away.

"Lady, I don't give a fuck what he does either. You're family as far as I'm concerned. You're welcome to follow us up to Alaska or wherever the fuck we end up anytime, if you can stand the cold."

Jesus, he's right. I really might have to follow him up there to stay together. I have no idea what I'll do for work, but keeping Ty in my life means everything. That's what love is, and I'm watching it spill over onto the old servant in his embrace, looking at me with tears in her eyes.

"I'll pack my best sweaters, Tyler."

"You got it. Now, we'll get the hell outta your way so you can get back to work. Hopefully it's just about the last you'll do in this house. Come on, babe." He pulls away and I follow him, shooting one last smile over my shoulder at Joan.

I've never seen her look so happy. To be fair, I've never seen her do much of anything except clean up after us, but the gratitude flashing in her face doesn't lie.

You can't buy that kinda loyalty, and it makes my heart swell. It's sweet to see my man do the right thing too, proof that the heart hiding in his rough exterior doesn't only open to me.

We head for his room and shut the door behind us. I inhale deeply, amazed that it's still got his scent after all these weeks away. Good thing too. His masculine richness helps calm me down. It's hard to worry about us being back here, staring down the barrel of a gun, when he truly surrounds me like this.

He steps out into the middle of the floor and starts to get undressed. It's amazing, really. He's so chill. Deciding to follow his example, I stand up from his bed and strip, enjoying the nighttime coolness against my body.

"You're magic, babe," he says, stepping close to me. "Gotta be. There's no other explanation for why the hell you look just as beautiful when we're under the sun or moon or rolling rain. Shit, even when we're back in this God forsaken place..."

I blink, then feel a big grin coming. "Hm. When did you turn into such a poet?"

He wraps his strong arms around me. If I'm forever beautiful in his eyes, then he's forever huge, forever hard, forever a superman in mine.

I can't imagine anything that'll ever break his brute strength. Being in the ring with Fat Boy came close, but he won, using the same persistence that's natural to him.

One hand runs down my back, fingers spread, before they stop next to my ass and give me a sharp whack, ending in a possessive grab. He's growling, tickling my cheek with his stubble, pressing his lips to my ear.

"I'm in an artsy-fartsy mood tonight. Call it nostalgic. This might be the last time we ever fuck in this bed. Better make it count, *Sis*."

My breasts flatten deliciously against his chest as he pushes me to the bed. The kisses keep coming, hot and feral. We're tired after the long journey in, not to mention the stress, but I'd be certifiably insane to pass up sex.

It makes me feel alive, reminds me of everything we've built. When he pushes between my legs a second later, grabbing my hips and wiggling them to take his cock deeper, I see our whole future.

And yes, it's really a *future* together, more than just endless naked romps. I see us growing old together.

This thing is more than temporarily losing our minds on a hot, forbidden summer tryst. This crazy affair's going to last forever. I don't care who says it's wrong, or how often they scream it in my face.

I'm going to do it. I'm going to build a life with this man, just as soon as I can stop losing my mind on his dick every night we're together.

He's thrusting hard now. His hips hammer into mine, and he leans down one breast, dragging my nipple against his teeth. He catches it and sucks hard, letting another growl slip, vibrating me right to the bone.

God, I love fucking him. Only him. With Ty, I'm not even curious about anyone else. I don't care that he's the only man I'll have for the rest of my life. Instinct tells me no other man comes close, and giving him my V-card was just the start.

I'm going to give him everything. *Everything.*

The thrusts deepen. My pussy tingles with delight, creaming and tightening on his cock. My hands go over my head, helping me push my body up to meet his. We're colliding, fucking at a more frantic, anxious pace than we did on the yacht, but it's just as amazing as ever.

Ty's teeth form a tight ring around my nipple. The energy hits the bolt coming up from my pussy and my nerves ignite, crying for release.

It comes a couple seconds after he kicks his thrusts into overdrive. I'm no longer attached to a gorgeous man. There's over two hundred pounds of rock solid fuck pressure between my legs, slamming me deep, filling me to my breaking point.

Oh, God. Oh, Ty. Oh – fuck!

My head snaps back and I come, reaching desperately for a pillow to stuff into my mouth before I scream so loud the house lights up. Snarling, Ty drills hard and steady, baring his teeth before he holds his swelling length to my womb and lets go.

The loud clap of his balls on my ass stops. Next thing I know, he's filling me, pouring his liquid heat into my core. It makes me come so hard I shake, whimpering into my pillow, keeping it between my teeth so I don't chip a tooth as they grind together.

Orgasm doesn't describe it. This is a climax, a crescendo, a peak so high I'm bound to wind up a little battered when I jump off it. And I do, falling straight into the wonderful mass of man surrounding me, spilling himself into me, driving his seed to my depths.

This is the medicine we need tonight. It's clear when he finally pulls out, and my heart doesn't slow to a dull thud. I should be dreading tomorrow.

Instead, I'm more content than ever, wrapped up in his arms. He holds me tight while I press my thighs together, trying to keep what he's given me inside. I don't want to lose his heat.

I don't want to lose him.

"I love you, Ty," I whisper in the darkness, nuzzling his shoulder.

"Love you twice as much, babe." I blink, surprised by the challenge, and he smiles. "What? You gotta be crazy if you think your heart pumps harder than mine. I'm more than twice your fucking size."

I snicker and roll my eyes, settling in on his warmth. Yeah, he's still a fire breathing asshole when he wants to be.

But he's *my* asshole, damn it, and I'm willing to put up with his crap for all the joy he brings.

"You useless fucking cunt! If you're not going to help me find them, then get the fuck out of my way!"

I jerk up like the house is burning the next morning. At

first, I think the harsh, deafening words are a nightmare, and then I think they came from Ty. But he's sitting up next to me, eyes wide open, tight lipped.

That can't be Gary...can it? Holy fucking shit.

"Wait! Please, wait, Mister Sterner! You can't go down there!" Joan's voice sounds small, muffled, desperate. It cracks like tears are piercing through it.

"Get dressed, babe." That's all Ty says right before the staircase down the hall thunders.

He doesn't wait for me to move. Ty jerks me out of bed and grabs my clothes off the floor, throwing them into my hands. I try to follow his lead, dressing as quickly as I can, but the world won't wait.

Angry fists start beating on his bedroom door.

Ty doesn't have time to put his shirt on. He stands in front of me like a wall, ready to destroy anything that comes through the door to threaten us. And it does a second later when the door blows open, so loud I think the hinges snap.

"Oh, God! Fuck. *Damn it!*" Gary's beet red face stops and stares at us. He takes one look at us half undressed and stumbles backward, smashing his trembling fists against the walls. "It's true, it's true, it's goddamned true..."

I notice he's holding a newspaper or magazine in one hand. Ty steps forward, his lips quivering like a dog getting ready to bite.

"Something you wanna say, *Dad?* Had a funny feeling you'd greet us like this after we came home. Didn't put a scratch on your precious *Stingray,* in case you're worried.

You're gonna give us the same respect."

He rips himself up in a flurry and stands tall. For a second, I think he's stupid enough to try getting through Ty, into the room, but he stops. The newspaper flies out of his hand and hits the floor where we're standing.

"I've got nothing else to say to you that these goddamned jackals haven't said for me, you ungrateful little idiot. I've got nothing to say to this fucking whore either!"

He shoots an accusatory finger toward me. Despite standing behind Ty, I want to dig a hole into the floor and hide forever. Seeing this billionaire aim his long-bottled hellfire my way makes my heart want to stop.

Still, I have to see what the hell's got him so riled up. Before Ty can lunge and beat his father to smithereens, I reach in front of him, snatch up the paper, and give it a good shake.

BILLION DOLLAR BEDFELLOWS! GARY STERNER'S SON SEXING HIS NEW SISTER, EX-REP. AMANDA FROST'S DAUGHTER!

WHO EVER SAID LOVE, POLITICS, AND MONEY CAN'T MINGLE?

Okay, now my heart really does stop. I barely have the energy to tug at Ty's sleeve and whisper his name. His eyes dart down to the tabloid and skip over the awful headlines.

We're both staring at the same thing – the pictures. Several are from our unforgettable Fourth of July holiday.

There's Ty and me walking around the beach, hand in hand, smiling as we hold our ice cream cones. Then we're on the deck of the ship, locked in a passionate kiss. The real killer is the one that's half blurred. We're both naked and horizontal on the deck while fireworks light up the sky, a thousand word picture carefully shot by some kinda camera with an amazing zoom from the marina.

I want to gag. I want to die. Mostly, I just want to bawl, and the tears are coming, stabby and brutal.

We tried so hard to keep our relationship under wraps for our own sakes. Obviously, it wasn't hard enough.

"You piece of fucking shit!" Ty explodes, eyes fixed on his father, ripping the paper out of my hands and crunching it in his fist. "Who the fuck did you hire to tail us?"

Gary snorts. "Jesus! You think *I* did this? My God, I really raised a dipshit for a son. Why the hell would I destroy myself when I have your careless, degenerate tryst with your sister to do it for me?"

Ty doesn't move as his dad steps toward us, this time crossing the threshold to his room. I cover my face just as Gary stabs a finger in his chest.

"You're the one who's getting off easy. I've had to live with this nightmare for days. The butt of every late night talk show joke and gossip rag. Poor Mandy, she's heartbroken. She'll be lucky to hold a state rep seat again before she's hit sixty with this kind of scandal. And it's all because you pissed off Jacobsen."

"Jacobsen?" Ty shakes his head.

My heart slams against my ribs. I feel like I'm going to faint if this was my fault.

"Martin Jacobsen, dummy!" Gary stabs his son in the chest again with his rigid finger. "You know, the big environmental nut. The same man your sick little sister couldn't hold down a job with. Apparently, some knuckle dragging animal got mad because Martin's son asked her out, and fractured the kid's jaw. I know the Neanderthal was you, Tyler, and don't you fucking deny it."

Gary looks like he's about to blow up and shower us in his gore. Ty looks at the floor, too stunned to speak, undoubtedly feeling the same ruthless ice crawling across my brain.

"Do you know I was supposed to meet the Vice President of the United States next week to talk technology?" Gary growls, shaking his head. "Now, my own goddamned shareholders won't talk to me. It's your fault, Son! Yours, and this sorry little bitch's too! This marriage was a big mistake. Mandy was supposed to bring me closer to the sun, not let her whore of a daughter burn me down."

His eyes hit me again, blazing with the same nuclear blue fire I've seen in Ty's. I'm stumbling backwards in slow motion, the tears blurring everything.

I feel trapped, pinned down. It's just as bad as the night Karl tried to force himself on me, before Ty burst in to save me. Gary's icy stare *violates* me, forces me to realize that the damage is already done. Ty can't save me this time when we're already fucked.

I'm struggling to breathe as Gary moves again. I watch in horror as the billionaire thumps his finger on Ty's chest, this time closer to his throat. It's the last spark before the powder keg ignites.

It happens in a blur. Ty screams, grabs his scrawny dad by the arms, and picks him up. One savage throw later, Gary's on the floor. There's a sick crunching sound, and I see his foot's twisted unnaturally, a look of sheer horror on his face.

Gary shudders, holding his hands up over his face as Ty closes in.

"You can treat me like dog shit all day, but don't you dare say shit about my woman again! This isn't her fucking fault, old man, and you know it!" Ty stomps forward, puts his foot on his father's chest, and holds it there until he screams. "This is yours! It's your greed, your little business wars, all this Machiavellian horseshit you call a life."

My God. I'm afraid he's really, truly going to kill the billionaire asshole in front of me if I don't stop him. I rush forward, tugging at his giant arm, making nonsensical pleas. Pulling on Ty feels like I'm trying to move a thousand pound statue.

Gary's got his hand out, and there's something in it. At first, I think it's just his phone, but it's actually some kind of pager. I'm still screaming as Ty stoops to the floor, picks his dad up, and hurls him against the wall.

Above us, somewhere on the second floor, a woman screams. It's got to be Joan or Mom.

A second later, boots are clattering down the stairs. When I look away from the slow motion murder going on in front of me, there are two big guards in black, men I've seen before with their golden security badges stenciled neatly in their dark shirts.

"Shoot him! Shoot him!" Gary screams, twisting his neck as Ty's fingers reach for his throat. "For Christ's sake!"

My brain wants to shut down. That's when another big guard joins his comrades, and so does Mom, stepping down behind him. Her jaw drops when she realizes what she's seeing, and we both share a look that says it all.

This. Can't. Be. Happening.

"Claire? Gary? Oh my God." She blinks, inert for the next three seconds. "Everybody stop!"

No one's listening. The third guard fumbles for something at his side. I can't fucking stand the thought of Ty getting killed in front of me by this monster, but my brain won't let me move, can't fully comprehend there's a gun coming out and it's going to shoot the love of my life.

It's just like a movie.

Father and son are still screaming, struggling as my instinct comes back. I leap in front of them. Something bright and impossibly fast hits me in the stomach, right above the belt, and everything becomes a howling white light.

My whole world turns into needles. All my muscles become crackling ice. I've never felt anything like it — not even close. I can't scream or cry or even breathe. I never imagined being shot would be anything like this, and then I realize it's because it isn't a bullet going into me.

I never find out how many bolts the Taser screams

through my body. It hurts so bad I'm certain I black out for a few seconds.

When I come to, my body feels like it's been drained, cooked. I don't know if I've been out for seconds or hours.

All I hear is Mom screaming nearby. Ty's on top of me, shaking, the electric probe he's pulled out of my skin bouncing in his fingers.

Gary roars incomprehensibly as he's pushed aside. Mom and Joan somehow reach me through the commotion. They grab me by both arms and start dragging me down the hall, toward the thick glass and the pool.

I keep waiting for Ty to look at me, but he's shaking like he's grabbed an electric fence, his huge arms and legs twisting unnaturally. Then I see the other guards around him, holding their Tasers. He's been hit by no less than two, maybe three of the goddamned things, and he's still screaming, trying to fight it.

"Get. The. Fuck. Away. Claiiiiiire." His voice drones, loud and anguished and freakishly calmed through all the lightning wrecking his body.

The last thing I see before my brain shuts down is the love of my life, kicking and bellowing until he hits the floor. Then, he doesn't move at all.

When I wake up, I'm lying on a sofa. I'm in the big family room upstairs, the first place I ever saw Ty, shirtless and magnificent, before I realized the asshole from the club was also my brand spanking new stepbrother.

I never believed Prince Asshole could become Prince Charming then. Now, I can't believe I'm going to see him alive, and it terrifies me.

My muscles jerk when I try to sit up. Huge fucking mistake. It's like the world's worst sunburn, except it's all on the inside.

"No, dear. Lie down. Doctor's orders. Try to stay calm. You're okay." Joan speaks softly, and I realize my head is in her lap. "Just rest. Any movement right now will be *very* painful."

I manage to open my mouth, but the words won't come. When she sees me struggling, she reaches for a tall glass of water, and holds it to my lips. I must end up spitting about half of it out, all over myself.

Joan dabs at my lips with her apron. I'm more ashamed and confused than ever, wondering how long it'll be until my throat muscles work again. *Hell, how long will it be before I can walk?*

I don't know how long I end up lying in her lap like an injured kitten. Time passes in a haze. My body hurts too much to think too hard about what the hell just happened. It doesn't all come back in any coherent way until I hear the voices screaming. I try to make out what they're saying, but it's too far away, and it stops after a couple minutes.

"Come on, Joan. Help me get her into the car. We're leaving right now." Mom steps out of the kitchen, her voice bright and sharp with the same ferocious spark I've heard her use during House committee meetings.

My mouth moves like a fish when Mom's over me. I

can't remember if I should be disgusted or relieved. She runs a gentle hand through my hair, and whatever anger I've got stewing dissipates.

"You're going to be okay, baby. Just give me a couple hours to get us away from this freak show. We'll stop at a real clinic on the way to Seattle too, I promise."

I think I groan. I'm not really sure what's happening until I hear more footsteps come storming into the room.

Mom looks up, her face tense and angry. "Jesus, you really have the balls to show your face again? After everything you and your lunatic son did to my poor daughter? I told you – we're done. Stay the fuck away from us!"

"Oh, please, Mandy. We both know he'll be locked up for a long time. He's cut off. Over. I'm not responsible for his shameful actions, and you're a fool if you think otherwise."

Her heels click loudly on the floor. Joan holds my head up higher, and I sense her suppressing a smile. I'm just in time to watch my mom slap the billionaire across his face.

"*We're over*, Gary. Don't make me say it again."

"Well, you've had your chance. I can accept that. What I'm not going to let you do is walk out of here having the last word." The billionaire moves his lips sourly and smiles. "Thank God for the prenup. If you really want to feed the media frenzy and ruin this family, then I guess I can't stop you. I hope we can at least be partners in Washington – assuming you ever make it back at all. Oh, and if you ever scratch me with the tenderly manicured fingernails I paid for again, I'll have my men escort you out. They're plenty eager to move around after everything else that's happened today."

I don't want to hear anymore. I've already seen the real Gary Sterner, and this is just an overload.

He's suave. Cruel. Arrogant. Maybe it's just the pain in my body fogging everything, but my soon to be ex-stepfather looks like the devil himself.

"Don't you fucking dare!" Mom snaps, before she turns around to face us, clapping her hands. "Joan! Is she all set? Let's go. I don't care how much overtime I'm paying you, we need to get out of here *now*."

"Consider these hours off the books, Miss," Joan says smartly. She looks at her old boss and frowns. "I know perfectly well what he's capable of. I suggest we all go."

I try to just breathe and rise above the pain while they carefully drag me to my feet. It takes longer than it should for both of them to hold me, walking me out the huge entry door. As promised, Gary's goons are outside, eyeballing us.

Mom gives them a wild look and helps Joan guide me very carefully down the long marble stairs. The soft black car has its door open for me to lay in the back, waiting to swallow me up.

This is the last time I'm going to see this house. Thinking about it chokes me as I'm loaded in and held by Joan.

It's a relief. The best and worst summer of my life just ended.

The huge mansion disappears through the windshield,

and that's when I start thinking about Ty. I don't have a clue what's happened to him, only that he's going to be *locked up.*

What the hell does that mean? It can't end this way. It fucking can't!

My heart bleeds in my chest, and I have to focus very hard on breathing so I don't have a panic attack. I need to hear his voice as soon as I'm able to hold a phone. I need to know he's okay.

I'm ready and willing to wait my whole life just to taste his lips again, but I start sobbing uncontrollably at the terrible idea that he's been ripped away from me, no different than the memories of his rough lips on mine.

X: Frozen (Ty)

When I wake up, it's like every fucking bone in my body's been broken and fused together again. At first, I think feeling the brutal concrete underneath me means my spine's fucked up and misfiring, but then I stretch.

My palms graze cool, hard stone. I sit up and growl as the worst hangover in the world crashes into my skull. Nope, the hard ass floor ripping at my skin isn't just in my head.

I look up. The prison bars in front of my face tell me where I'm at.

The motherfucker really went and did it. I'm sitting in the county jail, locked up tight, a world away from ever being able to spit in my old man's bitter fucking face again. Of course, spit's too soft for what I'd like to do if I ever get a crack at his wicked ass again.

I don't give a shit about being exiled like this. He hurt my girl, so I hurt him. I did all I could to get his goons off her, and it wasn't enough.

Seeing her twitch when the Taser's probe sank into her skin was the worst goddamned thing in the world. I felt my soul leave my body, bathing me in darkness.

And that's where I saw it – it's not just my bastard

father's fault. It's me. I'm the fucking cancer who hurt her, the senseless fuck who dragged her into this situation and nearly got her cooked alive. If I weren't so smashed from getting throttled with current myself, I'd wrap my hands around my own throat and squeeze 'til I pass the fuck out.

It takes me a couple minutes to stagger up. In the cell next to me, a nasty looking old dude laughs, smiling with his rotten teeth.

I walk to the edge of the cell and put my hands on the bars. Fucking shit. Now I know exactly how a monkey at a zoo feels.

Whatever, I barely give a damn that I'm locked up. What really bothers me is what went down before fifty thousand volts friend my nerves and I blinked out like a busted lightbulb.

I deserve to rot in here for what I did to her. Claire's *fucked,* and it's all because of me. Well, me and that cowardly little pissant she was working for.

I'm used to half the world pointing their fingers and laughing like the criminal in the cage next door. Shit's pretty damned natural when you're a billionaire's son, and I doubt it'll get much better now that I'm officially disowned. But Claire shouldn't have to live with this shit, shouldn't have to claw her way back with a fraction of the resources I've always had.

I'm willing to risk having my body shredded along with my reputation. But I can't stand pulling her into the grinder too, without even knowing it.

Goddamn it. My muscles pulse warning aches every time I

move. Too bad it doesn't stop the urge to take my fists to the walls and start beating them 'til something gives way, either the bricks or my own damned bones.

I can't fucking let her go down like this. I have to get outta here, have to make sure she's all right. Then I'm gonna do the soul killing thing I should've always done for this chick who's got my heart in her pretty little hands.

There's only one thing that's *right*, I know it's my only choice because it hurts so fucking bad.

I'm going to clean up loose ends, and then I'm going to disappear.

It only takes a day to talk to some asshole judge, and the badges running this facility. Actually, my boys from the club do most of the talking, and one of them just happens to have some powerful family ties in the local police force.

Thank fuck money doesn't mean much in this world. Yeah, you can buy your way to freedom or lock somebody up with enough dollars in the hopper, but an old police chief or two can buy even more on street cred.

Dad's gonna rage himself blind when he finds out how easy it was for me to walk outta here free, and I don't give a shit. I want to finish what I started in our old house, slamming my fists into his demon face, but it won't solve a thing. Driving home, busting down the gate, and wringing his scrawny neck won't do shit to help my woman.

As far as I'm concerned, my family's dead and buried. All I've got left is her, and not for long. Not after what I'm about to do.

I'm out in a heartbeat, dumping the tight neon prison clothes wrapped around my skin. Ed, Mike, and Tommy pick me up. It doesn't take long to ask them for a big favor, and every one of them is game.

We're gonna pay the too-stupid-to-live fuck responsible for those pretty tabloid pictures a visit.

We stop by a gas station on the way to fill up our ride, plus a few canisters. Then I'm outside the asshole's building, a nice swanky condo Daddy probably bought. The trees aren't the only thing that's green in the big environmental lobby.

My guts churn, thinking how easily I could've been beholden to the same shit, falling in line to run Spree like my bastard father always wanted, dragging anybody I damned well please through the mud.

Not anymore. Not ever again.

Dan the Boss Man comes home late. His jaw's still hanging a little crooked from our last encounter. Fuck if I don't wanna tear it right off.

I pull my hoodie up and wait about a minute after he's gone in inside. A shy, leggy blonde runs up the stairs, and I'm right behind her. She jumps when she sees me, and I don't say a word, just take the door she's nervously holding for me and my crew.

We're in. And we've gotta move fast in case the girl decides to squeal on four big dudes climbing up the stairs with several big plastic shopping bags. She'll really flip if she sees the red canisters inside.

I let Mike go first when we're outside the fucker's door. He gives me a nod and works the lock, exercising all the skill I expect as my newest and last ever security appointee at Club Zing.

The latch pops open and we all file in. Dan's several feet away, standing at the kitchen counter, fixing himself a shot of some amber colored booze.

"What the fuck!" he screams, dropping the glass.

It's a helluva commotion, but it's too fucking late. I grab the asshole before he can make a run for the balcony. My hand pinches his jaw shut, and I give his teeth a rattle through his cheeks that lets him know I'll pop the sonsofbitches out if he does anything stupid.

Oh, except, I guess he already did.

My free hand tugs back my hoodie. I've got him in the living room, next to a big black recliner, and my guys all grin behind their matching hoods. Dan the Man starts squirming, trying to scream into my hand. I knee him in the guts and knock the wind right outta him, realizing I've got no patience for this horseshit.

"Shut the fuck up, kid. You know why I'm here. You just couldn't let it fucking go, could you? You had to snap our pics when our heads were turned and leak it to the paparazzi!"

Slowly, I draw my hand away, and tears start foaming at his eyes. "It wasn't me, Sterner! I promise, I swear – I vow to Christ!"

"Yeah?" I blink, barely even amused. "Who the fuck, then? You're telling me it was the tooth fairy?"

"My dad found out what happened. He wouldn't go down without a fight, he wanted to destroy you, wreck Spree's reputation." Dan clenches his teeth, as if he's afraid to let out the rest. "I begged him not to put a PI on your tail, but he wouldn't listen. He hired some photographer from Hollywood, some guy who's damned good at getting celebs in compromising positions. I begged him not to, Sterner, I *fucking begged.* Please don't do this...please, please, please."

He closes his eyes softly. I let out a long sigh.

It's a cute story, and the asshole's a mighty fine actor. Only problem is, my boys tell me Martin Jacobsen's been laid up for more than a month after a golfing accident. Slipped disk or something, the kinda pain that makes you too paralyzed to get pissed enough to fuck with someone else, much less hire some jackass to follow Claire and me down the coast.

"Sterner? Tyler?" His voice is so soft. "You believe me, don't you?"

"Sure, bud. I read you loud and clear." I tighten my grip on his mouth, covering it as he starts to squirm. Then I look at my three guys and nod. "Burn this fucking place to the ground."

My guys rip the gas cans outta their bags and pop the caps. Half a minute later, the living room reeks like a fuel tanker, and they're spreading out across the condo, pouring gasoline on everything.

The asshole in my hands completely flips his shit. He's shaking, biting, clawing at me like a rat in a trap. I just hold him down and make him watch. Tommy stops above what's probably his favorite chair and empties the rest of his canister on it.

When all three boys are finally standing next to me again, I pull my hand off his mouth. "Have you lost your fucking mind!?"

"You wanna find out?" I growl. "Everybody in here's gonna throw their fucking matches if you don't shut the fuck up. We'll pull the alarm in the hall as a courtesy to your neighbors, and let you roast. You'll have this building all to yourself while it goes up in flames."

Blood drains from his face. "Jesus. God. I'm sorry I lied. You were right. I'm sorry I sent those cameras, Sterner, I'm *so goddamned* sorry."

"Sorry? We're past apologies, fuckface. The only thing that's gonna save your ass from burning is making sure you never, ever do it again."

He starts shaking his head. "Oh, no. I promise I won't. I'll swear on anything you want, on my own fucking life!"

Sighing, I grab him by the hair, lift his head up, and smash his forehead sharply on the floor. He sits up, dazed and confused, trembling as he takes the scene in. I'm not listening to anything 'til he gives me the look that says he knows we're mad dogs ready to bite.

I count to ten. Finally, it's there, clear and tiny as the pinpricks in his eyes.

"I'll level with you, Dan. I'm about to move a long ways away and I won't be here to fuck you up personally anymore." Grabbing his head in both hands, I crane it 'til he's looking at my guys. "That's why I brought these boys along as a reminder. They're local. They'll be watching and waiting for you to fuck me, to fuck over Claire, and if you do...well, the matches come out next time. Maybe we turn your home to cinders, or just your old man's offices. Or maybe they just take you out to some pristine, isolated section of Cascades wilderness and blow your fucking brains out."

He's shaking bad. Good. I can't fuck up again, threatening this asshole. I need him to believe every last thing I'm saying, make him fear for his life. Scaring his sorry ass straight's the only way to keep my girl safe for good.

And honestly, that's my only damned problem. Nothing else is. Not Bellingham, not my old man, not even Club Zing. Whatever happens to this stupid, sneaky little fuck isn't neither. I don't give a shit if he's traumatized and starts pissing his bed every night – that's for the shrinks to sort out.

"You can't do this, Sterner...you can't kill me..."

"I fucking can, asshole, and my boys *will* if you fuck up again. If you just simmer down and let go of my girl, live your life nice and quiet, I don't give a damn what you do. Bury my old man's company goddamned deep if he's really fucked up the environment like you claim he has. I don't care. This begins and ends with Claire. That's all this is about. And I hope for your sake you're smart enough to realize this is your last chance."

"Oh my God, I am, Sterner. Thank you for this chance.

I won't disappoint you, I won't screw up again. I won't –"

I knee him in the guts so he can't talk, then push him into a thick puddle of gas dripping off his soaked recliner. "Just shut the fuck up and get somebody in here to clean this shit up. Let's go, boys."

We're gone. If I were a betting man, I'd say he'll never so much as think the name Claire Frost or Ty Sterner without smelling petrol.

The easy part's over. Now for the one that rips my fucking heart out.

One Year Later

Has it really been a whole goddamned year? Every last one of my boys had tears in their eyes when they dropped me at the harbor where the Alaska ferry docks. They hugged me like brothers, and I embraced them just the same, told them to take good care of my club, because it's theirs now.

A little legal wrangling helps make sure my old man will never get the place back in his name, and he'll never siphon much money away from it either.

Despite the warm sendoff by my crew, it's not them I'm thinking about when the ship pulls away from Washington's shores. It's not like it gets better when I land in Anchorage and start to settle in.

Their faces don't haunt me at night when I'm tossing and turning, or come to me during the day when I'm in the choppy Pacific, screaming at my new guys to reel in a catch before the old fucking net snaps.

I've tried to forget about Claire every way I know how. And it's all a miserable failure.

Every. Fucking. Way.

There are so many times when I just wanna pick up the phone and call her, assuming her old number still works. But fuck, she's gotta be heartbroken when she realizes I'm not locked up, and then shattered again when she finds out I'm gone. Weeks ago by without any contact, and soon that turns into months.

I never reach out. I fucking can't. And it guts me.

I can't be responsible for hurting her again. I'll kill myself before it happens.

Some nights, when I'm watching the snow fall down for what seems like forever, I get down on my hands and knees, praying her ma will just shake some fucking sense into her, help her scrub every waking memory of me outta her brain.

But I've read the headlines, and I've got a feeling the Congresswoman's got bigger worries, now that she'll have to work three times as hard to ever find a way into Washington again. Her politicking is just as fucked as Spree's profits.

My first winter here's the worst. It blows in lightning fast, not long after I find a place in the city to hunker into while I plan the rest of my life. I'm cooped up in a little place in Anchorage, drinking myself half-blind every night, working up the energy to drive and hit the slopes when Jack Frost stops trying to turn everybody's digits black.

Snowboarding helps me get used to the Alaska cold. Useful for handling the weather, yeah, but it doesn't do shit to help me forget.

Neither does bar hopping. A few times, I try to approach some chicks, and God knows it wouldn't take much work to haul 'em into bed.

I'm still Prince Charming. When you're built like I am and you know how to melt panties, you're set picking babes for life.

Alaska has tough guys aplenty, but the women have never seen a specimen like me. I can practically hear their panties splashing into a puddle at their feet as soon as I say "hello."

It doesn't matter how drunk I am or how hot the girl seems. They all end up looking like ash by the time they're ready to pucker up and grab a ride to my place. I make up some bullshit about eating bad fish every fucking time, and I bail with my tail between my legs.

Maybe it's partly true. My poor guts are twisted up so bad I think my stomach's trying to hang itself. I'm sick – completely fucking ill – suffering withdrawals from losing Claire way worse than any junkie misses smack.

I can't get a handle on my guts 'til spring comes, and I'm able to get outside. There's work to throw myself into, and I work like a fucking dog with my first fishing crew, learning everything I can from the grizzled vets I've brought onto my ship.

We're out there for weeks, making hay while the precious summer sun shines across the cold Pacific. I get hooks in my hands and swept overboard a couple times. I've finally found something that makes my muscles beg for rest, and it makes me fucking stronger

Except it's not strong enough to burn away the memories of how we loved and fucked last summer.

I fight not to drown in this crazy new business, pitting men against nature's worst. And I muster everything I've got not to fucking die in my own lonely anguish, killed by my own black heart curdling my blood on those long, dark nights when we're sailing through the rain, exiled from everything I ever cared about.

I'm lost. Out there with backbreaking runs and constantly shifting waves, I start to question whether or not she was even real, or if it was some shit I just imagined so I wouldn't go insane leaving behind my billion dollar family fortune.

But there's no doubt about the last thing I've brought from my old life. The ring was in my pocket the morning we got our savage wake up call. It followed me to jail, and then to Alaska, haunting me like a goddamned vulture because it's everywhere except on my woman's hand where it belongs.

Fuck. *Fuck*.

Fishing season ends and we're about done counting our cash. It's no billion dollar empire income, but it might be seed money for a few new clubs in Anchorage, assuming I decide to go back to the night life and don't kill myself alone on those hellish waves.

I'm sitting on the dock late evening, holding the little

black box in one hand. My grip's so damned tight I think it's gonna snap, assuming I don't flip my shit and hurl it out to sea first.

Not that it'll do me much good if I did. I know damned well I'll dive into the cool water and swim after it. I'll fucking suffocate beneath the Pacific before I surrender the last thing I've got that ties me to that woman, to the summer I'll never forget.

I can't believe how much time's passed, and how much it doesn't matter. It's one whole year since I left the lower forty-eight forever, and it's still slitting me wide open. I've fought like hell to forget her, and I can't anymore.

I do the only sane thing left.

I walk home and hit the website of the fanciest Alaskan airline I can find. I place my order, print out a ticket for a one week trip in her name, and then I'm at the post office, scrawling a quick note before I stuff everything in a big flat envelope.

My boys said she still lives with her ma near Tacoma, and I've got the address. Hoping their info's right is all I can do.

So is hoping she doesn't just tear the envelope open, see what I've sent her, and throw it in the nearest trashcan. I sure as fuck would if a big, stupid man left me high and dry for a whole year, without even a note by pigeon.

Actually, I know that's a load of bullshit. If she's been hurting a fraction as bad as I have, then I know she'll want to see me one more time, if only to slap me across my face.

And I'll fucking let her too. Anything's better than suffering in silence, living this dead, dull mystery I try to call my life. I'll turn the Alaska shores red with my blood, my rage, my explosive need to have her under me again before I give up.

I drop it in the mail and punch the old blue box once, telling myself it's only a fucking week. It might as well be another ten years.

I've given her my hand, and I hope to fuck she takes it. But if she doesn't, you'd better believe I've got another ticket with my name on it, straight to Tacoma, or wherever the fuck else I need to be.

I'll chase her to the ends of the earth, anything for closure, whether that means tasting her lips on mine again, or listening as they cut me to tatters.

XI: Reset (Claire)

One year.

One complete course of the sun across the zodiac, burning me alive, leaving me in darkness. The Taser hurt me so bad I'll never forget it, but losing Ty numbs my body a thousand times worse, and it lasts far longer than the sting of lightning coursing through my skin.

For an entire year, his loss, his silence, hurts. I can't let go until the next summer starts to fade, marking the onset of the chill that's bound to last a lifetime.

I'm so ready to let go. I'm all set to slowly, painfully forget him after hundred hour conversations with Dana during our phone calls and weekend getaways to Portland. Mom's gotten her crap together too, and the stuff she learns at her long meditation seminars flows to me, encouraging me to hold onto my sanity through the heartbreak.

She talks all about Zen this and Buddha that and yoga breathing exercises. It's refreshing not to hear a thing about politics, except when she apologizes and beats herself up over the stupid marriage to Gary, the one that was going to help send her all the way to the White House someday.

Mom feels guilty. She does everything she can to help, and I can't say I turn it down. We're into the holidays before I finally come out of my coma long enough to take work seriously.

I refuse to take another job with her connections. It blew up in my face last time with Cascades Now! and I don't need another disaster to make me think about Ty.

Of course, I can't *stop* thinking about him.

He reaches through my chest and tears my heart out every night. Every fucking day. I dream about the tropical warmth I found in his arms all winter, and sweat remembering our heart pounding sex when spring comes.

I've picked up some consulting work, mostly line editing documents and things like that. It's not much money, but I get to work from home, and I'm doing it on my own.

The clients like what I do, and I adore them because they keep my brain on channels that aren't set to constant heartbreak. I try to bury my nose in career books when I'm not proofing for cash. It usually keeps me going until dinner time, when I shut down to eat and cleanup for the day.

Then the memories come back to torture me. That's when I miss him, and wonder what the hell happened to make him give up on me for good.

Was it all just a lie? Did the charming, brash, stinking rich asshole I first met screw me over once again?

I could accept that. It would hurt *less* to admit I misjudged him, made a terrible mistake, and had a fling with a remorseless bastard who at least gave me some spine tingling sex before casting me aside like another toy.

It happens. Bad boys rule this world, and sometimes they're *bad guys* too.

But the fact that I don't know is what haunts me. I don't understand why he's cut me out of his life. I wonder if he's hurting like I am.

The memories are brutal. I remember how softly he'd growl in my ear after we made love, how good his lips felt against my skin, and how we went from being bitter step-siblings to best friends in a few tumultuous weeks. It's the miracle of a lifetime, and its loss is devastating.

I keep working. I distract myself. I throw myself into whatever I can to take my mind off Ty, taking breaks with Mom over long cups of coffee, or driving down to Portland to see Dana. I feel bad about the trips, where I do nothing except rehash the disastrous silence with him. I'm sure one day she'll pull a muscle wearing that sympathetic grin while I'm dumping all over her.

But they both help. Really. They put gauze on a gushing wound that needs a tourniquet, but it's better than nothing.

Mom teaches me all about clearing my mind, banishing the nightmares in my life with a body work and breathing regimen for dulling the pain. Dana reminds me I'm never alone, shows me a good time, and constantly tries to get me to approach guys at the bars.

All I do is smile and keep my distance. I'm not going down that road again, and it's not an option, even if I want to. There aren't any places in Portland quite like Club Zing. And among all the bars and lounges and restaurants we frequent, there's no man like Ty.

There's arrogant playboys, desperate dude-bros, and divorced charmers with salt and pepper hair galore, looking for their newer, younger wives. They're all special in their own way, yeah, sometimes even a little hot. But not one man I see has that rare mix of fire and ice, money and heart, violence and tenderness.

Everything I want begins and ends with Tyler Sterner, and nobody else offers it.

Something different happens on the last trip to Portland. I don't know why it doesn't kick in at the bars, and sneaks up on me when I'm making my way home to Tacoma instead.

I'm in the car humming along to a love song when I just break down. The lyrics fall to pieces in my throat, and my voice breaks. I cry so hard I'm close to pulling over before I continue my drive.

It hurts like hell because Ty's love is missing from my life, but that's old news. What hurts even worse is that I want to find love, and I realize I'll *have* to do it without him if he's gone for good.

And I know he is.

For the first time, I feel it in my bones, and I don't wonder if it's some cruel physiological aftershock left by the Tasing a year ago. It's a year ago to the day, isn't it?

The next two days, I barely think about Ty at all, a sudden scary first.

I'm taking a break from my editing to walk to the mailbox when it shows up. As soon as I feel the envelope in my hands, my heart plunges to my ankles. The handwriting makes my knees give out, and I barely catch myself against the door for support.

God damn it.

I want to scream and curse, fall to the ground, tearing at the last summer grass until I've dug a rabbit hole to Wonderland to leave this world forever. I can't believe I have to open this fucking thing.

The package comes right when I was about to *let go*. I don't even have to see what's inside to know I never will. I'm mentally doing the math, trying to figure out how much it'll cost to get to Alaska before a freshly printed airfare voucher falls into my hand.

One crazy call to Dana later, and I'm on my way. I don't tell Mom what's up, only that I need to go up there, but it's not hard to see that she knows.

She doesn't curse me out or beg me to stay like I expect. Instead, she just wraps her arms around me, squeezes me tight, and tells me she loves me.

"Do what you need to do, and come home happy," she says. "That's all I ask, honey."

"Mom? Who the hell are you?" It's scaring me. The woman staring at me with her big, beautiful eyes is someone else.

Okay, maybe there's more to this Zen-yoga-breathing stuff than a way to escape her guilt.

"I'm family, Claire. It's taken me a long time to realize that I need to be putting my daughter first. I care about what's going to make you happy – even if it's a little crazy. Life's too short for nothing but climbing the ladder."

Her words echo in my head when I'm on the flight up. I'd just started to remember that there's a ladder to climb at all, and now I'm on the verge of throwing it all away again for this man who's burned into my heart.

I can't pretend I'm not scared. I eat a simple snack and down some anti-nausea stuff on the plane. If everything in Ty's note holds true, he'll be waiting for me at the docks this afternoon, just a short taxi ride from the airport.

I've got some emergency funds and a hotel room lined up in case it's a disaster.

But hell, who am I kidding? I can't imagine any disaster worse than this last year apart.

Just *seeing* him again promises to be the best thing that's happened to me since leaving Gary's house of horrors.

There's a uniquely northern crispness in the air when I step outside for the first time to hail a taxi. A pudgy older driver smiles at me with a few missing teeth, and I hop in. It's hard to keep up with the sparse small talk while he takes me down toward the section of the harbor I've asked for.

The trip takes a little longer than I expect. I hand him his cash, get out, and start moving fast. It's bewildering to see the choppy Pacific from a whole new angle, flanked by Mount McKinley and its towering cousins.

I walk fast, trying to keep my wits, searching high and low. I want to see him before he sees me. I can't let him surprise me. I can't just walk back into his life as nothing more than a moving target.

Luck's on my side today. At first, I almost walk right past the hulking man sitting on the pier. It's the tattoos that catch my eye.

Of course it's him, sitting shirtless and magnificent, despite the cool. I recognize the immense stripes flowing down his arms and over his shoulders instantly. When he turns, the tiger on his chest looks at me, as if it remembers how I moaned and shuddered beneath him those hot, unforgettable nights.

My legs ache. It takes everything I've got to move, steer myself toward him.

Ty's arms are folded and his face is an impenetrable mask. But I recognize the cosmic fire in his eyes, the magnetic energy in his baby blues that grabs me by the heart and draws me toward him, step by painful step.

Jesus, I swear he's filled out with new, rugged muscle. That's why I didn't recognize him at first glance. The tight slabs chiseled to his bones are even tighter now, rougher and more natural. He even seems taller.

His eyes are the same, and they draw me into his world instantly.

"Hey," I say sheepishly, as soon as we're close. I jerk to a stop just outside his reach.

"Hey yourself." The distance doesn't stop him.

It takes him all of two seconds to close it, and he's right up in my face, so close my blood boils. I don't know whether to jump up and kiss him, or jump off the pier and drown myself in the icy Alaskan waters. The fire roaring beneath my skin blazes hotter than everything I've known before, even the ones he kindled a year ago.

"Cannot fucking believe you're here." His mask breaks, and he flashes me a big, broad grin.

My body tenses as he lunges forward, throwing his arms around me, lifting me high off the ground to look into his eyes. God, it feels good to touch the sky with this giant. I never forgot how much I missed these arms, but *nothing* compares to having them around me again.

"Christ, I missed you, babe. It's like seeing spring returning to this God forsaken place."

My heart flutters. It's hard to speak, my throat's so damned dry. "*Ty*. I can't believe it either. I can't believe it's you."

I allow myself to squeeze his shoulders. A million emotions explode in my belly. Anger, fear, love, and lust. It hits my brain at once in a big sloppy wave, and I fight not to pass out.

He tries to move in for a kiss. As much as my body lights up when his skin's on mine, I can't do it. I jerk my head away. He senses the resistance and sets me down, his broad smile fading.

"What the fuck? Don't pretend you haven't been missing these lips all over your body."

"I have," I snap, feeling anger gaining the upper hand. "Really. But you don't realize I've missed hearing your voice just as much as feeling your lips. *Why* didn't you call? Why'd you let us slip apart?"

"Because I fucked up. Twice, Claire." He takes a pace

back, collecting his thoughts, and then he's looking at me again. I don't know if I should melt into a puddle or turn to ice beneath those gorgeous eyes. "Once was thinking I did so much goddamned damage that I had to let you go. My fuck of a dad ruined you, and he did it because of me. I lost half my soul seeing you hurt. Seeing those probes shoot lightning through your body was the worst damned day of my life."

"Mine too! I was glad to be out of that house – believe me. But you were supposed to come after me. I thought we really had something on the ship that summer. Do you remember the Fourth?" I pause and swallow a hard lump as he nods his head sadly. "You abandoned me, Ty. You didn't keep your promise."

His eyes flash brighter. "Babe, you didn't let me finish. I fucked up *bad*, and I'm man enough to say it to your face. My first mistake was running. Mistake number two was thinking I could ever let go. I lied to myself. I thought I could forget you, thought I *had* to, anything to keep my crazy shit from fucking up your life."

"Yeah? Then I guess you never understood I *wanted* it in my life. All of it. I wanted you. You're wrong, Ty, and I can't believe you thought I'd just skip away and get on with my life. Did you really think I'd be able to get over you just as easy?"

My heart thuds. I'm starting to think this is a bad idea, that coming up here at all to confront everything I should just leave behind is stupid. He hasn't changed. He's still the same selfish playboy prince who pulled me to his lips that first night at Club Zing.

"I'm not done yet!" he holds his finger up to my face and gives it a shake.

His whole arm flexes. I can't help remembering what those hands did to me all summer. If they weren't busy running across my body, plunging inside me, prepping me for his dick, then they held on tight while he fucked my brains out.

"Asshole." It slips out, and I can't stop it. "You're still the same man I met."

He blinks, and the rage seems to leave him. Ty lowers his hand. "Yeah, babe, I fucking am. That's the point. I'm the blind ass fuck who thought I could be somebody else. I was supposed to remake myself up here, become a blank slate, rip my own heart out and throw it away. I thought I could live with losing you, and the ticket you got in the mail last week's proof I was wrong. I know how bad I fucked up now, and I've come to terms with it. But I can't take back the past and apologies won't do shit. All I'm offering you is to pick up where we left off, babe, knowing like nothing else I'd rather be *dead* than ever dream of letting you go again."

I try to step away, but he won't let me. His arms wrap tighter, fuse tight, hook me to his immense slab of a body.

The choice is clear – it's either break down in his arms, bawling like a baby, or hit him as hard as I can and run. This time, there can't be any looking back.

Guess which one I choose.

Ty's face hits my fiery palm, and there's a crack like

thunder. I'm so shocked I can't think about moving my feet. He stops the impact dead, and I can feel the heat beneath his stubble, blood rushing in to cover the shock. I'm too stunned by the fact that I've done it to remember how to struggle away from him.

"You got that shit outta your system, or what?" He says coolly.

I shake my head. I don't know. Maybe I feel a little better now, sure, but something tells me I'm never going to get the huge hulking splinter named Ty Sterner out of my heart.

My head starts thrashing side to side. Ty squeezes me so close it hurts, shoves his face against mine, and swallows me with those beaming blue eyes. "What the fuck's the matter? Talk to me!"

"I don't know if I love you or hate you," I whimper, voice breaking. "You're an asshole because I can't let go, no matter how much you hurt me. Part of me wants to flee, get as far away from you as I possibly can, and never set foot on Alaskan soil ever again. But I can't forget you, Ty. I can't let go. And that hurts more than anything."

He looks at me, his eyes beaming and amused. I can't look away.

"That's what I thought, babe. We're both fucked – screwed by our own beating hearts in the best way possible. And if this is being held captive, then lock me up and throw away the key. Didn't you hear me the first time? I'd rather be in the fuckin' ground than here without you, even if you're crying and fighting like hell in my arms.

We've talked this shit out as far as I'm concerned."

He isn't wrong. Only problem is, I don't have a clue where we go from here, assuming I don't keel over first from the shame of ripping myself open and exposing it to him like this.

"We good, babe? We got an understanding?"

Very slowly, I look deep into his eyes and nod my head. Everything inside me is way too twisted up to say a word, especially my heart.

"Good. Now, let's shut the fuck up and let our lips say the rest."

Our first kiss in a year sucks the air from my lungs. His lips lock onto mine and I don't move at first, but it doesn't take long to feel the familiar, unstoppable heat rolling through me in one massive front.

My knees shake. My nipples throb. The V between my legs swells open, wet and empty and aching, screaming for him to throw me down on this dock and fuck me like he did last summer. I don't care if there are cameras watching and we end up all over the internet.

Luckily, that's not likely, considering our little scandal is yesterday's news.

My mouth splits open, and I let his tongue inside. A few seconds later, we're twined, kissing as hungrily as the last night in his old bed, harder and stickier to make sure we never have to miss this again.

We're not just making up for lost time. We're entering our future, and the asshole's right like he usually is.

I can't stop wanting him. I can't let go. I can't pretend

I'm not in love.

He made a mistake. He apologized, in his own screwy way. And now I feel the hatred, disappointment, and sadness steaming out my pores, leaving me like pollen after a good hard sneeze.

Ty's hands roam my body. I flatten my hands on his chest and let myself feel him. It wasn't just my imagination earlier – he's even harder now, stronger and more masculine, impossibly *developed* in a way ninety-nine percent of males on this earth will never be.

Jesus. God help me.

One hand pushes down his washboard abs with a mind of its own. I can't stop myself from moaning into his mouth as I touch the hard ridge rising in his jeans, huge and wanting, just the way I remembered it.

"Damn it, Ty," I sputter, breaking the kiss for oxygen. "I missed you so fucking much. I missed *us.*"

"Yeah, I can kinda tell with the way you're squeezing my cock. Keep your panties on a little longer. There's something I gotta do here before we fuck."

My eyes go wide and crazy as he lets me go and drops to the ground. His knees crack against the old wood hard when he crouches, and at first I can't figure out what the hell's going on.

When the little black box appears in his hand, I almost join him on the pier, and all the blood goes rushing out of my head. The world opens up and goes dead silent, condensed into this moment, with nothing except the churning sea and distant ships.

Not until he opens his mouth and pops the top with his thumb.

"I bought this thing in Lincoln City on the Fourth. It was a perfect fucking day – all except the asshole paparazzi snapping us. I was gonna give it to you before we came up here together, and it was still in my pocket the day our parents tore our world to shit. It's all I had to remember you this past year, and it still counts for a goddamned lot now that you're here."

"Ty..." I can barely say his name.

He holds up a hand, begging me to stay quiet. "There's a few less diamonds on this thing than I'd like, but it'll do the trick just the same. Marry me, Claire Frost. I want us bound together so tight we'll need an asshole judge to undo us if one of us goes crazy and ever thinks about walking out again. And I know it'll never happen. I need you to be my wife even more than I need you under me right now."

My heart swoons. The ocean's blustery echoes are like a sharp breeze, and everything starts spinning. I go down, fly through the air, landing in his powerful arms. For a second, I think I'm going to black out, but then everything goes bright and he's staring at me, just as strong and loving as he's always been at his best.

There's my Prince Charming, handsome as he is swoon worthy. Beneath the asshole, the best man I'll ever know and love is still there. I can't even dream about saying no.

"Babe? Shit, are you okay?"

"I'm great," I say softly, throwing my arms around his

neck and pulling him to my lips. "I'm trying to tell you yes, Ty. Let's get married."

My hand covers his as it holds the ring. We stay just like that, kissing for a long while. His lips speed up as soon as I say the words, pulling the energy from my body.

Great, I guess he's found a new way to leave me breathless without even taking me to bed.

We kiss through sunset before he finally takes his hand off mine and gets the ring out. It's a perfect fit for my finger, a little gold loop with a diamond surrounded by studded seashell fragments, a piece of forever.

"Jesus, Ty." It's going to take some time to get used to this beauty on my hand, and now's not the time when his lips are all over me. "I love you, love you, love you so much."

"Love you too, babe. Now, let me show you how deep that love goes somewhere we won't freeze to death."

Grinning, he helps me up, and we walk to his truck, hand-in-hand. Screw the hotel. We're heading for his condo.

Maybe I can survive the Alaska cold after all.

There's hardly time to take in his new place before our clothes are on the floor. I get a quick glimpse of the living room and kitchen, then I'm in his arms, being carried to the bedroom.

That heavenly smell I remember from his old room in Bellingham engulfs me. If I was wet before, I'm totally soaked now, trembling as my body realizes how badly it needs this, and how long it's been denied.

We're kissing as he pulls me onto the bed with him, dropping me out of my dress. I help undo my bra before I start working on his pants and the shirt he threw on since we got into his truck. Ty joins me with his god-like naked perfection half a minute later.

His cock pops out when his boxers drop, throbbing with long, hard, manly heat. I'd forgotten just how fucking *huge* he really is. He takes my hand and wraps my fingers around his length – not that I need much urging.

"Fucking shit," he growls. "Your hand feels ten times hotter with my ring on it."

Lightning tingles up my spine. I get on my knees and start to suck him, deep and fast. It's a joy to give head to this man after such a long break.

I breathe steady, working him as my own hot cream trickles down my thighs. He fists my hair in one hand and runs a rough finger over my jaw with the other. The callouses on his hands are way thicker than anything I remember, and it makes his touch hotter.

I don't know what the hell he's been through since he moved up here. But he must have suffered, hurt himself on nature's thorns, worked himself raw trying to forget me.

God. My fingers glide down his length to the base and cup his balls as I work my tongue. I wonder how the hell I survived a full year without this.

He lets me suck him for several minutes before he pulls out, giving me a gentle push until I'm lying flat. His hands grip my thighs and pull them apart, making room for his incredible mouth.

"Gush for me, babe. It's been a *fucking year*. I want your juices all over my goddamned bed by the end of tonight."

I moan a reply, and then I can't say anything at all as his face moves in. He buries his head between my legs. My clit sings with the first wondrous strokes in more than a year. It's like the thing comes back to life after a long, depressed sleep.

The rare, anxious nights with my bullet vibrator can't hold a candle to him.

Our bodies remember last summer, and it's like it was only yesterday as soon as we're naked. Ty doesn't miss a beat with the way he works me over, sliding his thick tongue up and down my folds, licking me until I'm flushed and steaming carnal heat. My legs hook over his shoulders and dig in.

It's all I can do, besides clawing the hell out of his sheets, to stay sane when he starts sucking my clit. I'm shaking in less than a minute.

My climax washes over me in a wave so sudden and sharp, it drowns the past year's longing and turmoil. My heart pounds to the swirl of his tongue inside my pussy, dipping up to draw circles around my clit, making me hum with release.

I come hard. I open my mouth and scream, wondering if he has any neighbors. If he does, they're going to realize there's been a big change in his life soon.

Thank God. I'm so fucking thankful we're together

again I can't put it into words. Luckily, our bodies do all the talking, and they've got *plenty* to say.

Opening my eyes, I regain my vision to him licking the last of my cream off his fingers. The bed sinks beneath his weight as he gets behind me, drawing me on top of his huge body.

My head turns and we kiss. My tongue plunges in and out of his mouth, teasing him and loving it. I want him inside me so bad it hurts. Growling, he fists my hair and brings his lips to my ear, snorting hot breath.

"Open your legs and sink that sweet pussy down on my dick. We're fucking all night, baby. Hope you slept on the flight in. Remember to breathe."

Yeah, I hope I can, because the rough edge in his voice says he isn't kidding. As soon as my thighs shift apart and I've got my knees over his, he stops rubbing his cock against my ass and shifts position, driving up into me.

My pussy stretches full and pulses pure pleasure, grateful to be filled with the only cock worth fucking. My hips start to buck, sliding up and down his length, pulling him inside me as his thrusts deepen.

Ty locks onto me tight. He holds me down, fucking me so hard my breasts feel like they're going to fly off. Those yoga breathing exercises Mom taught me come in really handy now. It's the only reason I don't pass out when he starts going full throttle, flinging me around like a ragdoll with his thrusts, hammering his dick so hard and deep his balls swing up and slap my skin.

My breasts wobble and roll wild. He covers one with a

rough hand and squeezes, all the better so he can fuck me harder, faster, meaner.

He fucks like an animal, and it carries me straight to heaven. I know there's something more behind it too, a feral tenderness I feel when he rubs his stubble across my cheek, or sucks at the skin on my throat. His teeth nip, hard and playful, one more sensation my body can't handle as it spirals toward overload.

"Ty. Ty! You're going to make me –"

He cuts me off with a sharp pinch to my nipple. I forget how to form words again as my body tightens up and convulses on his cock. I feel my walls pinching him tight, begging him to release, flood me with his hot, molten seed.

"You like that, Claire? Yeah, you fucking missed this. Just like I missed pumping my balls dry in your hot cunt, *Sis*."

That word. *Holy shit.*

It's the fucked up, taboo, filthy nickname that sends me over the edge, into a whole new pleasure zone I've never experienced.

I don't care that we're not technically siblings anymore. Our parents are divorced, leaving their mistakes behind. But without their screw ups, we wouldn't be here, fusing our bodies together.

He'll always be my step-brother, my best friend. My lover, my husband, and everything else a woman needs, everything there can be on some crazy cosmic level. And my twisted pussy will always love hearing him say *Sis*, clenching on his dick like a vice when he reminds me how we met, right before he pours himself into me.

With a growl, he comes. His jets pump scalding fast, filling me to overflowing. His pulse joins mine, and we're hooked together, thrashing in ecstasy, one earthquake shaking two bodies.

I'm so damned soaked by the end of it that I wonder if I'm really melting. There's a huge, cooling puddle in the middle of the bed, right where he pulls out, and sweat drips off us both in rivulets.

Ty kisses me, gently rolls out underneath me, and then walks to the window. He flings it open. The fresh Alaskan breeze feels like the sexiest shower in the world as it sweeps in.

Then I realize if nobody's heard us before, they'll hear us for sure next time. I sit up, tucking my arms across my breasts.

"What's up, babe? Thought we were both gonna die of heat stroke for a second."

"I like the fresh air, but do you really want to leave that open?" I point to the window.

He looks for a brief second, then stares at me and grins. "Sure. Might as well put Alaska's chill to good use. That wind's only gonna get a lot colder. It'll pummel us all winter like a motherfucking freight train before Jack Frost has had his fill."

"Um, I know this building's pretty fancy, but you've got to have a few neighbors. Don't you see a problem here?"

He tips his head back and laughs. "The two guys a few doors over will be gone hunting caribou and black bears all month. As for old lady Connelly next door, she's got her TV cranked up so fucking loud half the time that I'm sure she's half deaf. I don't give a fuck if anybody hears what's going on in here."

"I do!" I stick my tongue out. It's impossible to stay mad.

Still laughing, he topples into bed again, shadowing my body in his huge muscles. His cock rubs enticingly against my still wet pussy. One groan later and I start to forget all about the neighbors.

"I can't believe you're making me do this," I sigh, grinding back on his dick.

"Shit, you serious? Did you really think I didn't want the whole damned world to know we're tight now that we've made it official? We let some media shits come between us before. I'm not making that mistake again. I don't give a fuck if everybody in Anchorage hears what's happening in this bedroom."

"I do!" I say again, trying to fight him a little harder. I should know better. It's over before it's begun with his cock teasing me like this, tight against my entrance.

"Save that shit for the altar, babe. We're keeping that window open all winter with the fucking we're doing. I've missed a whole year of this pussy, and if you're still caught on trivial shit, then we'll have to screw twice as much as I was planning to un-fuck your head. Now, bite your tongue and put your legs on my shoulders. Nothing's stopping this dick from owning you tonight."

I smile and let it go. He's right about one thing – there's

nothing stopping this utter *dick* of a man from claiming me and fucking me until I'm a limp, steaming mess.

By the time he pushes inside me and I let out the world's loudest, most shameful moan, I remember I love the asshole, not just the good guy underneath. Lucky me, we've got the rest of our lives for him to drive me all kinds of crazy.

XII: Big Day (Ty)

Nine Months Later

My greedy dick steals more blood from my brain every time I look at her. She's fucking magnificent in that long white dress, and I almost forget about how bad I want to rip it off and lay her down. If only being up here at this makeshift altar didn't hit me right in the feels.

I look at our "priest," really a Buddhist monk we've chosen to marry us here in Denali. The thin man smiles and says the words I've been waiting for. "You may now kiss the bride."

Thank fuck. I'd been worried I'd freeze up and forget a few crucial words.

Our little audience explodes as I lift Claire's veil back and taste those lips. Having her pressed up against me, tight and salty and hot as fuck makes this all real.

She's officially my wife. I suck the air outta her precious lungs and leave her panting for more. Damn if I don't enjoy a long buildup, and I tease her mouth with everything I've got, hand on her ass, heart thudding like a goddamned jet engine in my chest.

It's late spring in Alaska, and the high afternoon sunlight glows down on us approvingly, as if the whole world's decided to celebrate along with us. Damned straight.

When I pull back, her cheeks are rosy red, the same hue they usually turn before we fuck. I gotta give her one more grin and look away before my cock rips right through my expensive trousers.

She leans into me. "Tonight."

Fuck! My dick does a hard jerk in my pants. I grab her by the hand and we walk down the aisle, listening to our small crowd clapping and cheering for us.

All my boys are there. Tommy, Ed, Mike. They're the only remnants of my old life in Washington worth keeping.

On Claire's end, there's her ma, an aunt, and several cousins I just met yesterday. I can't believe how much the power hungry Congresswoman's changed, and I can almost believe she's given up her dreams of going back to DC. Hell, she's the one who got us this monk to make things official, and I can't say it's a bad idea with all the eastern spice we're inviting into our lives.

She's brought Joan too. It's nice to see the old housekeeper again, and even better that they'll be working for us after the honeymoon. Claire's ma kept her gainfully employed after blowing my dad's estate, and now she's coming home to work for me, just like I promised.

I'll need all the help I can get to keep things running in the household too.

I'm due to open the doors on Club Tao next week, Anchorage's first full service bar and lounge, complete with an authentic West Coast feel. My boys are up to watch me tie the knot and make sure things get off to the great start.

We stop near the curb, not far from where our limo's parked, and wait for everybody to come up and give us their congrats. One big plus about having a slim guest list means it doesn't take long to see everyone.

I'm goddamned thankful for that. The sooner we have our dinner and reception means the sooner we'll take off for the high end resort at the park's edge. After that, we're fucking the whole week away, whenever we're not taking long walks into the wilderness and staring at the stars with champagne flutes in our hands.

Claire's ma comes up and kisses her. She throws her arms around me and I hug her back.

"Congratulations, Ty! Welcome to the family."

I outta cringe hearing that shit again. She said the same damned thing on the day we met, but this time it's happy. It's real. I study her face carefully for any lingering bitterness. There's nothing.

She's learned to live and let go of her mistakes. I can do the same, even when we're getting married in the same national park where Mandy tied the knot with my bastard of an old man.

Don't worry, he's got his comeuppance. Even if I'd sent that fuck an invite to wedding, there wouldn't have been a response. Spree's in somebody else's hands now.

I hear he's busy selling off his properties and drinking like a fish. Even the family estate on the coast is up for grabs, part of a whirlwind auction to raise sorely needed cash.

Turns out, the fuck got into a multi-billion dollar dick waving contest and tapped his company's money behind the shareholders' backs. The experimental shit Dad tried to fund to take a private rocket into lunar orbit ate up everything, and the fucking thing exploded on the launch pad, killing two engineers.

The media ruckus blew his finances wide open, and it only took a week for the board to come for his head. Now, he's CEO of nothing, and he'll be lucky to live a quiet, comfortable life of mediocrity on whatever the hell he's got left.

It's not much. Looks like it's up to me to rebuild the family fortune, and his greedy old ass won't be getting a dime.

Maybe I'll make an offer for the *Stingray* this summer, assuming the new club takes off and I can stand letting my lawyer send him a letter. Or maybe I'll leave him to die alone. His bullshit stole a whole year away from my woman, never mind watching his goons fry her before my eyes, and that's fucking unforgivable.

I don't miss his sorry ass. Everything I need's right here at my side. I swing Claire's hand in mine, letting out a possessive growl.

"Ready when you are, Mister and Missus Sterner." A neat dressed chauffeur I've hired holds the limo's door open for us.

Claire looks at me and smiles, flashing her bright

white teeth. "Oh, Ty. I never thought this would go so perfectly."

I smile back at her as we slide into the car, breathing in the rich scent of leather. "I did. And you'd better hold on tight because it only gets better from here."

The dinner and dance lasts long into the night. By midnight, I can't fucking wait anymore. I let her kiss her ma one last time and share a laugh with her best friend, this chick named Dana. Then I pick her up, throw her across my shoulder, and head out to the car.

"Floor it," I tell the driver, stuffing an extra tip into his hands.

He drives like a secret service agent ushering the President through some war zone, and I pull Claire onto my lap, pressing my lips to hers.

"I hope you've got something hot on under that thing, babe. I'm not wasting any more time with you changing once we're back in our room."

"Lucky for you, I've come prepared." She puts her hand on my dick, pulls up the hem of her dress, revealing the hottest pair of soft white stockings I've ever seen.

Fucking shit. Pounding her into the mattress with this lingerie accenting her would be hot as hell alone, but there's another reason my balls won't stop blazing like hot coals.

"You're sure you're clean? All that shit's outta your system?"

"It's getting there. The doctor said it might take

three or four months before everything works right. You know it's normal for a lot of couples to try for a year, right?"

I slam my glass of whiskey down in the cup holder and grind my cock on her ass, fisting her and jerking her ear to my lips. "Fuck that. Statistics don't mean shit when we're this serious. Get it through your pretty head right now, babe, and burn it there. I'm filling you every fucking day 'til something takes. We're fucking all night, every night, and we're not taking breaks 'til you tell me you're knocked up."

She flashes me a mischievous smile. "Oh? Maybe I shouldn't tell you anything, Ty. Sounds like you'll cut me off cold turkey when the job's tone."

She's such a fucking tease. I slide my hands up under her wedding dress and finger her panties, reaching for the softness between her legs. She's soaked.

"Just a couple more miles, babe. You're giving me the best wedding present a man can hope for."

"And it'll keep giving for the rest of our lives," she says, right before she closes her mouth over mine in a sultry kiss.

I suck her lip and kiss her like I own her, because I fucking do.

She's right about us, building our future piece by piece. I've always wanted a big family. Since her, I know I *need* it. We both come from fucked up places, missing a mother or a father or sometimes both, but us?

Well, shit, we can do better. And tonight, we're

gonna start, laying down roots by putting my first born of many inside her.

The car pulls up while we're still wrestling lips, hot and heavy. It's a quick walk into the fancy lodge and a ride up the elevator. I carry her the whole way, barely ever pulling my lips off hers.

Upstairs, I kick the door open and carry her over the threshold. Very traditional. Something about that feels nice, a small beacon of sanity in our huge, crazy ocean.

She's laughing as I pull her onto the bed and run my hands all over that dress. I feel like I'm gonna fucking die if I don't get it off, and I try to do it without tearing the damned thing to shreds. I let her help, if only to get her naked faster.

My tux is a lot more familiar. It comes off in a blink as soon as she's naked, except for those knockout stockings. I press my seething, tattooed skin against hers and spread her legs wide, pulling them around my waist and hooking them tight.

"Fuck me, Ty. Fuck me good and deep," she begs.

That's all I can stand. I can't wait a micro-second more to push inside her. My dick thuds like it's trying to leave my body as I push up into her.

I'm growling into her mouth next time we kiss, savoring her hot, wet heat as long as I can. But the fire churning in my balls won't stop 'til I move my hips. We fuck hard and deep, finding a whole new passion in this babymaking fuckery.

When she starts digging her nails into my neck, I

grab her hair and jerk her head upright, exposing her neck for my lips. I suck her skin just like I fuck her.

I can't get over marking this woman. I'm jealous, possessive, and crazy as fuck, and I want the world to know. That pretty ring on her hand isn't enough. I won't throttle anything back 'til I see her belly stretching with my seed, and she's got a whole wardrobe of turtlenecks to cover the love bites I leave on her flesh.

Shit, she's marking me too. Her nails rake deep down my back, harder when she starts to moan and thrash her hips into mine. Her whole body's begging at a primal level for my come, and I'm gonna give it to her.

But not 'til she's an insane, sexy, sputtering mess. I slam her harder, rocking her whole body, grinding myself into her clit.

"Oh, Ty – Ty! God. *Fuck!*" The wet heat wrapped around my dick pulls tighter as she starts to come.

I lose my shit and move my body like a runaway train. Her pussy sucks so hard at my dick I nearly lose it, but somehow I keep fucking her through her first climax of the night, never slowing down a single beat.

Those silky stockings brushing my sides feel damned good. When she's done coming and scratching my back to pieces, I flip her over, mounting her from behind.

Her sweet ass bounces each time I thrust, so deep my balls slap her little tender flesh. I'm gonna shake her all the way down, watching her tits swing beneath her. This is a full blown animal fuck, and it's gonna end the way animals mate too – breeding her.

My dick leaks inside her just knowing I'm gonna knock her up. My balls are about to split and spill, but I keep my control, plowing her with deep, long strokes that shake the entire fucking bed.

She's clawing desperately at the sheets now, ripping a pillow near the headboard and stuffing it into her mouth. It's the only thing that muffles the screams pouring outta her mouth.

I grab onto her thighs and pull them up. She's halfway in the air and I'm fucking her deeper, reaching all the way to her womb, feeling my balls ready to erupt.

The second orgasm hits her, and it's her pussy's death grip that does me in. I can't fucking hold it anymore.

"Scream your fucking brains out, babe," I tell her, lightning striking through my nuts. "I'm gonna fill this pussy up. Here comes our kid!"

There's shrill, sexy music coming from her pillow. My hips go wild and I growl, slamming her completely into the mattress and holding her there, shooting the first thick rope up her smoldering cunt.

Fuck. Shit. Christ.

This woman sucks the life outta me, and then some.

I lose my load and flood her, feeling the remnants gushing out around us. Her pussy's still massaging my dick as my brain throbs pleasure. I don't stop thrusting, rooting myself inside her 'til my balls pulse every last drop they can.

Everything ends, just like it began, in one feral

kiss.

"I love you, Claire. Love you 'til I'm nothing but dust and bones," I growl, touching my forehead to hers.

"And I love you, husband. Even when you're being the world's biggest dick." She smiles.

Cue me slapping her ass playfully as we roll, pulling her on top of me. "Shit, babe, I don't care. We're cool, just as long you keep loving me for having the world's biggest dick."

"Whatever." She smiles, rolling her eyes. "You're a cocky, sex crazed asshole, but you'll always be my Prince Charming."

"All for you, Little Miss Perfect."

We both smile and laugh. I spread her legs and push into her again. There's no fucking way I'm going soft tonight.

My cock's hard and happy, and so's my heart. I can see our whole future unfolding while we rock the bed, warm and beautiful as the rare Alaska summer.

It's glorious.

Thanks!

Want more Nicole Snow? Sign up for my newsletter to hear about new releases, subscriber only goodies, and other fun stuff!

JOIN THE NICOLE SNOW NEWSLETTER! – http://eepurl.com/HwFW1

Thank you so much for buying this book. I hope my romances will brighten your mornings and darken your evenings with total pleasure. Sensuality makes everything more vivid, doesn't it?

If you liked this book, please consider leaving a review and checking out my other erotic romance tales.

Got a comment on my work? Email me at nicolesnowerotica@gmail.com. I love hearing from my fans!

Kisses,
Nicole Snow

More Erotic Romance by Nicole Snow

COWBOY'S STRICT COMMANDS

RUSTLING UP A BRIDE: RANCHER'S PREGNANT CURVES

FIGHT FOR HER HEART

BIG BAD DARE: TATTOOS AND SUBMISSION

MERCILESS LOVE: A DARK ROMANCE

LOVE SCARS: BAD BOY'S BRIDE

RECKLESSLY HIS: A BAD BOY MAFIA ROMANCE

Outlaw Love/Prairie Devils MC Books

OUTLAW KIND OF LOVE

NOMAD KIND OF LOVE

SAVAGE KIND OF LOVE

WICKED KIND OF LOVE

BITTER KIND OF LOVE

Outlaw Love/Grizzlies MC Books

OUTLAW'S KISS

OUTLAW'S OBSESSION

SEXY SAMPLES: <u>OUTLAW'S KISS</u>

I: Cursed Bones (Missy)

"It won't be long now," the nurse said, checking dad's IV bag. "Breathing getting shallower...pulse is slowing...don't worry, girls. He won't feel a thing. That's what the morphine's for."

I had to squeeze his hand to make sure he wasn't dead yet. Jesus, he was so cold. I swore there was a ten degree difference between dad's fingers in one hand, and my little sister's in the other. I blinked back tears, trying to be brave for Jackie, who watched helplessly, trembling and shaking at my side.

We'd already said our goodbyes. We'd been doing that for the last hour, right before he slipped into unconsciousness for what I guessed was the last time.

I turned to my sister. "It'll be okay. He's going to a better place. No more suffering. The cancer, all the pain...it dies with him. Dad's finally getting better."

"Missy..." Jackie squeaked, ripping her hand away

from me and covering her face.

The nurse gave me a sympathetic look. It took so much effort to push down the lump in my throat without cracking up. I choked on my grief, holding it in, cold and sharp as death looming large.

I threw an arm around my sister, pulling her close. Lying like this was a bitch.

I wasn't really sure what I believed anymore, but I had to say something. Jackie was the one who needed all my support now. Dad's long, painful dying days were about to be over.

Not that it made anything easy. But I was grown up, and I could handle it. Losing him at twenty-one was hard, but if I was fourteen, like the small trembling girl next to me?

"Melissa." Thin, weak fingers tightened on my wrist with surprising strength.

I jumped, drawing my arm off Jackie, looking at the sick man in the bed. His eyes were wide open and his lips were moving. The sickly sheen on his forehead glowed, one last light before it burned out forever.

"Daddy? What is it?" I leaned in close, wondering if I'd imagined him saying my name.

"Forgive me," he hissed. "I...I fucked up bad. But I did it for a good reason. I just wish I could've done it different, baby..."

His eyelids fluttered. I squeezed his fingers as tight as I could, moving closer to his gray lips. What the hell was he saying? Was this about Mom again?

She'd been gone for ten years in a car accident, waiting for him on the other side. "Daddy? Hey!"

I grabbed his bony shoulder and gently shook him. He was still there, fighting the black wave pulling him lower, insistent and overpowering.

"It's the only way...I couldn't do it with hard work. Honest work. That never paid shit." He blinked, running his tongue over his lips. "Just look in the basement, baby. There's a palate...roofing tiles. Everything I ever wanted to leave my girls is there. It was worth it...I promised her I'd do anything for you and Jackie...and I did. I did it, Carol. Our girls are set. I'm ready to burn if I need to..."

Hearing him say mom's name, and then talk about burning? I blinked back tears and shook my head.

What the hell was this? Some kinda death fever making him talk nonsense?

Dad started to slump into the mattress, a harsh rattle in his throat, the tiny splash of color left in his face becoming pale ash. I backed away as the machines howled. The nurse looked at me and nodded. She rushed to his free side, intently watching his heartbeat jerk on the monitor.

The machine released an earsplitting wail as the line went flat.

Jackie completely lost it. I grabbed her tight, holding onto her, turning away until the mechanical screaming stopped. I wanted to cover my ears, but I wanted hers closed more.

I held my little sister and rocked her to my chest.

We didn't move until the nurse finally touched my shoulder, nudging us into the waiting room outside.

We sat and waited for all the official business of death to finish up. My brain couldn't stop going back to his last words, the best distraction I had to keep my sanity.

What was he talking about? His last words sounded so strange, so sure. So repentant, and that truly frightened me.

I didn't dare get my hopes up, as much as I wanted to believe we wouldn't lose everything and end up living in the car next week. The medical bills snatched up the last few pennies left over from his pension and disability – the same fate waiting for our house as soon as his funeral was done.

Delirious, I thought. *His dying wish was for us, hoping and praying we'd be okay. He went out selflessly, just like a good father should.*

That was it. Had to be.

He was dying, after all...pumped full of drugs, driven crazy in his last moments. But I couldn't let go of what he said about the basement.

We'd have to scour the house anyway before the state kicked us out. If there was anything more to his words besides crazy talk, we'd find out soon enough, right?

I looked at Jackie, biting my lip. I tried not to hope off a dead man's words. But damn it, I did.

If he'd tucked away some spare cash or some silver to pawn, I wouldn't turn it down. Anything would help us live another day without facing the gaping void left by his brutal end.

My sister was tipped back in her chair, one tissue pressed tight to her eyes. I reached for her hand and squeezed, careful not to set her off all over again.

"We're going to figure this out," I promised. "Don't worry about anything except mourning him, Jackie. You're not going anywhere. I'm going to do my damnedest to find us a place and pay the bills while you stay in school."

She straightened up, clearing her throat, shooting me a nasty look. "Stop talking to me like I'm a stupid kid!"

I blinked. Jackie leaned in, showing me her bloodshot eyes. "I'm not as old as you, sis, but I'm not retarded. We're out of money. I get that. I know you won't find a job in this shitty town with half a degree and no experience...we'll end up homeless, and then the state'll get involved. They'll take me away from you, stick me with some freaky foster parents. But I won't forget you, Missy. I'll be okay. I'll survive."

Rage shot through me. Rage against the world, myself, maybe even dad's ghost for putting us in this fucked up position.

I clenched my jaw. "That's *not* going to happen, Jackie. Don't even go there. I won't let –"

"Whatever. It's not like it matters. I just hope there's a way for us to keep in touch when the hammer falls." She was quiet for a couple minutes before she finally looked up, her eyes redder than before. "I heard what he said while I was crying. Daddy didn't have crap after he got

316

sick and left the force – nothing but those measly checks. He didn't earn a dime while he was sick. He died the same way he lived, Missy – sorry, and completely full of shit."

Anger howled through me. I wanted to grab her, shake her, tell her to get a fucking grip and stop obsessing on disaster. But I knew she didn't mean it.

Lashing out wouldn't do any good. Rage was all part of grief, wasn't it? I kept waiting for mine to bubble to the surface, toxic as the crap they'd pumped into our father to prolong his life by a few weeks towards the end.

I settled back in my chair and closed my eyes. I'd find some way to keep my promise to Jackie, whether there was a lucky break waiting for us in the basement or just more junk, more wreckage from our lives.

Daddy wasn't ready to be a single father when Mom got killed, but he'd managed. He did the best he could before he had to deal with the shit hand dealt to him by this merciless life. I closed my eyes, vowing I'd do the same.

No demons waiting for us on the road ahead would stop me. Making sure neither of us died with dad was my new religion, and I swore I'd never, ever lose my faith.

A week passed. A lonely, bitter week in late winter with a meager funeral. Daddy's estranged brother sent us some money to have him cremated and buried with a bare bones headstone.

I wouldn't ask Uncle Ken for a nickel more, even

if he'd been man enough to show his face at the funeral. Thankfully, it wasn't something to worry about. He kept his distance several states away, the same 'ostrich asshole' daddy always said he was since they'd fallen out over my grandparent's miniscule inheritance.

All it did was confirm the whole family was fucked. I had no one now except Jackie, and it was her and I against the world, the last of the Thomas girls against the curse turning our lives to pure hell over the last decade.

A short trip to the attorney's office told me what I already knew about dad's assets. What little he had was going into state hands. Medicare was determined to claw back a tiny fraction of what they'd spent on his care. And because I was now Jackie's legal guardian, his pension and disability was as good as buried with him.

The older lawyer asked me if I'd made arrangements with extended family, almost as an afterthought. Of course I had, I lied. I made sure to straighten up and smile real big when I said it.

I was a responsible adult. I could make money sprout from weeds. What did the truth matter in a world that wasn't wired to give us an ounce of help?

Whatever shit was waiting for us up ahead needed to be fed, nourished with lies if I wanted to keep it from burying us. I was ready for that, ready to throw on as many fake smiles and twisted truths as I needed to keep Jackie safe and happy.

Whatever wiggle room we'd had for innocent mistakes slammed shut the instant daddy's heart stopped in the sharp white room.

I was so busy dealing with sadness and red tape that I'd nearly forgotten about his last words. Finishing up his affairs and making sure Jackie still got some sleep and decent food in her belly took all week, stealing away the meager energy I had left.

It was late one night after she'd gone to bed when I finally remembered. It hit me while I was watching a bad spy movie on late night TV, halfway paying attention to the story as my stomach twisted in knots, steeling itself for the frantic job hunt I had to start tomorrow.

I got up from my chair and padded over to the basement door. Dust teased my nose, dead little flecks suspended in the dim light. The basement stank like mildew, tinged with rubbing alcohol and all the spare medicine we'd stored down here while dad suffered at home.

I held my breath descending the stairs, knowing it would only get worse when I finally had to inhale. Our small basement was dark and creepy as any. I looked around, trying not to fixate on his old work bench. Seeing the old husks of half-finished RC planes he used to build in better times would definitely bring tears.

Roofing tiles, he'd said. Okay, but where?

It took more than a minute just scanning back and forth before I noticed the big blue tarp. It was wedged in the narrow slit between the furnace and the hot water tank.

My heart ticked faster. So, he wasn't totally delusional on his death bed. There really were roofing tiles there – and what else?

It was even stranger because the thing hadn't been here when I was down in the basement last week – and daddy had been in hospice for three weeks. He couldn't have crawled back and hidden the unknown package here. Jackie definitely couldn't have done it and kept her mouth shut.

That left one disturbing possibility – someone had broken into our house and left it here.

Ice ran through my veins. I shook off wild thoughts about intruders, kneeling down next to the blue plastic and running my hands over it.

Yup, it felt like a roofing palate. Not that I'd handled many to know, but whatever was beneath it was jagged, sandy, and square.

Screw it. Let's see what's really in here, I thought.

Clenching my teeth, I dragged the stack out. It was lighter than I expected, and it didn't take long to find the ropey ties holding it together. One pull and it came off easy. A thick slab of shingles slid out and thudded on the beaten concrete, kicking up more dust lodged in the utilities.

I covered my mouth and coughed. Disappointment settled in my stomach, heavy as the construction crap in front of me. I prepared myself for a big fat nothing hidden in the cracks.

"Damn it," I whispered, shaking my head. My hands dove for the shingles and started to tug, desperate to get this shit over with and say goodbye to the last hope humming in my stomach.

The shingles didn't come up easy. Planting my feet on both sides and tugging didn't pull the stack apart like I expected. Grunting, I pulled harder, taking my rage and frustration out on this joke at my feet.

There was a ripping sound much different than I expected. I tumbled backward and hit the dryer, looking at the square block in my hands. When I turned it over, I saw the back was a mess of glue and cardboard.

Hope beat in my chest again, however faint. This was no ordinary stack of shingles. My arms were shaking as I dropped the flap and walked back to the pile, looking down at the torn cardboard center hidden by the layer I'd peeled off. Someone went through some serious trouble camouflaging the box underneath.

I walked to dad's old bench for a box cutter, too stunned with the weird discovery to dwell on his mementos. The blade went in and tore through in a neat slice. I quickly carved out an opening, totally unprepared for the thick leafy pile that came falling out.

My jaw dropped along with the box cutter. I hit the ground, resting my knees on the piles of cash, and tore into the rest of the box.

Hundreds – no, thousands – came out in huge piles. I tore through the package and turned it upside down, showering myself in more cash than I'd seen in my life, hundreds bound together in crisp rolls with red rubber bands.

Had to cover my mouth to stifle the insane

laughter tearing at my lungs. I couldn't let Jackie hear me and come running downstairs. If I was all alone, I would've laughed like a psycho, mad with the unexpected light streaking to life in our darkness.

Jesus, I barely knew how to handle the mystery fortune myself, let alone involve my little sis. I collapsed on the floor, feeling hot tears running down my cheeks. The stupid grin pulling at my face lingered.

Somehow, someway, he'd done it. Daddy had really done it.

He'd left us everything we'd need to survive. Hell, all we'd need to *thrive*. Feeling the cool million crunching underneath my jeans like leaves proved it.

"Shit!" I swore, realizing I was rolling around in the money like a demented celebrity.

Panicking, I kicked my legs, careful to check every nook around me for anything I'd kicked away in shock. When I saw it was all there, I grabbed an old laundry basket and started piling the stacks in it. I pulled one out and took off the rubber band. Rifling my fingers through several fistfuls of cash told me everything was separated in neat bundles of twenty-five hundred dollars.

I piled them in, feverishly counting. I had to stop around the half million mark. There was at least double that on the floor. Eventually, I'd settle down and inventory it to the dime, but for now I was looking at somewhere between one to two million, easy.

It was magnitudes greater than anything this family had seen in its best years, before everything went to shit. I smoothed my fingers over my face, loving the unmistakable money scent clinging to my hands.

No shock – sweet freedom smelled exactly like cold hard cash.

An hour later, I'd stuffed it into an old black suitcase, something discreet I could keep with me. My stomach gurgled. One burden lifted, and another one landed on my shoulders.

I wasn't stupid. I'd heard plenty about what daddy did for the Redding PD's investigations to know spending too much mystery money at once brought serious consequences. Wherever this money came from, it sure as hell wasn't clean.

I'd have to keep one eye glued to the cash for...months? Years?

Shit. Grim responsibility burned in my brain, and it made my bones hurt like they were locked in quicksand. Dirty money wasn't easy to spend.

I'd have to risk a few bigger chunks up front on groceries, a tune-up for our ancient Ford LTD, and then a down payment on a new place for Jackie and I.

It wouldn't buy us a luxury condo – not if we wanted to save ourselves a Federal investigation. But this cash was plenty to make a greedy landlord's eyes light up and take a few months' worth of rent without any uncomfortable questions. It was more than enough to give us food plus a roof over our heads while I figured out the rest.

Survival was still the name of the game, even if it

had gotten unexpectedly easier.

Once our needs were secure, then I could figure out the rest. Maybe I'd find a way to finagle my way back into school so I could finish the accounting program I'd been forced to drop when dad's cancer went terminal.

It felt like hours passed while I finished filling up the suitcase and triple checked the basement for runaway money. When I was finally satisfied I'd secured everything, I grabbed the suitcases and marched upstairs, turning out the light behind me. I switched off the TV and headed straight for bed.

I sighed, knowing I was in for a long, restless night, even with the miracle cash safe beneath my bed. Or maybe because of it.

I couldn't tell if my heart or my head was more drained. They'd both been absolutely ripped out and shot to the moon these past two weeks.

I closed my eyes and tried to sleep. Tomorrow, I'd be hunting for a brand new place instead of a job while Jackie caught up on schoolwork. That happy fact alone should've made it easier to sleep.

But nothing about this was simple or joyful. It wasn't a lottery win.

Dwelling on the gaping canyon left in our lives by both our dead parents was a constant brutal temptation, especially when it was dark, cold, and quiet. So was avoiding the question that kept boiling in my head – how had he gotten it?

What the *fuck* had daddy done to make this much

money from nothing? Life insurance payouts and stock dividends didn't get dropped off in mysterious packages downstairs.

He'd asked for forgiveness before his body gave out. My lips trembled and I pinched my eyes shut, praying he hadn't done something terrible – not directly, anyway. He was too sick for too long to kill anyone. He'd been off the force for a few years too.

I lost minutes – maybe hours – thinking about how he'd earned the dirty little secret underneath my bed. Whatever he'd done, it was bad. But at the end of the day, how much did I care?

And no matter how much blood the cash was soaked in, we needed it. I wasn't about to latch onto fantasy ethics and flush his dying legacy down the toilet. Blood money or not, we *needed* it. No fucking way was I going to burn the one thing that would keep us fed, clothed, sheltered, and sane.

Jackie never had to know where our miracle came from. Neither did I. Maybe years from now I'd have time for soul searching, time to worry about what kind of sick sins I'd branded onto my conscience by profiting off this freak inheritance.

Fretting about murder and corruption right now wouldn't keep the state from taking Jackie away when we were homeless. I had to keep my mouth shut and my mind more closed than ever. I had to treat it like a lottery win I could never tell anyone about.

Besides, it was all just temporary. I'd use the

fortune to pay the rent and put food in our fridge until I finished school and got myself a job. Then I'd slowly feed the rest into something useful for Jackie's college – something that wouldn't get us busted.

It must've been after three o'clock when I finally fell asleep. If only I had a crystal ball, or stayed awake just an hour or two longer.

I would've seen the hurricane coming, the pitch black storm that always comes in when a girl takes the hand the devil's offered.

An earsplitting scream woke me first, but it was really the door slamming a second later that convinced me I wasn't dreaming.

Jackie!

I threw my blanket off and sat up, reaching for my phone on the nightstand. My hand slid across the smooth wood, and adrenaline dumped in my blood when I realized there was nothing there.

Too dark. I didn't realize the stranger was standing right over me until I tried to bolt up, slamming into his vice-like grip instead. Before I could even scream, his hand was over my mouth. Scratchy stubble prickled my cheek as his lips parted against my ear.

"Don't. You fucking scream, I'll have to put a bullet in your spine." Cold metal pushed up beneath my shirt, a gun barrel, proof he wasn't making an empty threat.

Not that I'd have doubted it. His tight, sinister

embrace stayed locked around my waist as he turned me around and nudged his legs against mine, forcing me to move toward the hall.

"Just go where I tell you, and this'll all be over nice and quick. Nobody has to get hurt."

I listened. When we got to the basement door, he flung it open and lightened his grip, knowing it was a one way trip downstairs with no hope for escape.

Jackie was already down there against the wall, and so were four more large, brutal men like the one who'd held me. I blinked when I got to the foot of the stairs and took in the bizarre scene. They all wore matching leather vests with GRIZZLIES MC, CALIFORNIA emblazoned up their sides and on their backs.

I'd seen bikers traveling the roads for years, but never anything like these guys. Their jackets looked a lot like the ones veterans wore when they went out riding, but the symbols were all different. Bloody, strange, and very dangerous looking.

The men themselves matched the snarling bears on their leather. Four of them were younger, tattooed, spanning the spectrum from lean and wiry to pure muscle. The guy who'd walked me down the stairs moved where I could see him. He might've been the youngest, but I wasn't really sure.

Scary didn't begin to describe him. He looked at me with his arms folded, piercing green eyes going right through my soul, set in a stern cold face. He exuded a strength and severity that only came naturally – a born

NICOLE SNOW

badass. A predator completely fixed on me.

An older man with long gray hair seemed to be in charge. He looked at the man holding my sister, another hard faced man with barbed wire ropes tattooed across his face. Jackie's eyes were bulging, shimmering like wide, frantic pools, pulling me in.

I'm sorry, I hissed in my head, breaking eye contact. One more second and I might've lost it. The only thing worse than being down here at their mercy was showing them I was already weak, broken, helpless.

They had my little sister, my whole world, everything I'd sworn to protect. No, this wasn't the time to freak out and cry. I had to keep it together if we were going to get out of this alive.

"Well? Any sign of the haul upstairs, or do we need to make these bitches sing?" Gray hair reached into his pocket, retrieving a cigarette and a lighter, as casually as if he was at work on a smoke break.

Shit, for all I knew, he probably was.

"Nothing up there, Blackjack." The man who'd taken me downstairs stepped forward, leaving the basement echoing with his smoky voice, older and more commanding than I'd expected. It hadn't just been the rough whisper flowing into my ear.

"Fuck," the psycho holding Jackie growled. "I like it the fun way, but I'm not a fan when these bitches scream. Makes my ears ring for days. Can't we gag these cunts first?"

Nobody answered him. The older man narrowed

328

his eyes, looking at his goon, taking a long pull on the cigarette. My head was spinning, making it feel like the ground had softened up, ready to suck me under and bury me alive.

Oh, God. I knew this had to be about the mystery money the moment those rough hands went around me, but I hadn't really thought we were about to die until he said that.

Gray hair turned to face me, scowling. "You heard the man, love. We can do this the easy way or the hard way. I, for one, don't like spilling blood when there's no good reason, but some of the brothers feel differently. Now, we know your loot's not where it was supposed to be – found this shit all torn up myself."

Blowing his smoke, he pointed at the mess on the ground. I could've choked myself for being too stupid to clean up the mess earlier.

"You've got it somewhere. It couldn't have gotten far," he said, striding forward. "Look we both know me and my boys are gonna find it. Only question left is – are you gonna make this scavenger hunt easy-peasy-punkin-squeezy? Or are you gonna make all our fucking ears ring while we choke it out of you?"

I didn't answer. My eyes floated above his shoulder, fixing on the man across from me, stoic green eyes.

"Well?" The older asshole was getting impatient.

Strange. If Green Eyes wasn't so busy hanging out with these creeps and taking hostages, he would've been handsome. No, downright sexy was a better word.

My weeping, broken brain was still fixed on the stupid idea when Gray Hair grunted, pulled the light out of his mouth, and reached for my throat...

Look for Outlaw's Kiss at your favorite retailer!

SEXY SAMPLES: <u>BITTER KIND OF LOVE</u>

I: Shades of Betrayal (Alice)

When I felt the knife against my throat, I knew I'd fucked up bad.

Stinger wasn't coming to pull me feet from the fire either. Not this time, not when I'd run away from him and his club like the terrified girl I was.

He'd offered me the world, and I'd forsaken him. Now, I was going to pay the price.

"I'll ask you again, little bitch. *Where. Is. It?*" My interrogator's eyes were pitch black.

God, how many times had I seen eyes like that before? They were as black and dead as the last few months of this new life, lost to the world, abandoned in the deep cold darkness.

"I...I can't remember. I already told you that. I'm not lying!" I spat at the floor and looked up, trying not to shake.

My eyes passed over the patches on his cut: NERO, PRESIDENT, 1%, WRECKING CREW, SLINGERS

MC. Skulls wearing cowboy hats and smoking pistols menaced their way out of the leather. Above it all, his black eyes devoured me, darkness set in a bald head and cheeks pocked with scars.

Sick irony twisted my stomach. I'd fled to Idaho to get away from biker gangs intruding on my life, only to have a truly feral MC threatening to make sure I never had to worry about intrusions ever again. And all because I couldn't give him something I didn't know I had, that fucking map my father hid before they murdered him.

"Bullshit!" Nero lowered the knife and gave me a good shove against the wall.

Behind him, another man laughed, giggling like a hyena while he scratched his arm. Nero's head whipped back and he gave the psycho an evil eye.

"Shut the fuck up, Hatter." He drew in a heavy breath before turning back to me, bathing me in those inverted spotlights he had for eyes. "Your amnesia act's not pulling the fucking wool over my eyes, girl. Maybe it worked before, getting every fool from here to Missoula to swallow your shit, but I'm not biting. I know the Rams kept you for days in that shitty clubhouse after we killed your old man and ripped through his fucking truck. Don't tell me the Feds took it. I won't believe that shit for a second."

I looked up at him, hatred swirling in my veins. My fiercest look didn't faze him. All it got me was the knife at my throat again, cold and threatening as ever.

"Who the fuck took it, slut? Did you bring it out here

when you decided to move West and shake your pussy on stage? Should I rip apart this whole fucking house looking for it?" Nero looked up at his men and snapped his fingers.

His crew moved behind us, stomping into my tiny kitchen. Crashes blasted my ears as they turned over the table and started to open every drawer and cabinet they could find, hurling out the contents, killing the grim silence with a ferocious clatter.

Shit. He knew damned well I wasn't hiding anything in plates and cups, didn't he?

Maybe it was a new, sick form of torture. I didn't give a damn that they were destroying what little I had. It was the noise that got to me, the thunderous explosion of dishes, silverware, glass, and food hitting every surface within striking distance.

The one called Hatter added his high, insane laugh to the chaos too, a soulless cackle that drummed into my bones.

"Okay! You fucking win! I'll tell you everything I know. Just please...make them *stop*," I screamed, jumping in his arms, wishing I could get his gross hands away.

I nicked my neck on the knife while I was thrashing around. Nero tucked it away, satisfied with my surrender, but not before I felt a warm trickle of angry blood pooling in my cleavage. He blinked, his eyes wide, allowing me to hold one hand to the wound while he clapped his hands and yelled at his men.

"All right, boys! Keep your peckers down and stop

ripping shit to kingdom come. Our little raven's gonna sing..."

He smiled, reaching up to run the back of his hand through my black hair. I twisted away, stopping just short of slapping his stupid hand. Jesus, it was tempting, but I knew I'd get pure hell if I laid a finger on him.

The crashing stopped, replaced with wintry silence. Hatter's sick laughter faded into their heavy, excited breaths. They came tromping back to their boss, surrounding us in a cruel circle that would've made the biggest badass in the world sweat bullets.

My memory gathered itself while I stared into Nero's cold eyes, collating all the terrible things I'd forgotten for months. Everything I'd tried to escape forever.

I was an idiot to think I could run from it. Evil things always caught up with me, no different than this pack of vicious murderers.

"I watched Dad die in their clubhouse. The Rams kept me prisoner," I said, remembering the worst days of my life. "I couldn't have been there more than a few days..."

"You gotta do better than that, little lamb. That shit's the first thing I learned through the Grizzlies grape vine, and it's fucking useless!" His last word exploded in my face like a bomb. "I want those fucking routes. I need your old man's map. Don't give a shit hearing about the Rams' escapades while you were chained down like a bitch."

Don't shake. Don't cry. Don't give him anything except stark, bitter truth.

"The Prairie Devils picked me up. I was with them

for...damn, it must've been several weeks. They held onto me while their drama with the Rams dragged on. This man, Stinger –"

It hurt to say his name.

Stinger repulsed me, fascinated me, and stirred more conflicting emotions than any man I'd ever met in my life. I couldn't handle him. I ran, as fast and as far as a bus ticket and a little cash could get me, hoping I'd never have to say his name again.

Nero held up a hand, hissing through his teeth. "I already told you, bitch, I don't need to hear all these little details. I don't give a fuck about hearing how many times they used your tight ass. If you don't spit out something useful in the next two minutes, Hatter and Wasp here are gonna use your holes instead. And I can guarantee they'll give you a pounding a whole lot harder than anything those Prairie Pussies gave you..." He turned the blade in his hands, bored beneath his rage.

I shouldn't have said his name. I'm not worthy to even think it.

My heart sank, thinking about the only man who gave a single crap about me since these demons killed Dad.

Stinger was a total angel, a guardian, handsome as he was strong, determined to keep the brutal world off my back. He protected me, the total opposite of what these idiots thought about the Devils, and I repaid him by fucking off without even saying goodbye.

"It doesn't matter," I whispered, the worst lie I'd told all night. "I didn't see much. The Devils had their own crap going on – one of their brothers almost went to prison.

They barely told me anything about their business. Just asked me a bunch of questions until the Rams hit them that night."

"Yeah, yeah. Poison," Nero grunted. "I know all about what those sloppy motherfuckers did. Didn't off a single Prairie Pussy, did they?"

I shook my head, remembering my last night with the club, nearly all the men laid up and suffering. The tainted whiskey did a number on their stomachs.

But it wasn't the club that mattered. It was *him*, and I was right by his side, holding his hand while he writhed in pain, then laying next to him – repaying the same favor he'd done me the first night I left hell.

Then there was the kiss the next morning, when he was still delirious...

I closed my eyes. It was too damned much.

I was an idiot, and the world didn't offer second chances.

"You're right. None of them died," I said, reluctantly forcing my eyes open.

"Fucking amateurs," Nero growled. "So, what, then? The Pussies cut a deal with the Feds, I know that much. How did the Rams die? That fucking thing had to be at their clubhouse. I know they fucked us over. And I know the Feds didn't tear them a new asshole. Their dicks are too limp these days for massacres and media spectacles. Who killed them?"

I swallowed the painful lump in my throat. Nero stepped closer again, catching the glint in my eye that told him I was holding back.

"You coming clean, or what? Fucking tell me, bitch! You got one chance, and you're losing it by the second." He grabbed my shoulders and pressed me to the wall, hot breath spilling onto my face, carrying the faint and sickly stink of whiskey. "We're not gonna do this same old song and dance all night, girlie."

My feet dangled off the floor as he lifted me higher, hanging my face just a few inches over his repulsive mug. No matter how hard I tried, I couldn't look away, knowing if he wrung out the next bit, it would seriously fuck over the people who'd saved me.

And Stinger too – especially Stinger!

I'd already stabbed him in the back by running. I couldn't twist the knife by fucking over his club – could I?

"I get it." His voice went cold, the anger doused to smoky rage. "Cutting up that pretty skin or having a dick inside you doesn't rustle your panties too much. Hell, you're probably already fucking guys in your off hours at the strip joint, yeah? You got a body worth a few dimes, bitch, and having us steal what you're selling doesn't get you in a fucking twist."

I refused to answer. I had to keep my lips sealed, had to stay quiet. No, my memory wasn't perfect, but I'd be damned if I let it go.

"Let me tell you something." He let my shoes drop to the floor with a shove. "You've never fucked the way we do. You see my bro, Hatter, over there?"

He grabbed my face and twisted it in the right direction.

I was forced to look at the skinny, nasty freak behind him, the man who couldn't stop twitching and giggling like a lunatic.

"Show her your goods, brother!" Nero ordered.

Hatter laughed louder as he rolled his leather cut down his arms and pulled up his shirt. I gasped.

Crazy emblems lined his body like every biker, but they weren't tattoos. They were deep red scars, gouges in his skin. Several long lines of flame were deep red, nearly bleeding. The smoking gun on his chest was lined with thousands of little cuts designed to look like thorns.

The other two men laughed. I felt the blood draining from my face.

"This is what he does for fun," Nero said. "Likes to carve shit up like it's Thanksgiving dinner three hundred and sixty five fuckin' days a year. Not just his own skin neither. Fuck, you oughta take a good look at his dick...this man's the only bastard I've known in all my years who takes razors to his pisser."

The demon grinned and reached for his jeans, squeezing his crotch. Then he reached into the holsters near his waist and pulled out two matching daggers, holding them across the lump in his pants, giving me a smile straight from the darkest corner of hell.

Nero knew what he was doing. The bastard *knew* I'd take damage to keep my secrets, but not *this*. I couldn't fight the monster leering at me with his knives and manic evil, drool slipping down his chin.

No, no, Jesus Christ, no.

I couldn't let this sick animal have his way with me. I wouldn't survive.

Right then and there, I broke. My cowardly mind spun, ready to cough up anything to get me out of this. Anything to take away the pure fucking evil circling me in this room.

Hatter reached up, began to unzip his fly. I couldn't even stand to see it. Terror hit me like lightning, and I flinched in Nero's hands.

"Stop it. Stop. Call him off," I whimpered. "I know where the stupid map is."

"Okay," he said softly. "I'm gonna give you one more chance, bitch, and only one. *Who* killed the Rams? Who the fuck was there before the Feds rolled in? Who took it?"

"The Devils. The whole club combed the place over good before they gave it up to the cops. If anyone's got my Dad's stuff, it's them. The map's at their clubhouse, stuffed up in some office. Now, please...let me go."

Nero never smiled. He just nodded and did as I asked, letting me fall to the floor. He coughed once, watching me collapse in a sobbing heap on the ground.

Cold. Satisfied. Happy, maybe.

And why shouldn't he be? The bastard just watched me sell my soul.

"Come on, Shark," he said to the larger man in the corner. "Bitch finally gave us a gold nugget we can use. We'll call it in to the rest of the club and figure out the best plan of attack."

The man with the VP tag and the silver teeth nodded, and began to follow him out. I looked up, staring through my tears, wishing I could see through the walls, straight to the dense gray winter sky.

I'm sorry, Stinger. I'm sorry.

God, I'm so fucking sorry!

I saw it in my mind already. These assholes weren't going to waste much time. They'd show up not long after Christmas if they had to, a sneak attack. Nero and his men would burst in with guns blazing, brandishing their blades. They'll kill, torture, and burn anyone they had to for that damned map.

The Missoula boys would never see it coming. Blaze, Tank, Moose...Stinger.

They'd all fight like mad until their last breath. But it wouldn't be enough. They'd be flattened on the ground with holes in their chests.

I'd watched the club nearly get slaughtered in one ambush while I was there, and the Slingers promised hot lead instead of half-assed poison.

I thought about Stinger's strong face, lifeless and pale, a neat dark hole through his head.

Fuck. This couldn't be happening!

I couldn't let him or any of his guys die because of my screw up.

My hands stretched across my face and just kept going, pulling on my skin. I wanted it to hurt. My surrender was going to get a lot of good men killed, and probably their old ladies too. I might as well have put a gun to Stinger's temple and pulled the trigger myself.

I stopped stretching my face to total hell and looked up.

The other two demons, Hatter and Wasp, lingered. I wanted them gone like yesterday. I wasn't sure there would ever be a way to bleach their evil presence out of my rental.

After this, I had to leave. I had to get out and go far, far away.

Maybe I could leave the Devils an anonymous tip, a letter or a call to tell them what was coming...but first, I needed these killers *gone*.

Shit, why weren't they moving, following their nasty leader out the door?

"Hey!" I screamed, my life returning. Nero stopped with his VP at my front door and turned. "We're done here, aren't we? Take your guys and go. I gave you what I promised."

At last, I saw his smile, evil and crooked as the rest of him. "There's a special place in hell for traitors and cunts who can't keep their lips sealed. Don't worry, baby, your friends from the Prairie Pussies will be joining you down there soon. Daddy's waiting too. Old Mickey's paying for some seriously fucked up sins on Satan's bench right now, I'd wager..."

My eyes bulged. My lungs felt like they'd been filled with cement. I couldn't even shake my head or ask him what the hell he was talking about. It was all there in his savage face.

"I'm gonna give you boys an hour with this bitch. Have your fun and then clean up the mess. We'll dump her body off on the way to Montana."

Nero was out the door, his VP behind him. I took one look at the two smiling assholes closing in on me fast, trying not to let my knees turn into mud.

Run. Get away. Fight.

I hurled myself downstairs, heading for the basement, listening to their heavy boots clomping behind me. The last thing I thought before my screams pierced the darkness was Stinger.

I hurled my frenzied wishes, my prayers, my everything high into the cold, indifferent winter sky. I would've given anything for a miracle, anything for him to hear it and come for me.

Yes, I prayed, even when I saw what a total, undeserving bitch I'd become, the last girl in the world who deserved a rescue by the man who haunted her dreams.

But I wasn't stupid. The universe never, ever worked like that. I didn't believe in coincidence or miracles, and I definitely didn't deserve one after what I'd done.

Shit! It was so fucking dark down here, and I didn't dare turn on the lights and give them an easier time. I ran into the washing machine, its cold metal slapping my hands. When I looked up, the bikers' dark shadows blocked the hall, boxing me in.

When Hatter lunged, pulling at my hair, I lost it.

The screams, the prayers, and everything else went numb. He whirled me around, slapping me against the wall before I lost my balance and began to fall. Nothing broke it. Nothing caught me. Nothing except brutal regret as I hit the floor and they started tearing at my clothes.

341

That thing they say about your whole damned life flashing before your eyes right before you die? I thought it was crap – until it happened.

I remember everything, past and present flashing like strobe lights, colliding jigsaws in my head. Every piece of Stinger, I tried to cling onto, but I couldn't. It was all coming in a blizzard, churning too fast, the few good pieces always out of reach.

I'd lived on a merciless ledge, and I was an idiot to think there'd be anything different at my life's sudden dead end.

One second, I caught a fragment. Just one.

I remembered Stinger's warmth, his strength, his powerful arms wrapped around me, so real my heart stopped shaking to tatters in my ribs. And then it was gone in a wink, replaced with the savage wolves behind me, grabbing me by the ankles and ripping at my clothes...

Look for Bitter Kind of Love at your favorite retailer!

Printed in Great Britain
by Amazon.co.uk, Ltd.,
Marston Gate.